PIRATE'S PATCH

BAER CHARLTON

Cover by David L'Bearz

RMJ Manuscript Service LLC
Rogena Mitchell-Jones, Literary Editor
www.rogenamitchell.com

Published by Mordant Media, Portland, Oregon

Contents

00 Endgame

DISTRACTEDLY, BLAKE STUCK her index finger into the bullet hole. It was loose. She pulled it out and stuck in her thumb. It was still loose. Normally, her body would have healed the wound down to a snug fit on the smaller finger. She left her thumb in the hole punched by a large caliber slug. Her fingers weakly gripped the shoulder she now couldn't feel. The thumb would slow the oozing. Blake flexed the thumb around in the shoulder—the shattered chunks of bone moved roughly. She knew this body was dying.

She looked out across the ocean. The great raft of catamarans was a torn mess.

Nine of the ships drifted—partially cut loose and ablaze. The guns had long gone silent and given quarter to the ringing clash of swords. The two warring navies and marines were awash across the vast field of burning decks, bombed out bridges, and shattered masts.

In the distance, a dark mass squatted low in the water, as if silently watching the carnage. A pall of black smoke pouring from the mast and five open covers on the long deck of the nuclear sub—now a funeral pyre. Scattered about on the ocean, as far as the eye could see, were burning hulks, bellies of boats long turtled, and ships making last churnings before diving to the ocean floor—forty minutes away.

In centuries gone by, ships of the line or pirate ships burned to the waterline. The air reeked of burning tar, boiling blood, and roasting flesh. Mixed, it clawed the back of one's throat in an acrid burn from the cordite and black power. The oak of the decks could smolder for days. The smoke was a poisonous stew of sulfur dioxide creeping across the water. The nose would burn as the sulfur turned to acid, eating the lungs until pirate or Navy coughed out his guts. The lungs wept puss and blood in an oozing goo from one's own body killing them.

The modern world isn't as kind. Through the blood-matted strings of red hair, Blake could see the three catamarans drifting north were void of life. The bodies lay crumpled where they had stood when the carbon fiber ribbing started to burn. The high-tech ingredient used in making the rib cage of the large catamarans was also the most deadly. The chemicals giving the beams super strength yet flexibility when burned created a clear, deadly gas.

The results on a body were similar to tear gas—but only until the flesh-peeling nature of mustard gas. Long before the flesh peeled in large sheets, the chlorine and arsenic had finished their work. Modern sailors fear a boat fire more than a hurricane or tsunami.

The blood in the red hair flew as tiny droplets as the woman spun around. She stumbled. Her sense of balance continued to spin. She could feel the deck was losing its grip on her special boots. The slurry of blood mixed with oil and seawater kept breaking the special bond. Soon, her boots would become more of a threat than useful. She needed to take them off.

The crushing thump of a large explosion deep in the bowels of one of the ships caused Blake to spin. Three catamarans over, she watched as the guts of the gold refinery erupted and then fell back into the center of the boat. She knew the molten mass would drag the center down and thus draw the rest of the catamaran down also.

She watched it—stupefied.

Her lungs were battling with their own problems. Her body was losing its last fight. The butt of the titanium spear protruded from just below her left breast. The expanded point splayed tight against her back where she had pulled it to so it would be out of the way. She hadn't found anyone to pull it out of her back. The spear only went one way.

She leaned against the capstan to pull off her boots. The red boot came up, but the right hand only hung— useless. Three small rivulets of blood coursed their way to her fingertips and off. It was as if her lifeblood was running away. The last sword fight had bitten deep, severing tendons, muscle, and nerves. At least the arm had stopped aching from the morning's bullet wound.

Blake leaned back. There was nothing left to do. Ever Kind or not, eventually, a body can only take on so many holes, lose so much blood, suffer so many insults. Eventually, there is a final note played in the symphony of life.

She coughed. She didn't even try to cover her mouth. She could feel the blood running down her chin. She spat a wad of red onto the already red deck—it didn't show. The calm came. Her one good eye, rimmed with blood, twitched as it swept the sky. The columns of black clawed their way into what had started as a dark gray dawn. It never reached blue by the time the smoke of the battle had smeared the canopy of heaven from horizon to horizon.

Under the canopy, only hell reigned.

The surface effect boats had started arriving before dawn—guided by a beacon set by a traitor in their midst. The beacon had been a three-cycle marker. Fifteen seconds and its work was done—the damage complete. Over three hundred ships and boats had the dead reckoning GPS coordinates of the gold smelter in the center of the raft of eighty commercial-sized catamarans rafted in the middle of the ocean.

The flip of one switch and friend had become foe. A trusted family member became a traitor in fewer than the span of twenty heartbeats. It had taken less time than a loving hug, a lingering kiss, or a lover's goodbye. Blake had stood in the doorway and watched as the beacon tumbled from the other's hand, into the last cauldron of molten gold.

The tortured rending of a bent metal door howled behind her as the door opened. Blake looked out across the ocean. She did not want to look at the woman she came to trust, shared a bed, and had fallen in love with. Thousands of lifetimes, and still, she was never prepared. But this one hurt the worst.

The hand slid lightly along her shoulder. It felt so natural there. The fit was so right… until this morning. But she didn't move. The battle was over. All of her fight was gone.

"I can't get my boots off." Blake's voice was breathy, and the gurgle of the punctured left lung rattled wetly.

The dark-haired woman knelt. Setting her saber on the fouled deck, she gently removed each red boot and tall sock as Blake presented them. She watched as the bare toes curled and spread on the deck, any separation from the sailing ship and its deck—now removed. She looked up at the closed eyes. Cowboys want to die with their guns blazing and their boots on. Pirates want to feel the deck. Warriors search for the blaze of glory. Pirates take in the final peace.

She stood. "They have my daughter. I had no choice."

The redhead was a masthead, leaned against the capstan. The brunette ran her fouled hand through her friend and lover's blood-soaked red hair. Christine had fared well through the day.

She knew where attacks would be coming from. So even with the one act of a traitor, she had fought for and with the family. Her wounds would eventually heal. The treacherous heart… never.

One eye squinted hard, and the blood rolled out and down the cheek. Blake opened her eye. Her green searched the depth of the dark brown of the other. Her voice croaked in a whisper as she nodded.

"I figured as much." She tried to make a deep sigh. "We'll find her."

The brunette shook out her long black hair. The two could pass for twins, except for the color of their hair and the color and heights of their boots. She stooped and took up her short saber.

Stepping close, she leaned the point just left of her friend's breastbone. The tip dimpled the skin between the bottom and next rib. She leaned in close.

Blake took a long breath. "You know what will happen when you kill me."

Christine kissed her deeply and then gently. Her tears mixed with the blood from Blake's eyes. She pulled back only slightly.

"Yes, but it is not what you think will happen. Focus on my daughter. Focus on Noi. Take care of my girl."

The brunette drew back the sword slightly and then slipped the point in under the redhead's ribs. The blade sliced the heart in half—a metaphor of a broken heart.

Blake stiffened and then leaned forward and kissed Chris one last time. "We will see you soon."

The brunette's body shuttered with tears as she held the body of the redhead against the capstan and then let it gently slide to the deck. Her mind roared and then calmed. The searing storm hissed and then became calm. With luck, she knew Blake was now with her daughter—young, healthy, and in great shape.

Christine looked up at the angry sky. The incoming long-range helicopter could only be one person. She still had work to do.

She shook out her black hair, so it was loose down her back. She considered the weight of the lighter saber she had always used. She moved Blake's old heavier buccaneer saber about. She tested the balance in her hand and wrist. She smiled and rose as a tall man with long dark curls stepped out of the door and onto the deck.

He looked wistfully at the body of the redhead lying on the deck. "It was a good run."

Christine nodded. "She would have been two hundred and forty-seven years, next month."

Manny frowned at the brunette. "Blake?"

The dark hair shook sadly. "Still Christine in here—I sent Blake on ahead."

Hefting the sword, she smiled evilly as she nodded toward the settling helicopter. "Now, let's go kill us an immortal."

As they reached the lower deck, Christine pulled the cell phone from her back pocket. She smiled and showed the text to Manny.

"Here. Bad guy's dead. Love you. Blake & Noi."

01 Return to the Sea

DAYS OF DESPAIR are the spaces separating the times of excitement or thrilling terror. They are yards of bleached cloth on a dining table between past lovers and sworn enemies. They are the calm sea between two pirate ships becalmed off the Dry Tortugas. Running one's knife along the cloth is no more productive than stomping one's barefoot in the shallows. Both leave an ineffectual mark—quickly removed by movement—pulling the cloth or the next lap of water against your ankle.

Blake's head snapped up and scanned the knife-edge of darker blue separating the cool sea from an unruffled hot sky. Not even a bird disturbed the air.

Muttering a curse, she stomped on the sea and sand again. "Fuck. The gods hate me."

She looked down the beach at the approaching figure. Even at a distance, she knew she might not recognize the dark figure coming toward her—and yet the walk was certainly familiar and distinctive.

She ran her fingers through her deep chestnut mane. Looking over her shoulder, she considered pulling her knee-high boots back on over her leggings. At the moment—she missed her saber.

The man stopped a gentle throw of a knife away. His face was as animated as stone. With his whole palm, he wiped his brow up into his curly hair.

"I thought you were comfortable in the heat."

The man ignored her stab. With a sigh, he searched how to talk to this woman. "He still wants to talk to you, Miss…"

Her eyes rolled low. "I should have killed him when I had the chance." Blake's shoulders relaxed as she looked back down the other way to make sure they were alone on the beach. If this was the person she thought it was, she could trust him with her life—as she had many times in the past.

"You did, Miss. Four times… that I know of. The other seven were only almost…" He clasped his hands behind the small of his back as a small sidestep relaxed his stance. She knew he would never approach her with a hidden weapon—his position and honor would never allow it.

She looked back out to sea at the light sail on the edge. She let out a long breath and thought. "Tell me, Cole…" She turned to look at him. "It is still Cole, yes?"

He nodded slightly. His gaze passively attached to her.

She turned back to the sea as the small sailboat slipped over the horizon. "How old are you this time?"

"One hundred and seventy-four—or thereabout, Miss."

"Almost two centuries… and you still allow him to be your master." She looked back and stepped to the tall pirate boots folded on the sand. "Why is that, Cole?"

The man shrugged. "It works."

"So it has nothing to do with me killing you at Troy?"

He flattened his lips, noncommittal. "I was tired then. It became an easy arrangement."

"How many times have you two switched roles?"

The man took a shallow sighing breath. His eyes calmly closed in thought. "Not counting the crap you stirred up in Egypt… about five. Battling in the Roman Empire, we kept dying and switching. At times, it was confusing just keeping track of each other. Once he had to flow into a donkey." He knew he had overstepped as she started laughing. Finally, out of thousands of years of friendship, he allowed a thin smile. "It took us a month crossing the desert to find him a suitable human for him to flow into. He will probably never let me forget riding him for so long. Of course, a better map may have helped."

Blake smirked as she sat on the sand and pulled on her boots. "It's okay—he always was an ass. There was once hope for him, but then he killed his first wife and… well, you were there…" It was the first of few times Blake and Manfred were lovers or married. Few ever married another Ever Kind. They both knew there was only one way of ending the marriage… and murder was always messy—even in Mesopotamia.

She stood and brushed off the fine sand. "So what asinine crap does he want to stir up this time?"

"Other than pirates in the Pacific…?" The man smiled and shrugged. The muffled sound of trumpets broke the silence.

Blake snorted softly. "Why Cole, you learned to fart through a trumpet."

The man fished the phone out of his back pocket. "Pronto?"

He listened and then held the phone out to the woman.

She took it and thought a moment before raising it to her ear.

"Fuck you, Manfred—and the camel you were shit out of." She hung up and handed the phone back.

The man with the tribal lion scars on his cheeks smiled and stowed the phone. "Where will you head now?" They both knew he would find her anyway. The fifty score of Ever Kind around the planet always sensed where the others were.

Blake thought. "I've been away from the sea too long. I think I'll play around here for a while. If I see you soon, I'll kill you near a goat."

The man laughed at the old story from the early centuries of the Arab world. An Ever Kind died in a mantrap. The Ever Kind who dug the trap and set it had tethered a pregnant goat in the bottom of the pit. Upon dying, the Ever Kind in the trap had transferred or flowed into the nearby weakest mind—the unborn goat—and lived many years as the families favored milk goat.

"I'll give you a few months to become bored. I'll find you in October at Crane Beach on Barbados. Maybe you will be ready to listen then."

"Pirates in the twenty-first century… intriguing, but do we get to be the pirates—or hunting them?"

"I think he has in mind to hunt them by being the bait. With Manny, it is sometimes hard to understand—but I do know he has been bringing together a raft of catamarans in the Pacific."

Her one brow dented. "Cats? How big?"

"All the ones I have seen are double mast… about forty or fifty meters."

She thought about the unusual configuration and size.

"How large is this raft he is putting together?"

"The other day, he mentioned they were already over forty hectares." The man's cheeks glowed darker than his large toothy smile. Cole knew he had succeeded in sucking her in.

She pinched her mouth between her thumb and finger knuckle. It was more to prevent her from smiling and less about her doing the math. The thought of over sixty acres of ships rigged together at sea was beyond intriguing—pirates would just be frosting on the cake.

She dusted the sand off her butt and legs as she stood. She stepped to the tall black Nubian warrior and pinched his chin in her hand. They were eye to eye. "If I am not there yet—book my old residence. I want to see how these modern people can screw up a perfect set of rooms."

He didn't flinch. "Yes, Miss."

She released him and started to walk away. Turning back, she looked over her shoulder at the statue of a man in waiting. "And, Cole... if you don't bring Manny... I will find an ugly, three-legged, wether lamb to slaughter you over. Capiche?"

"Yes, Miss... Bring Manny or bring a three-legged wether."

"An ugly one... So ugly it hurts."

"Yes, Miss."

She laughed as she walked up over the sand dune to her car. *Who knows... this century could show some interesting possibilities.*

02 Grenada

THE JAIL REEKED from ages of urine, puke, and rotting bodies. The wall stones were cool and slippery as if washed with blood. Blake knew it was from the ocean—eighty-seven feet below. The storm surf pounding on the break rocks below had kept her awake most of the night.

A heavy breaker boomed up the stone cliff and rattled the lid covering the hole for a toilet. The air pressure lifted the lid as if a hand was crawling out. The air then whistled out of the small hole of a window set high in the wall. Blake knew if she counted a dirge marching cadence, the whole would repeat on the count of seventeen.

Three hundred years before, she was male—a free sailor. Her captain had been a gentle soul named Benjamin Hornigold. The man was fair. Some of his trials had lasted almost ten minutes while the crew argued over the man's fate. The menu consisted of keelhauling the sailor, hang him from the yardarm, or simply make him carry two cannonballs tied at his waist off the end of a plank extended over the open sea.

The day Blake and Hornigold had ended up in jail while suspended over the sea, the mutinying First Mate,

Edward Teach, put them ashore to be arrested. Teach took the ship and crew and set about making a name for him and the Bonnie. It wasn't long before the reports became stories and the stories became legends.

Young Edward became the most feared Pirate roaming the Caribbean. Even children safe in their nanny's arms in the center of jolly old England were terrorized by nightmares of being killed by the pirate Blackbeard.

Meanwhile, the now retired Hornigold and his cabin man, Blake Peele, lay about, imprisoned for unpaid taxes, stealing the mayor's wife and daughter, raising hell when in port, and for littering. The latter was of the bodies left strewn about the docks as the pirates massed a horrific sword fight to make their escape. Mr. Teach set on creating a massive diversion, broke anchor, turned downwind and let off a full broadside of cannonballs, grapeshot, and chain.

The city side of the banana docks had been slushed clear of standing men. Those pirates who could—rowed away. The two men left standing in the opening of the customhouse ended in the same dank room where Blake now sat watching the toilet seat once again shudder and flop.

The man who had saved them the first time was none other than the Federico Rotaño Esperanza Manfred, Viceroy of Venezuela and islands to the east of Grenada. His shoulder-shadowing campaign hat, cavalierly adorned with ostrich feathers dyed a repulsing pink, increased his stature. His velvet hat, doublet, pantaloons, and gloves countered in the color of hot blood. The ruffled blouse and stockings were pure silk from Cathay China.

Blake would have laughed at the dandy and his refinery, but the Ever Kind in him recognized the man as his first husband. The man had killed her on the shores of the river, near the Assyrian city of Nineveh eight thousand years before.

The Viceroy paid the hefty fine, promised bribes, and turned over the key to his superb apartments in the city. The mayor had long known about the apartments overlooking the profitable docks, which were the center of the Caribbean spice trade. He also openly lusted after the twin Valkyrie from the Dark Continent. The man held hope the two women would console him in the loss of his wife and simpering daughter.

The Viceroy had stood in the open doorway and said, "Will you be lying about all day? If not, it is time to set sail, cross seas, sink ships, and win some booty."

Hornigold was grateful for his release, but only wished to retire on Barbados. Manfred and Blake left the pirating to the wild new captivating Blackbeard. They knew there was more gold to be made by supplying ships and resupplying forts. They became an early crude form of the military-industrial complex. By the time they were powdering their wigs and drawing lines on their faces, they had their fingers on almost every ship sailing in, out, or on the Caribbean.

Blake notched the edge of her boot in the stone wall. She lay prone on the bed, such as it was. But with a mattress, it was better than the last time. She stared at the ceiling—two-person heights above.

The fort topped an old battery the French had built in 1600. Originally named Fort Royal, it quickly succumbed to the more common name after the capital city behind it—St. George. The jail cells perched half suspended over the boulders below needed no plumbing. The prisoners never complained. Moreover, if they did—nobody cared. There was always the second door if they did not like the accommodations. Lifting the whole seat provided a doorway of sorts to the direct drop to the rocks below. The fall took longer than a person repeating their name thrice over.

The main door to the set of three cells squealed open. Blake would have wondered about it being a little early for dinner, but then there had been no lunch served, either.

Bored, she picked at the cuticle on her left thumb. "I wish to speak to the Viceroy of Venezuela." She knew everyone on Grenada spoke enough English, but Viceroy was centuries outdated. She was bored.

A cane pushed at her shoulder. Blake rolled her head. She looked at the fat rubber tip and looked up the beaten and worn aluminum shaft. Seeing the old crone, she swung her legs over and sat up. She stared at the quietly waiting woman. There was something there. The old crone was Ever Kind, and yet...

The woman's rheumy eyes with milked cataracts rolled into the closing eyelids. The small hag sighed. Her voice was more of a croak than a human sound. "Are you going to lie about all day? There are sails to hoist, seas to cross, ships to sink, and booty to be won."

Not believing the person she was seeing, Blake rose gently. She didn't want to shake the dream, but she wanted a different perspective.

"Manfred...?"

The woman nodded as Cole came in from the anteroom. "All is taken care of, sir. And I must say, we need to depart before they invent more buildings the young Miss may have destroyed in her drunken state."

"I wasn't drunk. I had merely been drinking since—"

The old woman turned in her Chanel pantsuit. "Since two days before. Yes, we know. Now hurry along, dear. Our airplane waits, and the captain is antsier than Cole here."

Blake smiled at the sight of the medium-heeled pirate boots showing out of the bottom of the tailored suit. The block toe was the first giveaway. The sterling silver faux spurs were the second. The tiny woman was certainly Manfred. *This is a story I have to hear.*

She didn't have to wait long. True to the small woman's word, the engines were turning as the taxi pulled up beside it. One flight attendant stood in the doorway while the other waited at the bottom of the stairs. Blake took in the size of the jet. As she walked into the main cabin, she knew the area behind the separating wall of the jumbo jet would contain office space and bedrooms as well as the much-needed shower.

The small woman turned to the brunette flight attendant. "Please inform Captain Lewis he can depart when the tower allows, but we will be going to Los Angeles instead of Seattle."

"Which airport do you prefer?"

The woman pursed her lips. "Excellent question. Long Beach or Burbank will serve our purposes."

The flight attendant nodded and turned toward the stairs to the flight deck. Manfred turned and made her way toward the seating—and the bar. Blake watched and was almost certain the cane was more an affectation than a needed aide. The elderly woman may have been doddering before Manfred, but the effects of being the host of an Ever Kind were taking over. When they reached Los Angeles, the elderly body would be the woman she was five years ago.

As the flight attendants rose to attend the passengers, Blake rose and headed for the living quarters in the rear of the plane. She only hoped there would be enough water for a long shower—or they might need to make a water refill in Texas.

Blake had found the room she assumed was meant for her. The small closet held five lightly starched white pirate style shirts. The drawers contained a smattering of under-wear as well as a dozen black leggings. *Someone had done their research.*

She stood at the bar and splashed a couple of fingers of twenty-five-year-old scotch in the tumbler. She pulled an ice cube out of the bucket and swirled it twice around before throwing it in the garbage hole. She turned and evaluated the small woman sipping on a similar glass.

The woman smiled and put down her glass. "As I was crossing the street last year, I was struck by a bus. The woman I pushed to safety…" Her hands, turned up, passed down her sides. "I have found it has its upside as well. She was wealthy and well-traveled. Who else walks around San Francisco with their passport in their handbag?"

Blake snorted as she spread her arms and hands at the airplane. "Did the plane come as part of the package deal?"

"Um, no… this is mine. Or I should be more exact—ours." Her finger swirled, pointing out all three of them. "Well, actually, there are five in the corporation. The other two will be very quiet partners."

Blake raised an eyebrow slightly as she took another sip of her scotch. "Are they dead?"

"Oh, no, dear… they are also each one of us. They are

just doing other things to help our goals."

"And what exactly are our goals?"

Manfred stood. "You will have to excuse me. The bladder hasn't made much effort to adjust. Cole will continue."

Blake turned to Cole with the same raised eyebrow.

"He has since filled me in. If you would care to continue in the office, we can bring you up to speed."

An hour later, Blake swung around in the desk chair. "So, the short version is… we are building a giant raft in the middle of the Pacific to mine the garbage which has been collecting there since World War II." Manfred and Cole nodded. "So where is the pirate stuff? I didn't live for ten thousand years to become a dolphin garbage collector."

Manfred held up her two tiny hands. The osteoarthritis cocked her fingers severely. "Blake, Blake, Blake… If it was just a glorified garbage scow, sweeping the ocean for trash—I never would have devoted the last twenty years to developing the raft and all it can do." She leaned forward. "Look… what are you doing for the next twenty years?"

"I don't know…"

"How much of your life is twenty years spent on the ocean? Heck, we spent over sixty years terrorizing the Caribbean."

Blake's answer was muffled as she spoke into her glass. "Not much."

"Look, come out with us. See what we are doing. Spend a few months. If you don't find it worthwhile and maybe a little exciting—you can leave. I'll even sweeten the pot. If at any time you want to walk away, I'll deposit twenty million US dollars into any bank you want." Manfred leaned back into the chair and sipped her scotch.

"We part friends."

Blake looked at Cole. "Are you in on this also?"

The man nodded. "I brought this idea to him in the beginning. It's the right thing to do. We helped create the world that created the trash now floating in a giant swirl killing the living creatures and thus—the sea. We have a responsibility that supersedes the mortals. We alone possess the long view, and the long lives, to see the need and the balance of this kind of project."

"But… getting back to my original question—I get the nerdy science stuff—but where does the pirate stuff come in? Why do you need me?"

The older woman rolled eyes and head toward the only man in the room. "Cole…?"

The man shrugged his eyebrows and pursed his mouth. "You like killing people."

"Hey… I've only killed you two or three times. Where do you get off—"

He cut her off by pointing toward the tiny woman in the large armchair.

"Okay… but he doesn't count. We were married three of those times…"

The woman held up her tiny hand with the thumb curled in. "Four."

"What four?"

"We were married four times. You were so drunk on the bad date wine in Algeria, I didn't have the heart to tell you we had gotten married."

"Well, you didn't have to cut the head off the camel—"

"He spit in my face."

"He was our only ride out—"

Cole stood. "Enough."

The two froze with their mouths open. Cole never raised his voice.

"You two need to go take naps or something. Being killed is not the point. With us, it never is. It is the same as changing your pants or taking a different car." He turned back to Blake. "You have killed more of us than anyone else we know—except one."

She thought. "Jun."

Manfred and Cole nodded. "Jun."

Blake spat. "The biggest asshole in the world."

Cole nodded as the elderly woman rolled up on one butt cheek and farted. "The vote is unanimous."

"But what good does it do? If we kill an Ever Kind, he just flows into another body. Jun is Jun, always an asshole. He even made Genghis Khan look almost civil until he got crazy in the end… Oh, shit."

Manfred nodded. "Exactly, dear. Jun was a concubine and forced the Khan to kill her one night while they were in bed. After he had flowed into Genghis Khan, being the sick bastard he is, he had his sexual way with the dead body of the concubine."

Manfred sipped some scotch as she warmed up to the argument. "During the Boxer Rebellion, he went about beheading over a thousand peasants just to watch the blood fountain from the headless necks. He loved his job building the pyramids, but cracking a whip over the heads of the slaves wasn't enough—so he invented the flagella. It was centuries later, during the Inquisition, when he perfected it into the cat o' nine tails."

Blake held up her hand. "You don't have to tell me about Hitler—I was there."

Cole rolled his head and looked away at the ceiling. "Hmm, George should have learned a little more about building a bomb to fit in a briefcase."

"We only had so much time…"

"Children, children… What is past is past." Manfred sat forward. "But as you can see, Jun has that effect on all of us. Even a shark usually kills for food. But Jun is a sociopath or a psychopath—depending on how you look at it."

"Which… is the point, Manfred. There is no way to kill him permanently."

Manfred gently sat back into the chair as a smile grew on the old woman's face. Blake looked at Cole. The man had a smug smile on his face, and something she had never seen him display—his eyes were twinkling."

Her head snapped back to Manfred who was tossing back the last of her drink. "You figured out a way…"

"We're not positive, my dear. There is no way to try it out ahead of time… but yes, we think there is a way."

Blake looked back and forth at her two oldest friends. She knew whatever they planned—had been planned for a long time. Every detail thought out. Nothing, not a single item, was throwaway.

She swiveled a few times back and forth. With one final push of her boot on the desk, the chair made a rotation. Blake jammed both boots spread on the edge of the desk.

"And… that is why we are in the middle of the ocean."

The other two nodded softly.

Cole stood. Grabbing the bottle, he poured a finger into each of the three glasses. The other two stood, and Blake came around the desk.

They stood facing one another. Glasses of scotch hovered an inch apart. Blake smiled and raised her glass and tipped it in toward the others. "Here is to pirates and the spirit which binds us."

Three glasses clinked as the airplane engines slowed—preparing for the descent into Los Angeles—world's largest pirate den.

03 Too Hot for LA

BLAKE LEANED CLOSE to Cole's ear. The beat of the music was tribal and too loud. "This is the fourth male strip joint. What the hell is she up to?"

The quiet warrior shrugged his eyes and nodded his head toward the tiny old woman with the cane.

Blake admitted the taste in clothes was exquisite—and so—Manfred. Only he would luck into a body with exquisite taste in clothing. She may be old—with a worn out body—but still, an exquisite wardrobe. Before they had landed, the woman ditched the international look of Chanel for the younger, more hip, west coast look of Vera Wang.

The old woman stamped her cane and smiled like a gibbon monkey drunk on fermented bananas. The general appearance of the three said young couple takes crazy demented great-aunt out on the town for her to relive her burlesque days. Blake knew different—Manfred never indulged in trivial activities. Manfred was up to no good or was preparing for a very interesting evening.

Blake leaned back in her chair. Either way, she knew eight thousand years of friendship couldn't be wrong. She was all the way in on whatever was going to happen.

She turned to look back at the bar to see if there was a waitress or waiter for a drink. The slight movement gave her pause. In the dim light with strobe laser flashes slicing the air, she had to squint to see the change. There was now a thin gap between Manfred's back and the chair back. Blake's head ground around to follow the small woman's view.

The curtains on the left stage had just parted, and a figure stood in silhouette. The stance was familiar to all three. The legs spread to shoulder distance. The hands rested on the hips. The turnover of the boots at the knees they had all worn. The hat spread out to almost the edges of the broad shoulders. A single ostrich feather flew fluffy out the back.

Blake sat up and leaned forward. If the stage lit up and the man had a full thick black beard, he would pass for Edward Teach reincarnate.

The body swayed and swaggered forward. The movement spoke of sea legs. Three sets of eyes burned through the murky room.

A single spot hit the stripper. The baby-faced blond looked like he was a Navy recruit fresh out of boot camp with his last cheap haircut.

The old woman spat in disgust. "Bugger." She stood and glared at the other two. "So ends the night. I need to get drunk on much better scotch than they have here."

The livery car idled a few yards from the two large bouncers. Manfred had commented upon their arriving, "All steroids, and no brains."

The three stepped out of the doorway and looked about. Their driver threw his cigarette into the street and opened the back door of the limousine. Silently, the three looked about on the street and then entered the car.

The driver put up the separating glass as he started the car. Smooth as a boat leaving a dock, the car eased into traffic.

Blake turned on the small woman brooding in the other corner. "What the hell was all that about?"

The small head ground around and weighed the redhead. "My dear… have you never gone shopping for your next body? It may be crass, but I damn sure do not plan to resort to the nearest three-legged dog humping a child's ball in some front yard. And… I do have my standards when it comes to hair. Poof boy may look great selling butter or axle grease… but I doubt he could strike fear into an enemy or inspire a crew to defend an ethereal ideal. That, my dear, will take just the right look."

Manny sat a bit straighter in order to look out the side window. Her voice took on a wispy flavor as she addressed the glass as much as the other occupants of the backseat. "Besides, there is always tomorrow."

04 How About a Little Romance?

BLAKE FELT MORE than heard the wheels lock into flight position. She considered rolling over and sleeping another year or two, but curiosity got the better of her. As she pulled on her leggings, she cursed about being only a passenger instead of a bridge officer.

As the white tunic shirt fell down over her shoulders and stuck on her breasts, she realized it was the body Manfred was in she resented. It was old. It was tiny. It was frail. Everything she always knew or thought about Manfred—this body was not.

A tall blonde stewardess she had not seen before walked past as Blake opened her cabin door. The woman was muscular but moved in an athletic way.

"Breakfast is set out in the boardroom, Miss."

"Cole?"

The blonde turned only slightly. "I heard the shower earlier, but I haven't seen him yet. But Ms. Manfred said he might be sleeping late this morning. They were up late last night working."

Blake closed one eye and leaned against the bulkhead. "Okay, thanks. And, um, Ms. Manfred is…?"

"In the office, Miss."

Blake turned right toward the office. *Answers before food.*

The small, impressively dressed woman lounged at the desk. Blake recognized the summer chemise blouse as high dollar Jones of New York. The slipper shoes, showing almost no wear on the blood-red heels, lay crossed on the corner of the desk.

"No, dear, I do not intend to be patient. We have lavishly upholstered your bank account in the Caymans, Switzerland, and the one you thought the IRS didn't know about in Croatia. If you want them to remain private, along with the other three… or for your wife not to meet your other wives in two other countries I can think of off the top of my head—"

She was cut off but listened. She held up one tiny finger.

"Mr. Isley, I can assure you we have never resorted to threats or blackmail. However, we do expect certain professionalism in what people promise and what they produce. I am only explaining what information we can prove to be true. How we use the information is another matter if we are not delivered what we paid for when promised."

She lowered her eyelids in a facial growl.

"Yes, Mr. Isley. Tuesday would be an acceptable day to come tour our two boats. And we have our own livery in Seattle, so sending a car will not be necessary. Good day, sir." She pulled her feet off the desk as she tapped on the bud in her ear.

She rose, glanced at the paperwork on the desk, and turned back to Blake. She smirked with a satisfied smile. "I'm hungry. Shall we go dine?"

"Hmmm… Said the cat that just emptied the birdcage."

"Our two last boats are nine days late."

They entered the boardroom to find Cole in shorts and bent over the food. Blake had never seen the man without a shirt or long pants. The tiny keloid scars created patterns covering his entire body and down his legs, as well as most of his arms. She stopped to study the effect of the lighter skin pattern on his deep blue-black skin.

Manfred stopped and looked up at Blake. "You've never experienced Cole in all his glory, I take it."

Cole turned around with one eyebrow raised. "Enjoy it while you can."

Blake's head ground slowly askew. "Exactly how many bodies are we shopping for?"

"Two… now." The blonde sidestepped around Blake and continued toward the food. She looked back with a smile. "You never were good at this, were you, Samir?"

Blake stood stunned by a name she had not used for over two millennia. "Kanu?"

The woman poked the tip of her nose. "It was Estelle for the last… um… five or six hundred years?" She frowned at Cole in askance.

"Don't look at me. I was only El Cid's manservant, and nobody would kill me near him. Such a waste of good man meat…" The man sighed and forked up some roast beef to his small mound of eggs.

Manfred stood with her feet and cane forming a triangle. Others may have taken the stance as patience, but Blake knew it to be exactly the opposite.

Blake hung her thumbs in her wide belt and gently wing-nudged the older woman with her right elbow. Then she nodded her head forward. "Go on. You've been at it longer than I've been awake." The woman moved as Blake looked back up at the stewardess. "So it sounds like you changed hair color and are ready for a new name as well."

The blonde turned and took in the storm brewing in the face of the small woman. She stepped back and picked up her glass of juice—nodding Manfred in at the food. "This body had a great name, so I'll just keep using it. Besides, I've always had a soft spot for goat cheese and other soft cheeses."

As she passed, Blake read the small brass nametag— Brie.

Blake chased the spoon around the glass for the last of her fruit, nuts, and yogurt mix. "So there will be how many of us on the raft?"

"Ever Kind? Six on the raft, but there are seven more, elsewhere about the world."

"That is a lot of effort just for cleaning up the world."

Brie looked up from the bowl of fruit salad. "Didn't you tell her about Jun?"

Manfred pursed her lips and paused. "Some... she knows we are planning to kill him."

"So she doesn't know why she is here." The blonde sat down while sucking the fruit juice from her left hand as her right undid the scarf holding her hair.

Cole rumbled a low growl. "We were upfront with her. She's here because she's an exceptional sailor, as well as superior with a sword."

Brie shook her hair out about her shoulders. "Did they explain we could be facing thousands of south sea pirates? Did they explain we could easily be outnumbered fifty-to-one if things do not go right? Did Manfred mention you could end as a fish?" She faced Blake. "Did he explain the nuclear bomb?"

Blake stared at the blonde. Her face was passive and examining. The other was hard and burning. The other two recognized the old bad blood and were silent. Bad blood with Ever Kind could boil for hundreds of years and then one day ignite, and burn hot for seconds and then be gone. It was the way of their kind. *For everyone but Jun.*

Blake gently leaned back into her chair. "You never forgave me for killing you over the back of the young ewe, have you?"

Brie softly buzzed her lips. "It wasn't the first time I had been fucked in the ass or stabbed in the back. I guess it was the few years you spent milking me to feed the children—children you'd hidden from me…"

"You would have only molested them like you did me." The accusation was as hard as old stone. But the heat was the ashes of last winter's hearth.

Brie's hard face held and then broke into a wan smile. "You did keep me in the better pasture." Brie held her hand out, palm up.

Blake leaned forward and bounced the bottom of her fist in the palm. The two smiled—it was done.

"So you're good with all this?" Brie swirled her finger as if stirring coffee.

"I get to sail, I get to work, and I get to kill a bunch of nasty pirates—what's not to love?"

Manfred and Cole laughed softly as the blonde shook her head. "God, you must have loved the Viking era."

"I was with Leif. We mostly did hard sailing. But, yeah, it was a time of high testosterone. It didn't compete with the time of stupid tin cans coming down to Jerusalem, though. That… was a great time of killing." As the plane touched down, Blake turned to Manfred. "So, we've had breakfast. Where are we and what is on the agenda for lunch?"

"Denver and we are going to a book convention. If you behave yourself, I might just take you out to the Brown Palace Hotel for lunch." Manfred dropped a paperback on the table in front of Blake.

The cover was the usual torchy image for a bodice-ripper romance. Blake snorted. Romance now was code for soft porn—and depending on the writer—not so soft. She picked up the book. The title was Pirate's Passion. The red haired woman was in a white dress—more Hollywood than seventeenth century. Her large breasts were falling out of the ultra low cut neckline. It was standard fair… except for the pirate.

Blake pulled the book closer. The black wavy hair over a closely cropped goatee framed smoldering dark eyes. A rugged, chiseled face and rippling naked-to-the-waist body matched the perfectly tailored pantaloons disappearing into the knee-high boots. He was a perfect likeness of the young pirate in the Caribbean who had stolen her heart.

She looked up at the tiny elderly woman. All she could see was the pirate. Then her mind started thinking about the young captain who had commanded the Queen's barge on the Nile. The mental catalog of Manny flowed through her head. The rugged captain of the Byzantine warship, the close-cropped beard, but the flowing hair of the commander of Alexander the Great's fleet—Manfred had almost never changed. Blake never realized Manfred shopped as much for his new body as he did for his clothes.

She picked up the book and hefted it in the air. "And this author will be at this convention…?"

"As will the models making special appearances—for fans to pay money to pose with." Manfred smiled lustfully. On the pirate—it had been sexy, but on the small, elderly woman, it looked almost perverted. "After all, a pirate is a pirate, and we are all mercenaries."

THE CONVENTION HADN'T disappointed. The Saturday sessions of authors hawking their books, thinly veiled as engaging in a discussion panel, started at nine. The vendor room didn't open until eleven. Fans clutching books for autographs jammed the halls with fanatics dressed as their favorite characters.

The foursome walked in a tight group to protect the tiny, frail woman. None of them had taken up protective positions consciously; it was an ingrained reflex after centuries of war and battle.

Two zombies with machetes in their heads walked passed. Blake looked back at the couple in matching clothes and blades. Only their hair and body types belied them being male and female. They were holding hands and had the *walking together in love* look about them.

She turned back, musing more to herself than anyone in general. "When did zombies become a romance genre?"

Manfred snorted. "After vampires became sexy teens sprinkling in the sunlight."

Brie growled. "I think the term is sparkle. Deer, squirrels, and skunks sprinkle in the sunshine."

Cole never flinched but kept scanning the crowd. "They and the genre just need to be dead."

Blake remembered a story told one drunken night a few centuries before. "Ah, Cole, you're not still pissed off about Vlad putting you up for the night... or month, are you?"

"How and where he rammed the spikes was just rude. Very, very rude."

Manfred stopped as she scanned an area of writers. "Cole is just mad he didn't die fast enough to take over Vlad's body. Jun had paid a mercenary to get them close to the monster and then cut of Jun's head. As the body fell, Vlad—now Jun, turned and eviscerated the mercenary."

"There is just no honor in that asshole's spirit."

Manfred held up her hand. As one, they realized the woman taking her seat at the table was the woman on the back of the book. The doublewide banner behind her was an eight-foot tall poster of the book's cover art. The four moved as one with Manfred in the lead.

"Hello, may I help you? We aren't really signing for another half hour... but..." Even successful authors are hungry.

Manfred stuck her white gloved hand out. "Gwyneth Doubleday Manfred, Sidda Lee Rains told us you would be here a little early. I hope you don't mind."

"Sidda?" She squealed. "I love Sidda. She is such a nasty girl. She almost makes me want to go tour the pro bull rodeo thingy." She caught herself as she started to pant. "Um... How can I help you?"

Manfred smiled sweetly at the woman's gushing. "Yes, well, we have a business offer for you."

"I'm already under contract..." She hinted that for the right price, an arrangement could be possible. She twirled at her hair—possibly an aftereffect from referencing the other author.

"This will not affect your contract with them in any way. This is about… well… today. More specifically, right now. It has to do with your male model."

"Ernesto? What about Ernesto?"

Cole stepped up. "There were certain indiscretions… the authorities are aware he is appearing here today. We would like to head off any public embarrassments to you or the convention."

"What my associate is delicately trying to say is the man is wanted for questioning. The case involves underage young men, a goat, a donkey, and a kangaroo stolen from the Denver zoo. They were… hum… found in a hotel suite. We need to talk to him right now."

The woman blinked at the tall blonde dressed in a cheap pantsuit that would pass for FBI or the underpaid detective new to the job and female. "Oh my…"

Minutes later, the four stood outside room 341. Manfred knocked gently.

The door swooshed open as the man in a black European bikini brief stood talking on the phone. "… I told you I need them now. Without the costume, I am not the pirate. Comprende?" He took in the foursome. "Who the hell are you?"

Manfred gently planted her cane in the man's navel and pushed. "We are the ones who will be controlling the rest of your glorious career, Señor Romero."

The man stumbled back as he mumbled into his cell phone. "Get me the clothes or you're a dead man." He turned off the phone.

"Who the hell are you again?"

Manfred patted the air. "Please, take a seat, and I will

explain." As she sat down, she removed a small vial from her pocket.

Cole stepped to the sliding glass door leading to the veranda. Leaning over the rail, he noted the enclosure for the large dumpsters. The parking lot was large as well. Brie joined him. She pulled a small child's toy from her inside breast pocket. They both smiled.

Cole stepped into the room as Manfred was describing a new life of international largess for the model. Cole nodded once. Manfred opened the vial and raised it to her mouth. "Excuse me. It is time for my medicine." She drank the poison and screwed the cap back on. Cole took the vial and wiped it clean with a tissue as he returned to the veranda.

Handing the clean vial still wrapped in the tissue to Brie, the woman gripped the two in the leather pocket of the slingshot. Drawing it back, she sent the vial well past the parking lot as the tissue fluttered to the garbage enclosure.

They stepped back into the room as the elderly woman shuddered one last time.

Manfred stood and strode to the mirror. Finger flipping his long black wavy locks, he nodded. He turned and leaned back against the counter. "Well... all we have to do now is to wait for the clothes to arrive."

Blake was incredulous. "You aren't going to go pose for *that* woman are you?"

He waved the notion away. "Of course not, my dear. But you don't expect me to waste perfectly fine clothes, do you?"

"What about the body?" She pointed at the expired shell.

"Well, you know… an elderly admirer with a weak heart." Manfred smoothed down his body with the backs of his hands. "She got too close to her dream of a dalliance with this body and… well… you see the results."

Cole responded to the knock on the door. He took the cleaning from the man's hand. "You were late. No tip."

The plane was wheels up three hours later. Lunch at the Brown Palace had been as good as promised and almost as lavish as when Blake had sung there in 1873.

05 Puget Sound Training

BLAKE FOUND THREE weeks of book learning about how the six different configurations of the ships worked, torturous enough. The two months of sea trials to learn how the strange craft worked had become hell.

Blake rubbed the back of her head and the inserted implants. The three inserted devices worked in concert and became undetectable radio communications powered by their own bodies. Training the commlinks, and the people hosting them, had their funny moments as well as embarrassing ones.

Just thinking Manfred's name and visualizing his face caused the link to open from her side. Twenty miles away, and battling his own ship in the storm, Manny finished the link by saying her name.

"Damn it, Manny. This whore is bucking and sputtering like she's about to scuttle."

"They designed the cats for this weather. This is only a Category 4 gale. They're guaranteed to ride out a hurricane or typhoon, as well as a Cat-5 storm. Did you run out the gimbals after you retracted the pins?"

"Fuck…" Blake jumped to the other console. The pins

showed red—still in place and stressed. They still held the entire one hundred sixty-eight feet of the hull as a single unit.

"What? Blake, what is wrong?"

She growled at having forgotten the strangest part of the large sailboat. She forced her mind to go blank and see only white. "White." The radio connection ended.

She yelled at the two crewmembers on the bridge as she hit the large red button. "Pulling pins, prepare to push gimbals…" Six red lights turned green. "Now."

"Set one… extended. Set… two… extended. Set three… we have all green lights."

The small Asian woman with her arms outspread—bracing herself stoically—never moved her head as she read the monitors. "Mast one—coming back up to speed. Mast two—stable but still at forty percent—she's showing bearing heat. The upper vanes are being pushed harder. I think they're torqued."

"Feather two, what's number three doing… I can feel heavy vibration behind my left foot."

"It reads twelve percent, but it is constant. I think its shot."

Blake turned toward the bald Norwegian. "Damn it, Erik, I want visuals." She pointed at the six dark gray monitors. She knew the one wave had taken out three of the cameras on servo arms, but the other six squatted in small protective domes.

The man's fingers struggled to dance over his three keyboards as he tossed about.

Without saying a word, Erik's right arm and index finger shot out. No words necessary—they both knew where the door was.

You don't like it—go look for yourself.

At the last second, Blake remembered the harness.

The webbed tether pulled straight as she blew down along the side of the bridge. She caught the capstan at the end of the small building. Her muscles screamed in the howling wind. She hugged the capstan and worried her way around until she could see the tall mast. The blades running up the entire height of the masts were the sails. They should have been moving. The center mast was also the core of a generator. The blade cylinder was a field—rowed with rare earth magnets. The spinning bladed mast created an eighty-foot tall generator. Besides powering the controls, it also powered the electric motors driving the screws. The ship was a wind-powered hybrid.

The straight blades were a stationary corkscrew.

"Manfred."

The man's voice was calm. "I lost a mast. How are you doing?"

"I'm lying out here on the fantail enjoying a nice rum spritzer in this balmy weather." Blake marveled at the clarity of their conversation. She was barely able to hear herself over the storm, but she knew the inserts were picking up her voice from inside her head broadcasted through the skull.

"My remote shows your speed has dropped off drastically. How are your sails?"

"Well, the forward mast is holding its own. Number two is torn sheets in a dogfight." Blake looked up at the sound of metal tearing. "And number three... just sailed over my head." *So much for drag.*

"Wait... did you just say over your head? Where the hell are you?"

"I told you. I'm lounging about on a deck chair on the fantail."

"But you—"

"Look, Manny. I love you dearly, and you know I love having long stupid chats with you. But could you please be a dear? Call Erik and ask him to come pull me the fuck back in."

Manfred had not hung up, and Blake could hear him calling her ship. A moment later, the door cracked open, and two of the larger crewmembers pulled her toward the door.

"Thank you, Manny. We're going to hunker down, and we'll talk after this shit blows out."

Blake squinted to see the second mast through the storm. The gray pillar was there, but she could not make out if the vanes turned or not.

She pushed off from the capstan only to be blown back. A chunk of something hit her on the left shoulder. She spun to catch the noose made from thick rope. The one crewman was pantomiming to pull it over her shoulder— easy for him to say.

She thrust the harness line they held taunt. Letting the wind blow her stationary against the capstan, Blake wormed her head and one arm into the noose. As the noose took up slack and began to pull, she hooked her left leg around the thick rope. She sat down in the calmer wind of the deck and let the noose drag her.

Blake's eyes closed. The scene in her mind was over three hundred years before. The ship was coming apart piece by piece as the hurricane picked at it like a turkey after dinner. The rum was the warm sea—whipped into the air and slapping everything standing. The after dinner conversation was the howling wind. The Vendetta had been a good ship. Its two courses of cannons had provided them with ample caskets of booty—coin, bullion, and finished goods. The ruby necklace, meant for the Queen of Spain, she had worn for over fifty years. The deep ruby complemented the highlights in her dark hair and the color of choice of her boots.

The regular soles of boots didn't work on the high-tech deck she now slipped across. Manfred had said nothing as she originally stepped aboard. Three steps on the stable deck in dry-dock had found Blake on her ass. She scowled up at a laughing Manfred. The man pointed to his new deck shoes, which looked more like the high-top basketball shoes an NBA star would wear.

The company representative had explained the deck. Its design shed everything unapproved—water, oil, trash, as well as boarding parties with the wrong shoes. The soles of their shoes were just as high-tech as the deck. They not only didn't slip on the deck, but the two were in a constant struggle to bond with each other. She had made the mistake of standing at the rail for over an hour one day. Her feet almost came out of the lace-up shoes before they finally broke the bond.

The wind swirled off the side of the cabin and started to blow Blake away from the door path. She jammed her right heel on the deck and pivoted to the left. Two arms reached out of the doorway and grabbed at her wrists. As Blake also grabbed at their wrists, they dragged her over the step lip and into the calm of the bridge.

The manual winch's legs were stabbed into the holes gridded everywhere on the decks. They appeared to be round pieces of eight, but stick a rod into them, and the hole is six-inches deep and set in the metal composite crossbeams of the ship. Little of the equipment was stationary, and everything else used the holes. Once in, the automatic gripping takes over. Manfred warned her not to stick a finger in the holes—Ever Kind cannot regenerate body parts.

A couple of days later, the two catamarans rafted together. Manfred's cat was acting as the propulsion or a sailing tug.

"What the hell, Manfred. A shakedown cruise is one thing. Getting our ass ripped open by an arctic whore of a hurricane is another story."

The two stood at the edge of a gash sliced from the mast disappearing in the storm. The gaping hole was twenty feet wide and ran the forty feet to the pod separation. They looked out along the tear and mangled second mast.

"Got any ideas on the masts?" Manfred looked shyly out the side of his eyes at his occasional partner of many millennia. His acknowledgment of her being the better sailor had always been unabashed. Male or female body never influenced her as a sailor or as a pirate.

"Erik was explaining how they work while we waited out the storm. I get how you can sail even tighter into the wind than on a regular cat sail, but I still think there is some mystical magic going on."

"But apart from my special relationship with Poseidon or Neptune…?"

"Poseidon is the ocean, asshole. We're talking about the wind." She slugged him in the arm, but not hard. "But we thought of separating the vanes into ten-foot lengths. If one segment froze or got damaged, the other segments would continue to rotate."

She pointed at the twisted mast in front of them. "The reason number two obliterated was from a jam occurring in the bottom five feet. The high winds on the other seventy-five feet of vanes simply twisted it out of shape. If we divided the mast, only the bottom ten feet would freeze. The other parts would still spin normally. Also, the winds on the deck are not the same speed as those at forty or eighty feet higher. So if the pieces could spin independent of one another—"

"Everything would move at its own speed." Manfred smiled as he gently punched back at her shoulder. "We need to get that—"

"Erik is drawing up the preliminary CAD work as we speak. He'll send it ahead so they can start doing the engineering."

Manfred nodded with a half-smile. "He's a good man. Maybe a raise would be in order."

Blake growled. "I told him if he had it done and sent by dinner, I wouldn't whip him for at least a few days."

"How kind of you... It's almost like you're getting soft in your old age."

"Hmm, times change..."

06 A Raft in the Ocean

BLAKE STOOD IN the middle of the large deck on top of the bridge. It was one of the few areas set aside for nothing but exercise, pirate style. Blake had spent the last hour since dawn, sparing with rapiers and sabers with Cole. Even with the cool north Pacific temperature, her sports bra and leggings were drenched with sweat.

The side of the large container ship slowly edged closer. The electromagnet grappling lines had been shot out to the steel hull when the ship was a hundred feet away. The square mile raft of catamarans was slowly pulling the ship in. Along several hundred feet of the raft, large inflatable bladders, called muffins, were flipped over the side, and inflated. These would allow the two floating vessels to be tied harmlessly together.

"Does this feel like the day you commanded the tiny French barquentine off Barbados…?"

Blake snorted. "*Madre d'Cristo*, Manny." She turned to scowl at the man approaching in just his pants. "My barque carried a double line of cannons. She was no tiny skiff in the water. You just got lucky when you shot away my main mast."

He smiled at the verbal fencing that marked their relationship since she had burned her fleet on the shores of Troy. He had scoffed at the construction of the giant horse on wheels, chiding how the armies within the gates were not children to be fooled with a toy.

He handed her a new saber. It was an identical match to his. "You have to admit, the twenty berserkers on the swing-lines was a nice touch."

She hefted the sword in her hand—assessing the balance and weight. "But it is so hard to find good berserkers these days." She held up the sword. "Nice weight… but the balance is slightly off. I would prefer the balance to be on the hand side of the pommel instead of the outside."

Manny switched swords. He held the blade straight up and struck the pommel in his off palm. He weighed it and repeated the movement. Handing it back, he explained, "When you want the weight at your index finger for perfect balance, move the internal weight. But as you fight and need the weight out toward the blade, the natural swing will push it out."

"The weight is in the handle?"

"No, the weight is a four-inch rod of depleted uranium concealed in the tang. You get all the fighting weight dynamics of a three-pound Great Sword but in this lighter saber. The two-pound weight makes you faster and more nimble."

She swung it through the air in a series of fast eights. "It didn't shift…"

"It won't until you start hitting something." His hand swung out and around, spinning his body in an arch that would decapitate her. His blade met her blade rising to an upright post. His right foot stepped back into the dance where he started but with his blade now swinging swiftly toward her right knee.

The silver sheared through the air as the heel of her right boot connected with his jaw. He stumbled back laughing. "You learned well."

"I had the best teacher." Her upper sweep crashed against his blade and guard. She could tell it had been a while since he had to use both hands in holding a sword steady against a hit.

"I'm flattered." He spun his blade back and over the top toward her right shoulder.

"Don't be… it was Constantine the Unger." She parried the sword strike out as the tip of her blade landed on the hollow at the base of his neck. "Are there any pregnant goats on board?"

They both laughed at the original meeting of Manfred and Cole. Manfred did not like being the family's milk goat for fourteen years, but he had come to accept, and then like, the kind treatment from the family and young girl. When the goat stopped producing milk, the father killed it. Manfred had taken over the man's body. A border war had broken out, and Cole had begged Manfred to kill him so he could take a warrior's body.

Manfred could not bring himself to kill the young woman who had cared for him as a goat. Instead, he cut her hair, bound her chest, and taught him to fight as a young man. Cole did well and survived for many years as Manfred's man at arms. But as Manfred was first to admit, it was Cole who took bodies that would bring him into war, or at least battle. Of all the Ever Kind, Cole was the consummate swordsman and warrior.

As the two stood laughing, with a sword to the one

throat, coils of thumb thick rope hit them.

They looked up at the figure leaning over the rail of the ship. She raised her hand and arm and then clenched her fist and pulled her arm down.

Manfred stooped to find the end of the rope. He fed the end into one of the pieces of eight covered holes. At the sound of the click, he stood and shook the rope. It hauled up onto the ship. A moment later, the woman with a backpack swung over the rail and zipped down the taught rope. Hitting the deck, she stooped and pushed on the end into the deck. The clench released, she cast the rope back at the ship, and it disappeared up and over the rail.

The blonde saluted. "Permission to board?"

"It is always good to have you, Brie." The three shook and turned toward the gangway. Manfred looked back at the two women examining the new sword. Manfred continued as he walked. "Cutting edge technology makes it forty percent lighter than steel, and the insert edging will hold a cutting edge twice as long as A-4 held to 64-Rockwell. The weight changes from in your hand to just past the guard, or Riccaso. I have yours in the office."

THE REMAINS OF an extensive breakfast lay about the table. Cole had gone to supervise the last of the docking and beginning of the repair work.

"Does the ship contain all of the new masts?" Blake brought her legs up into the chair and crossed them.

Brie shook her head as she took a sip of coffee. "No, the rest are about a week or so behind us. They are doing the final construction as they sail. The ship is a decommissioned submarine supply ship. We bought it with the full machine shop and fabrication facilities intact. As they affect final assembly, they push them out and onto the top deck. Once they are standing on-station, this ship can crane their masts over and insert them into the cats. The supply ship will also be able to machine any of the heavy parts we might need for the raft or any of the sub-cats."

Manny put down the roll he had been nibbling on. "You guys made good time. Last I checked, we were at least a month out from smelting all of the metals we've farmed."

Brie nodded. "They are still smelting, but the supply ship is also bringing a new solar smelter. It's the one Olaf has been working on over at the university. He also sent more canisters for the mercury. He said you hit a pocket or something?"

Manny leaned back with his coffee mug wrapped in both hands. "There was a Category 3 gale which tore up the area southwest of the Kenai Peninsula. We were sweeping for metal items, which may have come from the Fukushima area. When the two teams ran the catching walls back out, they noticed a lot of mercury coming in from the sensors. They shortened the walls for a tight one-mile sweep and ran through the area putting out the most hits with the aiming floats."

Blake frowned and raised her hand. "Okay, I'm the new girl in the class... but... aiming floats? Catching walls?"

Manny smiled with the right side of his mouth. As long as Blake had known him—through many lives, many bodies, and both sexes, the one-sided smile was pure Manny. It was the one show Manny had that gave away his having fun. "Remember back in the sixties—"

The two women laughed. "Which century…?"

"Fair enough… the last century. Specifically, Santa Barbara. If I remember right, you were running a bar for the unsavory side of society."

Blake nodded with a half-grin of her own. "The Rat's Patoot. One of the drilling rigs had a massive leak."

Brie scowled. "Fucked up the beaches for several years… The surfers were getting pink eye, scaly rash, and something which is still around today, the Pacific cough… or Surf lung."

Manny pointed at both women. "To contain the oil slick, someone ran out miles of swimming pool lane marker floats. It worked so well a company in Houston started building a larger version. I think there was a California company who built the soft foam ones strung with twenty-foot flexible beads."

Brie snorted. "The kids at the swimming pools call them worms."

Manny pointed and winked. He shook his long wavy hair as he leaned forward. "We took the idea and expanded on it. The problem with what we are trying to round up is it's not on the surface—for the most part.

"Eighty percent of it does hang in the top twenty feet below the surface. We don't need to be perfect—just half-assed perfect. For our purposes, we'll settle for gathering half to sixty percent. In a few years, we might get back and get sixty of what is left."

Blake sipped her coffee and thought. "So the walls are sort of like fishing net?"

"More than similar… in fact, they are very much like a net. The big difference is the pattern, and how the net actually works." Brie held up her left hand and made a circle with the finger and thumb. "A net for fish is a lot of squares, which are basically smaller than the fish you are trying to catch. The krill and small fish get away by passing through the holes. What we want is for all the fish to pass through, but the tiny pieces of trash to be caught."

Blake lowered on eyebrow. "You want to catch the tiny stuff and let the big fish through… and do you have a bridge to also sell me?"

Manny put his mug down. "It's true. Like you, I was also a skeptic—until I swam through the test net."

"You swam…?" She laughed. She was picturing a wizened up old lady in a wetsuit flailing at the water. She started pantomiming what it must have looked like.

Brie got the giggles and Manny growled. "I had a better suited body back then."

Brie nodded as she controlled herself long enough to blurt out, "He was a dolphin…"

Blake roared as Manny sulked. "Bottle-nosed or pink?"

Manny spun in his chair. "Children…" He didn't get up and leave. Blake knew he was laughing silently. She studied her coffee because every time she made eye contact with Brie, it set off another wave of giggles.

"Come on, Manny… tell me how it works. If I'm going to spend the next fifty years out here, I want to know what I'm doing."

Brie coughed into her hand. "Hundred."

Blake looked at her in question.

"A hundred years… maybe more like two. We really fucked up the ocean this last century. Plastics are only the white tip of the Pacific Garbage Patch's toxic iceberg."

Manny gently pushed his chair around to face Blake. "She's right. The general bleeding-heart, chest-pounding, whiners have a concept in their minds, which is woefully misleading. They would paint an image of a large island of milk jugs, water bottles, grocery story baggies, and leftover Barbie dolls swimming in and out of colorful plastic play forts. All of which would be the size of a supersized Texas or Alaska—depending on which doomsday speaker you are listening to and how much money they expect to fleece from your person."

He raised his mug to his face and realized he had already drained it. "In any case, the concept is close but wrongfully distant from the truth. The area of the swirling mass is more in the neighborhood of Australia. The island of plastic is not of bottles, although many are here, but instead, shattered tiny pieces the size of the nail on your little toe. In a cubic meter, there may be suspended a child's handful of these pieces."

Blake's mind raced ahead. "But at seven meters deep, and spread over the three-million square kilometers… there are a lot of children with their hands full."

Manny soberly bobbed his head. "This is just the shattered plastic. We have found large sections of floating docks, small boats, a half-submerged high-end Mercedes-Benz car, huge quantities of floats, boat bangs, buoys, wooden furniture, a roof, containers such as thermoses and welding tanks. Last week, a team found a nicely carved king-sized bed."

Brie giggled. "Were the occupants still asleep?"

07 Jessie and the Gold

THE TORTOISE MUNCHED methodically on the thin roll of kale and bib lettuce. He chewed contentedly as if he had an eternity to finish the one meal. Blake studied the brown boxes on the shell. All of the squares glowed from attention, no obvious old dried scale showing. Each square was a soft muted dance of light to dark browns. Of all the tortoiseshell jewelry, glasses, desk accessories, and fine boxes she had owned or worn over the last thousand years, this singular tortoise was what all those shells had aspired to be.

Manfred pushed his hand forward another inch. The reptile finished swallowing and took another bite of the offered roll. The man's chin rested on his left hand, which was flat on the table. It was as if the man was trying to see eye to eye with the small animal.

Manny cooed softly. "Yes, my friend, you must eat to stay strong if you are to save the world."

The blonde leaned over next to the red mane of Blake's hair. "If I didn't know better, I would think he loves the little box turtle more than us."

Blake startled, slopping coffee on her front. She wiped

at the coffee, which was now blending with the sweat on the sports bra. "Damn it, Brie. How do you do that?"

Manny raised his eyes but not his head. "She is always masked. None of us can sense her. It's the reason she's the one in Singapore."

Brie kissed the top of Blake's head. "It keeps you on your toes."

"But how do you do it?"

Brie shrugged her shoulders and face. "I don't do anything. I'm just a black hole—nothing gets out. You guys, on the other hand, resonate as different colors to me. You are red with purple lightning flashes mixed with gold, and Manny is black with gold flashes glowing with an aqua hue." She picked up her full mug from the counter and took a sip before walking back to the table. "Except when he is a woman—then the hue shifts to more pinkish-aqua like a fire opal."

She sat watching the man and beast. "Jessie looks nice and healthy. I think we should get him laid before the war."

Manny snorted. "Find me a female as pretty as him, and I would."

Blake noticed the alluding to the small animal playing a much larger roll. "And Jessie is doing exactly what? And while you're at it… what war?

Manny sighed as he fed the tortoise the last of the greens. He seemed tired as he rose and sat back in his chair. "Jun… we are going to lure Jun out to us and engage him once and forever."

"Forever is a long time…"

Manny hummed. "Yes, but our little friend here is going to help us rid the world of the evilest person it has ever known—over and over. But if this all works out, this will be the last he is ever heard from again."

Blake snorted softly and then laughed. "You almost had me there, Manny. I mean, between the two of us alone, we have been killed almost every way possible—and yet here we are." Her arms were spread out. But when she saw nobody else laughing—her smile faded fast. She leaned in. "So how do you kill an immortal?"

"One step at a time… How about a real tour of the raft?"

Blake looked at Brie who held her palms out. "I've taken the tour. Besides, I have work to do before I leave. I've been here off and on for most of the last four years. Why don't you two go ahead, and I'll join you for lunch."

Manny stood. "Great. Give a call when you're ready, and we'll let you know where we are."

A FEW HOURS later, Blake stood listening to a tall brunette explaining the solar smelter. The two stood close because of the noise and wore matching insulated light-filtering smocks and helmets.

"Gold and silver melt at just under two-thousand degrees Fahrenheit. But there are also about five other metals that all melt in the same hundred-degree bracket. So we control the temperature through the matrix and can adjust to pull the melts off one at a time." She pointed to the large light concentrator.

Blake leaned closer as she yelled, "So, the Mercury and tin gassed off because they have a lower flash point, but these metals melt and run off through the separator over there?"

Christine dramatically nodded her helmet as she turned and waved them away from the sound of the light bombarding the ore. Blake thought back to the sounds made by beasts, which most today thought were just myths. The subaudible bombardment of the hydra came to mind.

They removed their helmets in the quiet of the office and changing room. "This is just the first and rawest form of separating the ores. The tin and mercury we usually keep together because it makes it easier to ship. Occasionally, like today, we have a call for pure mercury, so Todd is in the next unit separating this year's load, and we will ship five hundred liters of mercury."

Blake watched the tall woman's eyes dance and sparkle as she spoke. "You really love this shit, don't you?"

Christine's laugh tinkled with a huskiness of size. "I love all of this stuff we're doing out here. When Manny hit me up, I was on welfare and hustling for extra money. I wasn't beyond sticking up some dude for his wallet."

Blake laughed. "Manny…"

"Yeah. Who knew some dandy would have a dirk under his jacket."

She continued as she stripped off the aluminum-skinned smock to reveal a sports bra, leggings, and boots. A short bladed dirk hung at her hip. "Manny took me to dinner and actually showed me he cared. I told him about my daughter and the private school I needed money for. He told me about this… and a much better boarding school. I was hooked."

"So your daughter is here?"

"No, she's in Belgrade, Pennsylvania, at the Holst Academy. When she finishes there, with all of their science focus, she'll be ready to come here."

"How old?"

Christine hung the smocks and helmets on the racks. "She'll be fifteen next month." She sagged against the desk. "I wish I could spend a hundred years with her— here. I never thought to work for free… could make me so happy and fulfilled. Manny takes care of all of us in any way we need. So I sleep great and know there are no bills, and I'm not working toward a retirement date." She looked up and smiled. "We can always live here."

Blake smirked. "Rough commute."

"Only when we want to go somewhere, like for a vacation."

Blake could read the half smile. "Like going to visit your daughter?"

She nodded.

Manny stuck his head in the door. "Are you ready for a run out to a sweeper?"

Blake looked at Christine who waved her off. "Sure. How many days will we be gone?"

"If we take a cat, it will be a week or so… so we'll take one of the subs." The having-evil-fun smile was pure Manfred.

"Sub…? We have submarines to play with?" She looked at the other woman.

The brunette gently shook her head as she smiled. "Yes, we have big toys too."

"Oh, hell yes. Sign me up on the dotted line." Blake bounced her butt off the desk and strode toward the door. Christine gently grabbed her arm.

Her voice lowered. "When you get back, can we talk?"

Blake studied the dark eyes. "Sure."

"Also… I've watched you and Manny spar…"

"You want to learn how to use a sword…?"

"I'd like that… and the fighting."

"The martial arts?"

The woman nodded.

Blake smiled gently. "I start at sunup. Manny sleeps until later, so we would have a couple of hours to ourselves."

"I like stretching as the sun comes up. It feels like my body is waking up with the world."

Blake smirked in thought. "You would have made a great Ever Kind."

They held the other's eyes… and then Blake opened the door and followed the way Manny had gone.

For his ball's sake, he had better not be lying about the damn sub…

08 Running Silent

"HOW THE HELL did you ever get a nuclear submarine?"

Manny chuckled. "Don't you really mean… from whom?"

She leaned back with a skeptical look on her face and then watched him slide down the ladder into the guts of the submarine's conning tower or sail. She went next as the sailor closed the hatch from above. They would sink straight down from the catamaran.

Manny nodded to the captain as Blake entered the bridge.

"Flood and make depth three hundred meters."

"Aye, making depth three hundred meters."

The captain turned to his tattooed executive officer. "Kewika, as soon as we have a cushion over us, bring us up to cruising speed and head for sweeper six." He turned back toward Manny and Blake. "You might as well make yourselves comfortable. We won't be there until the morning."

Manny gave him a two-finger salute and waved at Blake. "Come on… I'll give you the nickel tour."

Blake stood her ground with a cold face.

Manny started and then stepped closer. He knew they were about to have words.

Blake jammed her thumb back over her shoulder toward the back of the boat. "I think the forest is this way, Pocahontas."

Manny froze. He ran through all the knowledge he had about Blake's recent history—or at least the last century.

"For now… the conference room is this way."

Blake's face was stone as she waited out her friend. Realizing what they looked like to the crew, she acquiesced. "Lead on…"

Manny dropped his head and turned. He knew they would have to talk about the nuclear missiles—eventually. As they walked out of the bridge, he started the conversation—very little was secret aboard the most secret of the flotilla. "This submarine went missing in 1999, off the coast of Brazil. The Russians looked for their boat and crew. After 9-11, they gave up the search as they too faced the new reality of terrorists and the shift in the world order."

They turned into the small officers' mess and conference room.

"By then, they wouldn't have recognized her anyway. In 2000, we hid her in the hollowed-out hull of a tramp cargo hauler moored in the bay of Singapore. Once inside, she was lifted, and the ship became a dry dock. By 2001, she was split open and began her transformation into more comfort and an expanded capacity to carry more cargo."

Blake coughed. "But still able to launch a nuke…"

Manny raised his eyebrows as he closed his eyes and rolled his head… bending to mitigating circumstances.

"Down the road, there will be a need—"

"For what? Mass destruction of the world? If I feel this right, Jun is in Hong Kong or in the area. If you nuke him, you also flatten and take out nine times the population of Hiroshima and Nagasaki combined. I get that we can't die… but the world and all the rest of the Ever Kind will chase you down and kill you over and over for eternity. It will make what Jun did as Hitler look like the Saturday before the Valentine's Day Massacre."

Manny held his hands up. "We are not blowing up the Hong Kong basin. In fact, we aren't even getting close. The nukes we have on board don't do the same destruction—"

She cut him off as she slapped her hand down on the table. Her growl was pure venom. "Fuck you, Manny. A nuke is a nuke and they all—"

"Unless it's an EMP." He leaned back as his hands came together in a steeple. He turned, and his right leg rose. He laid his right boot along the table and then brought up the left to cross it. He waited with a smug smirk. He could see the shift in her face as the ideas shifted, and her beliefs of what he was up to slewed to a different perspective.

"Where…?"

"Oh, about eight hundred miles northwest of nowhere."

Blake thought about the map of the Pacific Ocean. A thin smile crept across her face. "So… essentially, the midpoint between Hawaii, Japan, Korea, and the raft."

Manny sipped his coffee as he nodded. Placing the mug down between his hands, he played at gently pushing the handle back and forth. "As you taught in 1973, the EMP bomb doesn't have to be large to have a huge effect.

All we are looking to do is turn a large fleet of modern ships into a fleet of floating metal containers."

"No power, no communications, no GPS, nothing but wind power and old style sextons." Blake chuckled softly.

Manny chuckled louder. "An EMP knocks out all missiles and anything larger than a BAR, rifle, or hand weapon."

"How many of our guys know sword fighting?"

Manny shrugged his face. "Most of the crew, I would think. Why?"

"Christine, the brunette working the smelter, asked if I would teach her."

"You mean the leggy woman who likes the high boots like you?"

Blake nodded.

Manny rocked back with a laugh. "I hired her just after she had won an open competition in saber. She was the only woman in the last four rounds." He leaned forward onto the table. "When are you going to start because I can't wait to watch her hand you your ass."

"Fuck you, Manfred." She grabbed up her mug and let the steam swirl around her smoldering eyes. She watched the man over the rim of the mug. "She already told me about trying to mug you up a dark alley."

Manny laughed. "It was more like a dark booth in the back of a bar… but, yes, she could use some instruction. A toddler with a sharp rubber spork would have been more threatening."

Without moving the mug, she continued to probe for information. "So what exactly is… um… Brie doing?"

"She is being one of the most devious pirates we have seen in the last century. She is an international precious metals dealer—with little or no scruples."

"How is this being a pirate?"

Manny chuckled. "We actually are mining precious and semi-precious metals out of the ocean—just not as much as she has been selling." His smirk pulled up tight on the right side. "The mix is right for what we get out, but we have only provided about a tenth of what she has been selling in Hong Kong. The rest has come from other sources which are off the grid."

Blake cocked her head sideways and frowned. "What do you mean off the grid?"

Manny held his arms out with the palms up. "Same way we financed the raft and these subs."

The plural of submarine did not escape her. "Manny… how many subs exactly?"

"Only three… well, there's a fourth on the way next month. But it's for a great cause."

Blake closed her eyes and pinched the bridge of her nose. "Let's get back to the source of the metals."

"Remember the little mine we had back in Africa?"

Blake opened one eye and stared at the man. Gently, she raised her head as the reality of what he was saying became clear. "I thought we agreed the volume of gold in the Solomon mine would implode the world market and crumble many governments. The result of opening the mine would destabilize—"

Manny held up his one palm. "If… we sold the gold on the legitimate market."

Blake leaned in. It wasn't the first time they had argued over ethics—even as pirates. "We both know it will eventually make it to the world markets. The flood of gold alone would tumble half of the western economies. How much have you already…" Her eyes flew open, and she fell back. "Oh fuck me blind, Manny. You opened the Leeds and Hempfield catacombs, didn't you…"

"Only some. And the world order isn't going to collapse anytime soon. At least it hasn't done so in the last ten years… so I see no reason to do so now."

"How much?"

"Well, a lot less than you are thinking. You might say we leveraged the deal."

"Leveraged?"

"There are many of us chipping in on this project. So there are many," he crooked his fingers in the air making air quotes, "companies or people who are buying nothing more than air. They pay us with air money. We sell them air bullion. This way it looks like a lot more metal is being pushed around than exists."

Blake lowered her one eyelid. "That's not leveraging."

Manny winked with a smile and stepped over to the sideboard, pouring himself more coffee. "Over the last few decades, a lot of nuclear material and other nasty stuff have found its way into the hands of certain people which shouldn't have such toys."

"Terrorists."

Manny pushed his lower lip out and shrugged with a nod. "Only since Dick Cheney convinced the world to start Crusades number three. But let's take the terrorists—they didn't have the wherewithal to do anything with it, so we bought it with something they could use."

"Gold…"

"And silver, platinum, and arms which we made sure were only provisionally service worthy." He sat. "The American's were willing to pay top dollar to take control of all the nukes we could get our hands on… but more importantly, they were willing to go further if they didn't have to pay real money. So, we bartered for other things— things other people wanted and could supply us with items we wanted."

"So you traded an old leaking man-o-war for three light frigates, which you turned around and sold to other pirates." She referenced one of his earlier trading deals during the seventeenth century.

Manny smiled warmly. "Those were grand days."

Blake scowled. "So how much gold did you wind up dumping onto the market?"

He shrugged. "So far? Brie would have a better grasp on what exactly we've sold in reality and how much was just air. But I think we stand close to forty gold, fifty silver, some odd artifacts from various cultures, a little platinum, some chromium, and a bit of… Well, you get the picture."

"And all of this went into the black market instead of the legitimate markets?"

"Right… bringing us back to Brie." He ran his fingers through his long wavy hair and rubbed his face. "For the last five or six years, she has quietly offered pure precious metals into the gray markets of Asia. She's discreet, but not excessively discreet. About two years ago, a certain buyer bought a load of gold and mercury. We were certain they analyzed it with a mass spectrometer because he came back and asked where the metals came from."

"Did she tell him?"

"No, but about six months ago, he asked how much the mine could put out. She let slip the ocean is large, and we're only getting started. When the man showed more interest, she assured him the amount she brought to Hong

Kong represented only a fraction of the production."

"And… this guy works for Jun."

Manny gently lowered his head in acknowledgment. The slow smiles were mirrors of the other.

"So, when Jun gets really greedy—"

Manny swept his boots off the table and leaned forward. "He will amass the largest flotilla of pirates the world has ever seen. Evil attracts evil, and he will pool the worst of the world into one flotilla. They will have sails and large freighters. They have some old light coastal frigates from the days of Vietnam and other ships, which disappeared in the night. Mostly his fleet will be large cabin cruisers in the fifty- to seventy-foot range. There is a loose armada of sailors who are sweeping the open ocean south of Hawaii. By next year, they will start searching north. There will be an article in the World Dredging Magazine about mining in the free water of the north Pacific—which we will place at the right time."

"How soon do you think he will start moving this way?"

"Brie estimates he won't make a concerted effort short of two years." Manny stood. "Care to take a walk in the forest, little girl?"

Blake put her mug down on the sideboard. "Why, sir, I thought you'd never ask."

The original forest would have been a series of two vertical launch tubes running down the longest compartment on the boat. Two by two, there had been sixteen tubes—each containing a nuclear missile. Blake looked up at the four remaining tubes.

"All four?"

"Full. We'll only launch one. The other three will only

be backups in case we need them."

Manfred turned to a large monitor mounted on the bulkhead. At his touch of the screen, a shelf slid out with a keyboard and mouse. Blake only vaguely recognized the schematic as being a nuclear bomb. This was one hell of a lot more complicated than the one they had built at Los Alamos in the 1940s.

"I'm sure you recognize the general gist of this. It is important you pay attention to the weight." He highlighted an area.

Blake leaned in and frowned as she did the math. "It won't go off. It's too small."

Manny smirked. "Yes, normally, I would give you an excellent score for doing your homework. But first, what is the effective range if we detonate this reduced size—at fifteen thousand feet?"

She downsized the size and extrapolated the math. "Twenty to thirty miles across a flat sea—but if there is any storm—"

"Then we would simply wait." He keyed in a few codes, and a map of the northern Pacific Ocean appeared with concentric rings overlaid. "Optimally, we want to stop Jun here. If they're moving as a single flotilla—they will be moving at the speed of their slowest vessel. If it's sail, it could be as slow as ten or twelve knots. But my guess is they will use larger sailboats and more like our cats, so we're looking closer to twenty-five knots. This ring is our window, which gives us a six-day spread."

He turned and leaned back on the bulkhead. "Even if we launch in a tropical depression, there are good odds of knocking out at least seventy percent of his flotilla. Anything left with power or electronics... well..." He patted the tube. "We have three more shots."

"What about torpedoes?"

Manny smiled broadly. "Now you sound like the Blake I have known for so long. What about swords and knives when the cannons fail?" He nodded his head as he started back toward the front of the submarine. "The best we could get our hands on were some basic sixty-fives and a handful of Gant missiles which launch from the tubes. The sixty-fives we traded for some old N-49s. Even those are overkill."

"What did you do with the Gants, and I'm assuming you are talking about the cruise missiles?"

Manfred rolled his eyes as he opened the porthole into the torpedo room. The distinctive missiles lay racked in the top bays.

Blake patted his shoulder as she stepped past him. "Good boy. You done good." Her eyes sparkled as she looked at all the toys of destruction. "You done very good."

She looked at the detail painted on the nose of each cruise missile. She frowned at first and then rolled her eyes as she turned. She rotated around her finger pressed against the one nose. "This is the old signage for grapeshot. A Gant is a single warhead designed for deep penetration."

Manny's smile pulled to one side. "A Gant is great if you are taking out a warship of fleet size. But if you are targeting twenty small craft, it's a waste. The one factor in our favor is the advanced proximity detector."

He stepped over to the keyboard and monitor mounted to the bulkhead. With a few keystrokes, he pulled up a schematic of the warhead.

Pointing to an area, "This is the sensor. The normal setting explodes the missile nearby to soften the target before the spent uranium core penetrates the ship." He petted the large tube of steel and death. "The beauty of this chip is it's hardwired. This is the same unit used in the F-15 and F-16 to search, acquire, identify, and respond. The Gant only uses a small part of its talents. But for us, we reprogramed it to look out and identify the best flight path and approach to enlarge the spread pattern of an explosive release of a herd of firebombs."

Blake's finger tapped on the grapeshot insignia. "Firebombs?"

"Fulminated phosphorous bonded thermite—all wrapped up in a bomb the size of a baby's fist." He patted the thick missile. "Inside here, there are hundreds of them. When the mother blows, they will fly for a mile before the friction of the air lights them up. If they fire in a monsoon, the bombs will end up igniting the air itself. But heading for a fleet of sailboats and small craft with wet decks, they will hit and burn until they have burned their way through the bottom of the boat."

Blake rocked back with a single breath of sardonic amusement. "And so we return to our fireballs and catapults of the Phoenician fleet."

Manny turned to the other overhead. His hand wiped over the painted bellyband of a classical trim design. "The egg and dart pattern gave me the idea. In these, we have little eggs that contain a thousand spring-loaded flechettes. Over a square mile, the coverage will be close to three or four darts each square foot. If the area is scattered with tightly packed sails… they and anyone on deck will be taken away."

She looked down at the plain cylinders of gray. "And did you hot rod any of these?"

Manny snorted softly as he shrugged. "We didn't see the advantage. Anything under the size or weight of a cargo ship is overkill anyway." He looked up with his pure evil Manfred smile. "Besides, we wouldn't want to take away any of your playtime, now would we?"

09 Sweeper Number Six

THE MORNING LIGHT found Manny and Blake looking out at the long slow curve of the sweeper net buoys. The twelve-foot wide poly-foam canisters, at the segmentation points, were the only parts showing above water. Each divide of the mile-long arm was twenty-four feet long with colors running from muddied yellow to fluorescent orange to neon lime green.

"What do the colors mean?"

Manny snorted shortly. "The colors were only relevant to whom we stole them from," he glanced at Blake, "or bought them from. Early on, a few of the crew tried to put together a pattern, but if you ran short of green, do you substitute an orange or a blue?" Manny shook his head. "It got confusing, and they quit."

He pointed. "The sweep arms go out for a mile in each of the four directions. Solar powered robot tugs hold and move the ends of the arms. The arms slowly drag around the center processing float." He pointed to the large round platform they were standing on. "All the sorting is done inside the float. We separate the plastic by type, but the metal, we dumped in the holding bins. Christine and the other smelters do the separating in the smelting and refining."

"What about the beds and cars floating around?"

Manny snorted and pointed out a seagoing tug and scow barge. "All the large storm wreckage goes into the barges. When we have a half-mile of secure heaped barges, the *Roaring Boring Alice* or her sister tug take it to the reclamation depot in Tacoma, Washington. Most are just crap needing a nudge to get to the right landfill or turned into energy. But some is glass or metals for recycle."

Blake looked at him with one eyelid down.

"What?" He was already chuckling.

"What is the sister tug named… Polar Poop?"

Manny laughed. "You get to name the next one. But the sister is already the darling of the fleet. Cole named her the Northern Blights."

"I'm going to run you through when this is done, and then I'll find a three-legged sea turtle to kill Cole over. A young turtle at that."

Manny sobered. "I'd go easy on the turtle jokes around here. I'd have to check, but last I looked, we had rescued a few dozen with fishing line, nets, plastic bags, and other crap wrapped around them. But I do know we have over two dozen shells."

"Shells?"

He waved. "Come on. I'll show you." He led the way through the hatch as he explained. "When we find a dead turtle, we clean the shells and give them to Hodor. In her spare time, she does a little carving."

He turned and winked to show he was being sarcastic. They turned into a large mess hall.

Blake stared. Intricate sculptures lined the walls. All

of them retained a two-inch frame of the original shape of the large turtles—but the uniformity stopped there. Each shell was a three-dimensional image of endangered animals in their native habitat. The cuts and manipulations were delicate and lacey. These were not carvings Blake would associate with an artist named after a fourth-century berserker—especially one known for tearing apart villages and Roman legions.

"Well, Samir… has my handiwork improved?"

Blake reacted to the name she hadn't heard for the last fifteen hundred years or more. She turned to find not a hulking ogre of a man, but a tiny Asian woman of advanced years. The inscrutable pursed smile matched the twinkling deep set eyes. The hair was a mass of silver pulled back in a braid. The small hands waited, nested in each other's relaxed embrace—waiting with the patience of one who is older than time.

"Well, let me first say… you are easier to look at now than the last time I had to see your ugly mug."

Her smile spread as the woman cracked. The Asian woman's head cocked as she smiled with a shrug.

"If I remember right, you had brought a few thousand of your friends to play with my sword and bludgeon. They also had an uncouth habit of exploding with blood spraying everywhere. If you had come alone, I might have taken a bath…"

The two held each other's eyes, and then both shook their heads in unison. "Naah…"

They laughed as they hugged. Blake spun them around until they were side by side looking at the turtle shells. "When… where…?"

The small woman offered her hand at one of the tables. "I will get a pain in my neck if I have to look up to you. I am not young like you anymore."

Blake was about to tell her she was already past her two-hundredth year in the body but realized this person would only laugh at such a young age.

"I was a young merchant in Venice when Marco Polo came to me. He was taking the Silk Road to China. Few Italians rode the treacherous trade route, but we were young and in need of having an adventure. After the fall of the Roman Empire, I had lived many hundreds of years tilling the land, selling merchandise, building a church of stone, and sitting by the hearth of a loving home. I was be-yond bored, and I was in the sixteen-year-old body of a third son. I would inherit nothing but more labor."

Manny excused himself to go get coffees and tea. Hodor nodded.

"We fell in love with China and the court of the Ku-blai Kahn. Eventually, it lost its luster the second time back. We wanted to go home, but the Kahn forbade it. We finally convinced him to let us escort the princess Ko-kachin to Persia where she would marry his grandnephew Il-Khan. The road was fraught with thieves, robbers, and others who would do harm. I became one of those."

"So you became a robber?" Blake passed her hand through the air at the wall of shells.

Manny placed the drinks on the table and growled as he sat. "Shut up, Blake. Let her tell her story."

With her mouth hanging open, she sat stunned looking at Manny. Hodor gently pushed her jaw closed with her finger. "Drink your coffee while I talk... or were you in a hurry?"

Blake wrapped her arm around the woman's shoulders

and kissed her forehead. "I'm sorry. I forgot my manners." She could feel frailty of the woman. The centuries had taken all but the last meat.

The woman tepidly sipped on the tea and then carefully placed it in front of her. "Oh, yes… Nepal. I lived for a few years with the horde, but then I was soon drawn to a village down the mountain. One night a cart struck me. I fell and hit my head. In the house next to where I lay dying, a woman gave birth to a son. I would learn to carve ivory from my uncle. I learned from some of the great carvers of the time and became good."

She pointed a finger toward the shell exploding from the wall. "Stare at the bamboo shoot just to the left of the center. Let me know when you see an animal besides the tiger."

Blake found the large shoot and relaxed her eyes and mind. Her vision kept trying to slide to the right, and eventually, when she looked back for the bamboo, it was gone. She laughed.

"It's an elephant." Then, as the trunk had become obvious, so did another shoot. "Oh…"

The Asian woman smiled as she sipped more of her tea. She knew the revealed animals progressed through the rhinos, to the walrus and ended with the narwhale, all of them hunted for their ivory, except the rhino, whose tusk was nothing more than matted hair.

"In 1663, I succumbed to the lung disease, which took most of us carvers who breathed in the fine ivory dust. Everyone knew I was dying, and I rested in the back of the shop. The master's small daughter was applying wet rags to my forehead to give me relief." She held out her hands. "The master felt blessed to have a daughter with a natural ability to carve. But lucky for me, it was bad luck for a girl to carve the sacred ivory, so he put me to work carving wood, and eventually, turtle shells."

Blake sat back, taking in the tribute wall to all the animals that had touched the life of the woman next to her. "Have you been carving for all of these years?"

"I have always carved, but just not always in the public eye. For a long time, I was a successful businesswoman selling the art of others to foreign investors or wealthy Asian families. Some of my work is in many of the museums of China and Japan."

Manny cleared his throat. Blake had forgotten about him being there. His usual flamboyancy seemed only to smolder. The man sat quietly humble, and somehow, smaller than she remembered him.

Manny nodded toward Hodor. "About thirty years ago, I was in Hong Kong. I was bored and wandered into a shop selling carvings. I had sensed Hodor but was looking for the behemoth we had known of yore. Imagine my surprise when this small old woman opened her mouth and addressed me by a past name."

The woman leaned against Blake. "He lies. I came up behind him and told him all centurions must die. I think he wet his pants."

"I did not." Manny pulled himself up in his attempt to look indignant.

Blake whispered back loudly, "Did he also load the backside?"

Manny spun sideways with his coffee and ignored them.

"You women are horrid."

Blake reached out. "Ah, come on, Manfred. We know

you whipped around and started to thread her heart with your dirk."

"No, actually, he was a gentleman. He calmly asked if I had any suggestions for what he could do with his wealth." The older woman looked kindly at the man who was teasing at rejoining the conversation.

"She surprised me—but not by sneaking up on me. What started as lunch had carried well past dinner and a long walk along the shoreline. She thought about the problems Ever Kind and we humans were creating for the planet for centuries. The twentieth century turned out to be the perfect storm with plastic, light metals, and the disposable society."

"When I am carving, only a part of the mind is engaged in the work the hand is doing. The other half is free to think about involved questions. In this life, I have watched people go from having two or three changes of clothing to large rooms filled with clothes. A small carving of an elephant for good luck turned into a full tusk of the animal carved into a parade of little good luck charms. Then greed turned from a single large carving to collecting many for each room. Luck became no longer something to be enticed into the home but bought like a cheap whore."

Manny fiddled with his mug. "She showed me carvings in her shop with princely price tags, but they were lies. Carved cast plastic set in among the complex ivory figurines and scenes."

Hodor pushed her empty mug forward. "They test on the underside for real ivory. There is no carving, and it won't show. So the plastic is never disclosed."

Manny leaned back. "I didn't know about the plastic in the ocean." He pointed at the woman. "Hodor has thought about it since 1959. A man brought some plastic from the ocean and asked if it grew there."

"I knew it didn't grow there—but I was curious about how it got there." She glanced at Blake. "We hear many stories about the glass floats the Japanese used for over a hundred years. They float on the ocean currents and have washed ashore, even on the shores of England and Greenland."

Manny held his arms out. "And so, all of this…"

Blake smiled. "From a bored man stepping into a shop in Hong Kong."

The other two nodded. It was a truth the long-lived saw many times. The seemingly accidental happenstance in one's life and it changes so much—even the world.

Manny waved at the shells. "It was Hodor and her experience that suggested Jessie as the savior of the world."

Blake rolled her head toward the woman. "Yes, about that…?"

Hodor pushed her lower lip out and shrugged her one shoulder. "Can you imagine the world we could create if we can trap the most evil for only three hundred years?"

Manny snorted softly and tossed his hair. "Even then, we could always make him move into another tortoise… which could give us a millennia or more."

Blake lowered one eyelid. "But you said to actually kill… your words… kill an immortal."

Manny stood with a large smile. "Who wants to go swimming?"

Hodor pushed on Blake's shoulder. "Go. Swim. Leave saving the world until later."

Blake rolled with the push and stood. She knew when the conversation had ended. She knew Manfred and his ways. He made the diversion to have her meet the new Hodor. Cleaning up the ocean is a gigantic concept. Understanding where the idea comes from can be as powerful as the project itself—even if the solution is a lowly turtle or kelp.

BLAKE HAD BEEN scuba diving many times, but never in a dry suit. The whole idea was to wear insulation and climb into a suit to keep you entirely dry. It was as close to a micro-mini-sub as one could get. The water temperature is close to fifty degrees and if exposed, extremely uncomfortable for the twenty-eight minutes or so to die.

Manny explained the breathing rig. "This is similar to the rebreather unit you used in the Caspian Sea, except now we get a full hour to play with." He rotated the unit. "This is our depth monitor, but we won't be going below thirty or forty feet, so we don't have to worry about timing our ascent. It's just good for you to know your way around the unit for now."

"Oh good, I'm getting the resort certification class."

Manny gave her a mock stern scowl. "Your sarcasm can either get you killed or at least have your bottom well spanked later tonight."

"Can I bring a friend?"

Manny rolled his eyes. "Does your friend indulge in tall boots, spandex leggings, and have a sweet tooth for over-weighted sabers?"

They chuckled as they donned and secured the helmets and gloves. The suit was anything but spandex. Blake was hoping she didn't have to walk far in the inner space suit when Manny turned and struck his fist against a large red button. A klaxon horn had blown three bellows before the floor dialed open like a camera iris.

The water below the large floating cylinder was dark in shadow. Blake looked into the maw and thought about Jonah and the whale. She heard a muffled chuckle from Manny as he turned on the intercom between the two helmets.

"And he said, let me turn on a little light here..."

The black water became day as Blake watched a stairway slide down into the moon pool. The steps were large to accommodate the padded insulated booties and the swim fins. Manny's voice came from the back of her helmet.

"Just walk down to the bottom of the stairs and step off. The weight of the suit is set to keep us around the thirty-foot level. The lights on your helmet will go on automatically when they sense the water. If you ever want or need to turn them off, push on the rubber bulge over your right ear. The left side will cycle through a yellow light, red light, and ultraviolet. Some of the sea fauna is photoreactive to the ultraviolet, and it makes a great spectacle."

As the helmet lights came on, Blake could see the hanging shadows of the closest curtain. As they swam closer to the curtain, she could make out the separate cylinders of what looked like large kelp.

"One of the smart people long ago noticed the kelp forest in the Monterey Bay did a great job of trapping trash. The local aquarium studied the plants. They noticed the trapped trash slowly transferred from one leaf to the next. The garbage eventually moved to the surface where it blew away, or at least, moved away by the surface tides."

Manny easily swam through the soft hanging pillars. A hand's slice of separation, but the spines or tendrils were soft and pliable. As Blake followed, she thought about the inverted bottlebrush she had used in her bar for many years. Passing between these bottlebrushes felt almost erotic and pleasurable.

There was a brown flash to her right, and when she turned, a silver body slid through the space and then disappeared. The bright reddish-orange of Manfred's suit slid up beside her.

"You must have seen Dance and Flash. The harbor seal is Dance, and Flash is her best friend—a miniature bottle-nosed dolphin. The aquarium studied them but feared turning them loose because of the delicate ecosystem. So we brought them out here where they could play, work, and not disrupt the ecology."

Blake turned and then realized as she looked at the mirror of Manny's helmet—he couldn't see her frowning in question. She looked about inside the helmet for a trigger to talk. There was none. She hung in the silence of the water.

"If you're looking for a chin toggle—there is none. We are linked live, so please do not fart—I can hear you. In addition, our commlinks do not work out here or underwater. They only work on or in the raft."

Blake glowered. "Some days, Manfred, you amaze me at how crude you can be when you're surrounded by the beauty of pure nature."

He reached out and tugged on a tendril. "Nature my ass—this is pure T-Rex aftermath. This is some of the finest rayon to come out of Akron, Ohio, or Transylvania, Mississippi, or Saigon, Vietnam."

"The beauty of the two creatures shooting by befuddled your mind and you can't remember where your giant bottlebrush is made. You must be getting past your prime, old man."

"The 'Flashdance' wasn't lost on me. We just use three small companies to spread the wealth, and so nobody caught on to what we're doing. We make the bottlebrushes as continuous extruded and slitted lines. They are labeled oil pipeline cleaning rods. Only when they get out here are the mile-long rolls then chopped into the forty-foot lengths and attached to their twirlers."

Blake rested her thumb and index finger high on her hip and adjusted her body in what she hoped would convey her exasperation with the man. "Really, Manny... Twirlers?"

He turned and swam through the curtain at an upward angle. "Sure. We even have pasties too. Let's get on the working side of this curtain, and I'll show you."

As they slowed in open water, Flash and Dance turned a fast loop around them and shot for the surface. Manny held his hand out flat near the man-made kelp tree. With the stable reference line, Blake could see the cylinder was indeed turning—slow but nonetheless turning.

"Why the turning?"

"You see the turning, but there is also, at the core, a three-inch up and down. At the end of the three-foot bristles, the total movement translates to a wave motion of about six or eight inches. This rubs the tips together and moves the plastic chips." He moved in close and pointed. "Look here. This little white chip... right now, it is on the tip of, let's say... twenty feet nine inches."

They hung in the water watching a tiny white dot as it

gradually approached another cylinder. As it touched, it was knocked onto the bristle of the other cylinder.

"This new bristle is on the down post, and when it reaches over there, it will be on the top."

Blake harrumphed at the observation. "So merely going from the one to the next, the piece raised six inches."

"Right, and eventually, it will be near the surface where it will be swept by the pasties." He started kicking to rise in the water. Blake followed.

The two helmets surfaced, and Manny did a fast circle to make sure they wouldn't be run over. He pulled Blake to safety from what reminded her of a bloated, floating pool sweeper for leaves. She could feel the water movement. The yellow machine was exactly that.

Manny laughed. "We fed some steroids to a swimming pool leaf skimmer. But we also provided an electrostatic charge that attracts the plastic. Once the long bag is at full, we reverse the polarity, and it spits it out into the processing Keep."

Blake snorted. "I wondered what you called it."

"Hodor named it. Back as a berserker, she said they only feared the Roman outposts—the Keeps. They weren't large like a castle, so easily overlooked or missed, if not just dismissed outright. But as they found, the dismissed could become the undoing of a horde. Most of the Keeps had signal fires built on top. The signal was much faster than the fastest messenger, even on horseback. They also provided protection for the local farmers, so grains and animals were stocked against any siege."

Blake floated back and looked along the curtain line to the dark structure. This Keep may fit on a soccer field, but she knew it to be several stories deep.

"I'm probably missing something right now…"

Manny laughed. "Probably missing a lot."

Blake looked at the now clear facemask filled by the dark mustache and beard. She knew the man, no matter what the body—it consisted of layers on hidden layers. He had much in common with a Keep.

She nodded and then curled into a duck dive, kicking for the bottom of the curtain. The reddish-orange suit followed. Manny was getting hungry and not only for food.

10 Bang Bang in Singapore

BRIE WAS ENJOYING the view just over her left foot. The small weatherworn red freighter arthritically moved about to make its mooring. She had lain out on the deck about an hour after sunup. The text had woken her up.

The public deck of the Marina Bay Sands Resort covered one hundred acres floating a quarter mile in the air. The long deck was built to resemble a cruise liner that had come to rest on top of the fifty-fifth floors of the three supporting towers. Brie knew there were no tourists wandering around on the public deck two floors below her private deck. The restaurant wouldn't be open for breakfast until later, and nobody pays twenty Singapore dollars just to go look at the scenery.

If anyone were down there, Brie knew they were doing the same as she was—watching ship movements. The decrepit rustbucket of a ship was her favorite to watch. A few years before, she had watched the ship surge out of a mooring and give chase at a respectable flank speed of any large military ship. Someone in her bed had once bragged about the horsepower hiding below the rust. She never cared what the person's name was. They were walking dead when she would have corroborated they would have the right information and were headed for her bed.

Brie raised her dark glasses as she brought up her long-range spotting scope. She found the rusted freighter still fussing about the mooring buoy and then moved the scope slightly down and to the left. She studied the derelict containership with random stacks on its deck. The fantail marking was in faded and rusted away Chinese characters. She knew the words in English meant praying mantis. The back of her mind chuckled about the misspelling having made it a predator.

She watched the two ships for the next hour. Neither showed any obvious deck activity. The smaller ship never seemed to get the moorage right, and the larger appeared as dead as it had for many years.

She placed the scope back in its case. Taking a sip on her iced green tea with pineapple, she thought about the republics secret monitoring ship. She pulled her dark glasses off her head and shook out her hair. Putting her glasses back on, her distant vision improved threefold. Many times in the field, the twenty gold coins she paid for them had proved their worth many times over.

She raised her smartphone and placed both index fingers on the shared reader pad. The screen opened. She continued to hold the two fingers in place. The screen cleared and a new screen appeared. She thumbed the green bush icon.

If the phone rang on the other end, she didn't hear it. The voice on the other end merely spoke the word yes.

Brie stretched her neck in the sun. "Danny, darling, is there a reason the snoopy little troll would be having such a hard time mooring this morning, just off your port bow?"

She listened to the British man prattle on about how bad the fishing had gotten lately. In fact, it was so bad that he had just the night before watched a large prizewinning fish slip away into the dark waters just before his bedtime.

"Oh, so sorry to hear you lost the big one. So old age is setting in, and you're going to bed by eight?"

He assured her he would live to fish another day for another trophy. He cackled at the early bedtime. He makes it a habit of slipping between the sheets with the nine o'clock hour. After then, there wasn't any decent television, and he had read all the great worthwhile books, the last being the underwater adventure by Jules Vern.

"Give my love to mum and kiss the kibblings." She thumbed off the phone and switched to a secured text mode. The text would be routed through seventy countries before it made one bounce through a satellite over the northern Pacific Ocean.

"Package on the way. Enjoy the sardines. No word on Christmas vacation yet. Love Sis."

Half her job in Singapore was done. Her tan had not suffered the last six months of her watching the ship movements around the rusted hulk of the containership. The outside shell was nothing more than finely composed scenery hiding the true nature of the giant ship that was a floating dry dock.

The large fish that had gotten away the night before was the latest reconstruction of four nuclear submarines. The first three were from Russia and the last being a 688 or Los Angeles class fast attack sub from the United States arsenal which had gone missing on patrol two years before.

The highly trained crew had been lost on a mission the government would never be able to talk about. Some of the experienced crew was a lot more mature and experienced than the government believed. The other crewmen and two women were long-standing supporters of the Pacific project. The spy ship was believed to be lost somewhere in the Sea of Okhotsk, between the mainland of Russia and the Kamchatka peninsula—deep inside sovereign Russian territory. Stacked aboard were examples of some of the most advanced torpedo technology the Navy had sent to sea.

Two Ever Kinds, holding high ranks in the Pentagon, would eventually help any queries or reports on the submarine find their way to a shredder. They discreetly performed the same functions as their counterparts in China and Russia. For this project, many who were simply living their lives had come together to work for the common and long-term good—removing the one true evil in the world.

BRIE FELT REFRESHED after her laps in the infinity pool. She only stopped at the one end cantilevered a hundred feet out into space. It was the closest she could come to her experience as a dolphin and as an eagle while enjoying the body of a woman. If mermaids were real, she knew in her heart she would never be another kind of body.

"Excuse me, Miss Jones…"

She turned to see the young man standing at the edge of the pool. She had once guessed his age at a young twenty but had not been surprised when she found out his son was almost twenty. The smile never wavered. His hand held out a dark cell phone. She knew the hotel did not provide burner phones to their guests—even ones who lived a quarter of the year in one of the discreet penthouse rooms.

"Oh, thank you, Jake. You found my phone."

"Yes, miss." He bowed slightly as she pushed herself up out of the water and sat on the side. She was as far away from anyone eavesdropping as she could get, in a city of twenty million people. As she settled in and looked at the screen of the phone, she felt a soft bath sheet gently draped around her shoulders. She only turned slightly and nodded.

She raised the phone to her ear as she watched the Singaporean man stride out of earshot.

"Well, I must say, this is a pleasant surprise." Though her words said pleasant, her voice was all business.

"Sorry to interrupt your morning swim. I'm doubly sorry because I admire your taste in pools. I'm assuming you know who this is?"

From the moment she saw the black phone, she could sense it was Jun. Even though she was a blank to every Ever Kind, she could sense them in ways the others could not.

"I'm assuming I am finally speaking to Mr. Fat himself. Ming has a much finer voice, and she knows better than to disturb a woman before noon... unless brunch is in the offering."

"I apologize again for the early hour, but I am in the air right now, and time is not something I have a firm grasp on. Brunch sadly is not in the offering, but I did call to see if you would do me the honor of meeting me for a late lunch at Raffle's?"

She looked east towards the topic of conversation. "I could fit it in, yes. Shall we say two o'clock on the veranda?"

"If I may be so bold... I have a less public veranda with my suite. I'll leave word with the desk to expect you, Ms. Jones. I look forward to our meeting."

She hung up the now dead phone, his rude shortness expected.

She almost threw the phone over the edge of the building but knew the small phone could reach a critical mass. Puncturing a car's roof and killing the occupant never looked good. She flipped it in the air and let it sink to the bottom of the pool.

As she stood and walked away, the attendant smiled and leaned to look over her shoulder at the pool—presumably, where the phone now lay. She lowered her head and growled sweetly. "Rude man."

Jake snorted. "Yes, Miss. Rude when the phone rang too."

Brie stopped. She truly liked the staff and sensed them having her back when it counted. "Where did the phone come from, Jake?"

He stepped in closer and spoke quieter. "It arrived by special private courier about ten minutes before it rang."

"And he asked for me by name?"

"Yes and no, Miss. He said hand this phone to Ms. Jones—the blonde woman in the pool." He shook his head. "Before you ask, the answer is no. Other than from a helicopter or airplane, there's no other way to see who you are or that you were in the pool." He held her stare for a few heartbeats. "Other than our security cameras…"

The man was admitting to a breach of their own security. It confirmed at least his loyalty. "Can you look into it for me, Jake?"

The man nodded as he took her damp towel and substituted a fresh dry one. As he wrapped it around her shoulders, he leaned a bit closer. "Tonight, your housekeeper will attend you and turn down your bed at ten o'clock."

Her blue eyes sparkled to match her public smile of a wealthy pillow princess. The world took care of her wants and needs.

11 Brunch and Betrayal

THE FINE WEAVE of the wicker chair creaked softly as the woman shifted position. The introductions and first two courses had been social and casual. Brie could sense the true nature of the being starting to show through. She smiled inwardly—this is what she came for.

The man from Beijing, despite the custom-tailored silk suit, had a cruel face. The hard cruelty was more in the set of the eyes and jaw than the ragged scar running from above his eyebrow, down past his left eye, finishing short of his lip. Brie only guessed at a live fencing badge. The scar added to the tightness about the powerful and danger-ous man. There was nothing soft about Mr. Fat—even his handshake had been bone and steel.

"Ms. Jones… or is it Ms. Jorgensen… or should I say Ms. Gertzen? After all, your information footprint does give one cause to raise an eyebrow." The man patted his lips with his napkin, almost hiding his soft smile.

Brie froze and then nodded only slightly to admit his information and the skills of his people uncovering her true identity. Her eyes hovered, looking at the edge of the glass tabletop as if looking for answers. She looked up. "And what makes you so sure you have peeled back all the layers of the onion?"

The man leaned forward, his eyes never leaving Brie's gaze. By touch, his fingers chose a medium grape that he quietly wiped with his napkin. His right arm fell slightly toward the floor before rising with something dark and small in the fist. With a chilling snick, the small narrow blade appeared at the end of his curled hand. Methodically, he peeled the grape—collecting the skin on the blade. With the skill of an ambidextrous person of skill, he deposited the skin on the plate as he placed the perfectly peeled grape in his mouth.

As the blade disappeared with the same quiet snick, Brie knew, in the bottom of her soul, he was just as capable of peeling a human alive. The image and knowledge were not comforting.

His hand opened with a brief flash of black dropping back into the sleeve. His eyes never left his victim.

He chewed softly as he sat back. His black eyes studied the blonde. The smile was brief and small. "I will admit you're good, but not that good."

The Chinese man's eyes narrowed to slits. If they were vertical, he would have resembled the snake he was inside. "For someone who lives their life so in the open, you have a very hidden in the shadows reality. One would think you may have much more to hide than just your aging mother in London."

Brie leaned back as her eyes also narrowed. Her left hand came up, and her thumb and finger gently plucked at her lower lip.

If Jun were more observant, he might have remembered the fop in his court who had reflectively played with the bit of hair on the lower lip of his goatee. But then, he hadn't paid the young man attention when he was Louie XVI, and he didn't now. But he did read the eyes correctly.

"Oh, Ms. Gertzen, I can assure you your mother is fine… although… she might want to consider tempering her unhealthy taste for the rare Anise infused Belgian chocolate at her advanced age. One never knows when they may fall victim to clogged arteries… or worse." He selected another grape from the plate, wiped it, and slid it into his smirk unpeeled.

"What is it you want, Fat?" Brie held her voice and edge at subarctic. "You tapped into the Marina security, invaded my privacy, snooped around in my life, and now you are threatening my mother's life—"

Mr. Fat held up one languid palm. "Please, I merely pointed out her advanced age and love for chocolate which only comes from one chocolatier in the Victorian galleria in Brussels. It is not safe to be so… predictable. It is you who assumed it was a threat."

"What do you want?" Brie allowed her voice to carry an edge.

The waiter stepped out onto the veranda. The carts tremor was only a soft tinkling of the heavy metal covers against the covered plates. The two seated ignored him, but they were silently locked in a war of eyes. As the man finished arranging the plates, Mr. Fat nodded, and he retreated.

"Ah, the lobster looks magnificent." He looked up. "Please, Ms. Gertzen, eat while the dish is at the ideal temperature."

Brie didn't move.

Finally, Mr. Fat sat back. His arms rested on the large rolled arms of the chair. "In my culture, one enjoys a fine meal before engaging in the mean endeavor of business…"

Brie's right eyelid fluttered to cover half of her iris. Her voice was more growl than ice. "In my culture, one does not cyber rape a woman, show her the pew of an orphan and then pretend to be a scion of civility. Either we get to the point… or I'm leaving." She reached for her clutch on the corner of the table but didn't touch it. The micro camera in the design continued filming as the five microphones continued to work with clarity.

Fat raised both hands. "Okay, we'll compromise. We can talk business as we eat. But, please, eat. The lobster thermidor is exquisite and will only remain so at temperature."

"And… the business is…?"

Fat raised an eyebrow as he forked a small bite to his mouth. "Why, metals… of course." He shrugged and smiled as he chewed.

She eyed him as she took a bite. He was entirely correct. The lobster was divine, and their business was metals.

"We already do business with metals…"

"Yes, but you don't bring me all of your metal. In fact, my sources inform me you don't bring me all of even the gold." His face took on a threatening posture of inquisitiveness.

"Why would you want to purchase more of my gold… much less some of the other metals I broker? You can only handle so much weight before your market becomes saturated."

He patted at his mouth and took a sip of water. "There are many markets for certain metals. Even with gold, there are markets within markets. Even within markets, which are recognized as open and legal… and then there are the other markets. Markets where one must be a bit more… shall we say… creative?"

"The deep or black web…"

He nodded. "Such a disingenuous label."

"But apropos when we are talking about the nature of the business and people who troll those trade routes. It is the trafficking which does not tolerate the light of day or scrutiny."

"Let's just say… at times, there is a certain expediency only reached in those places which are sheltered from the usual overwatch by certain governments."

"We're not talking about gold anymore…"

He shrugged his lip and face. "We also are not talking about a series of conventional mines. Are we, Ms. Gertzen?"

"So what is it you want?"

Mr. Fat plated his fork and dabbed at his mouth. Gently folding his napkin, he laid it on the table—the lunch was done. Brie knew they had finally gotten to the point of the meeting.

He sipped his water and then leaned back in his chair. His vision was of the large old Dragon fruit tree blocking the sight and sound of the busy street. "Like the various markets for gold, there are also markets for even heavier metals. Ones which are not as benign."

"Isotopes?" Brie had not expected him to be searching out a market of nuclear material. She was certain the person or people watching at the other end of her purse's feed were just as surprised.

He nodded gently. "Isotopes."

"What makes you think I have any contact with…? I sell precious metals, not nuclear bombs."

She watched his face darken around his eyes as he leaned in. "This may be true, Ms. Gertzen, but the people you deal with—are not as pure. The mercury we bought from you last month had been exposed to low-level uranium. It was a low exposure, but nonetheless, exposed to weapon's grade uranium. The miners you are dealing with have nuclear arms." He had no way of knowing the miners who were watching the meeting had specifically exposed a small amount of the mercury to uranium for just this possibility. They had left Brie in the dark so her reactions would be natural.

"So… are you with the International Nuclear Regulatory Commission?"

His soft chuckle was evil. "Certainly not, Ms. Gertzen. If they knew about me, they would not like me."

"So why would you want a nuclear?"

He reached for another grape as the waiter took up the plates. "Tell me, Ms. Gertzen… we've been doing business for about six years now. How much do you know about me?"

She patted at her lips and folded her napkin as she nodded at the waiter's hand hovering near her partially eaten lobster. Laying the cloth on the table, she weighed the question. "You have offices in thirty-seven countries, your public net worth is well above Warren Buffet but less than Bill Gates, and you have a passion for riding horses but only bareback."

He hummed with a half-smile, "Hmm, how safe…"

"Excuse me?"

"Your answer… You chose the answer one would find

on the internet question site which everyone resorts to."

"Wikipedia…"

The man nodded slowly.

"What answer are you looking for?"

His eyes hooded as his smile showed more evil than happy. "One which would probably offend a lesser person—you didn't secure the suite on top of the Marina Bay by playing it safe, Ms. Gertzen. Let me see some of your… how is it said in your country… fire?"

Brie leaned toward the table. "Okay, if you want to play with fire… Without touching a single public asset, you could buy both Buffet and Gates today and recoup your losses by next weekend. You personally control at least a third of the international shipping and oil production. Last year, you personally brought three governments to the brink of financial collapse and are now toying with them to control arms flow in the regions. You control, but don't own, more gold than the United States warehouses. How am I doing?"

"You missed a country, and I would be financially solvent by this weekend, not next. Otherwise, your information is good enough to suspect I have a leak somewhere high in my organization." He sat back musing, "Which makes you an extremely dangerous person, Ms. Gertzen."

She snarled soft and threateningly. "Meaning—you need to leave my mother out of this."

"Oh, to the contrary… This means I need you closer… or where you and your mother are no longer a threat to me or my organization."

She reached across the table and plucked one of the grapes from his plate. His face darkened at the social offense. She smiled. "So which do you propose?"

He did not blink. "How much loyalty do you owe to the mining consortium?"

She leaned back in her seat. Her face and eyes shrugged. "We go back a ways…"

"But no family or binding circumstances?"

"None to speak of."

"Do they know about your mother?"

"Only you have found her." She made a mental note to remove the elderly woman soon. It was time for a new body anyway. The running joke between them was the woman had been the handmaiden at the signing of the Magna Charta. Her controlled rent in London was locked-in since then. The flat was large and provided Brie a place to live twenty years before. Brie had been a dashing Roger then with a tall American girlfriend. The two had married, but a drunk had ended Roger.

The blonde-haired woman passenger on the bus that fateful night leaned forward and pinched off a second grape. She noted the lack of a scowl on the man's face. The hook was set.

"How much do you know about their operations?"

"Enough."

"The fissionable material?"

"Rumors… but with some allusions to confirmation."

The man brought his hands together in a steeple, his forefingers bouncing against his lips. "How often do you go out to the facility?"

"They only bring me out about twice a year. Some years not, and I was just out there a few months ago to bring in the last load of metals."

The man fished for information. "And the only way in or out is by sea…"

She hesitated—frozen. Her heart skipped a beat, and then her body relaxed in being caught. She nodded only slightly.

The man's satisfaction was hidden by his hands. He leaned forward and experienced another grape. There was a mutual meeting of the minds.

She started gently drawing on the net. "We have discussed what you expect to get out of this deal, but we haven't discussed my interests."

"We discussed your mother—"

"Who pays rent for her flat?"

His one eyebrow ticked a fraction upward. "But if you owned the building…"

She rolled her eyes. "A few paltry coins of silver in a beaten old leather sack. We are talking gold and more here, Mr. Fat. Much more."

"The building in London is worth a few million pounds—"

She cut him off with a snap of her fingers. "The housing is rent controlled, it needs repairs which the landlord begs he cannot afford to make from the low rents, and once Mother passes on, I have no use for it. I rarely go to visit, and I never stay there when I do."

"But you do spend substantial time in Singapore."

"Last time I checked the penthouse suites at the Marina Bay were not for sale."

"Everything has a price, Ms. Gertzen… even the Marina Bay."

"I don't like sharing the floor with the other suite."

The man had found her price. "There is a single penthouse on the top. It even has its own private elevator. The pool isn't as large as the one below…"

"But between London and the top suite, I could muddle through… as long as I don't end on the orphan listing."

The man from Beijing bowed his head slightly as his eyes closed most of the way. He had set the hook and successfully reeled in his catch.

Brie sat silent, showing no indication of her same thoughts.

12 Vacations

THE FALL OF long red hair washed over the mane of darker. The curl in each was the same and could have come from the same head. The darker head stirred.

"Did you pack any swords?"

Blake chuckled. "No, silly. Why do you think we are picking up Noi at the college?"

Christine sat up and looked out the airplane's window. Breaks in the low cloud cover revealed only squares of farms, roads, and water. "Noi never mentioned sword fighting was available."

"She may be a little short for most of the sword fighting, but has she mentioned the gun club or any of the martial arts?"

Christine's head jerked around as she frowned. "Have you been talking to my daughter more than I have?" Her left hand fussed with the ice and remains of the Bloody Mary. She raised it slightly, so the steward noticed with a nod.

Blake laid her head back. "You don't know Manny very well." She rolled her head to look at her close friend and lover. "Noi is only one of our kids in special schools.

He gets almost daily reports on all of them. In our three or four times being married to each other, we only produced one child—so in a way, he's making up for lost time."

Christine's face softened—they were talking about kids—their kids. "What happened to your…"

"Son?" Blake smiled at the connection. "He was a fine young man. We trained him in the arts and the sciences of the time. His swordplay was good, he could outride me—his father—and was superb at his bookwork. His uncle was a mathematician and lived three houses down, so we had the best of tutors."

"I hear a sigh in there. I take it he did not live a long and wonderful life."

"No… he didn't." Blake nodded at the steward as he placed the two fresh drinks on the small tray between the two large seats.

The strikingly handsome attendant sparkled behind his glasses and beard. "Excuse me, ladies, but we will be serving the meal in about ten more minutes. I have roast lamb, Atlantic salmon, or Chicken Kiev."

Christine hummed as she picked up her drink. "I never made it to Kiev, so I'll have the chicken."

Blake stifled a giggle as she ordered. "The lamb sounds great. Thank you, Mike."

Chris dug a finger into Blake's ribs. "What are you laughing about?"

Blake chortled as she hid her face in the other's shoulder. "Did I ever tell you about killing Manny over the back of a three-legged ewe?"

Chris wheezed as she began to laugh. "Is this the one which turned out to be pregnant and Manny became the lamb instead of the ewe?"

Through the fits of giggles, Blake nodded. "He had to wait six months until we were hungry enough to eat him… and the only other body then was a little girl or a squirrel."

Chris's face was full in mock horror. "No… which did he take?"

Blake recalled the result and sobered. "The squirrel. He has always had a soft spot for not putting young girls in harm's way. He has experienced too many small girls who died before they ever had a chance to live."

"And why he is looking after our kids."

"Yes… and many other reasons which make up the complex person we call Manny."

Christine sipped on her drink as she weighed the new information. Putting down her glass, she looked out the window as she stretched her legs. "So, what happened to your son?"

Blake shrugged as she rolled her eyes. "When Napoleon rose to power at the end of the revolution, war unavoidable—Jamie's skill with the sword and horse quickly made him a light commander—somewhere between a sergeant and a lieutenant."

Christine folded into her seat. "Waterloo…"

Blake rested her head on the other. "If only he had lasted longer. We lost him in 1798, in Egypt."

"What happened?"

Blake rolled her head to look at Chris. The concern on her face was as real as if the boy had died recently. A child is a child.

"After Napoleon had finished wasting his time with the Masons on Malta, he got word the English fleet under Nelson had sailed back into the Mediterranean. Knowing he needed to fight from a protected space, he sailed for

Egypt and the mouth of the Nile. Jamie and the other marines landed near Alexandria. On the map, I'm sure it only looked like a couple of days to the city, but the landing had been less than just a mere disaster. The biggest problem was it was June, and what few horses survived the landing, the rest died from the heat, lack of decent water or food, flies, and mosquitos."

Chris pursed her lips. "So a cavalry officer was screwed from the start."

Blake nodded as Mike placed the food in front of them. "We learned later he had suffered a large wound to his one leg during the coming ashore. The wound had festered, and when they reached Alexandria, he was on a stretcher. Napoleon pushed his army into battle… and everything else got left by the wayside—including the wounded."

"And he hadn't inherited the… whatever it is?"

Blake took up her fork. "No—he was not Ever Kind. We don't reproduce… We only have children. And even then, it is rare."

Christine opened her mouth to say something. Her fork floated in the air—wavering, but only for a second. She bent to her meal.

Blake sensed the silence and left the woman to her own thoughts. Blake had buried his son a few years before and signed on with a trading ship headed for the Americas. When the ship reached the Caribbean, Blake was master of the ship. The crew not killed or thrown overboard— became pirates. Left to preying on Napoleon's ships as much as they did the Spanish, Dutch, and English.

With the desert, Blake started thinking about why they were even taking the trip—Christine's daughter, Noi. Chris hadn't seen her in almost a year, and they were going to surprise Noi for her sweet sixteen.

"Tell me about Noi…" She looked over at her friend.

The brunette leaned back in the seat and sighed. "What do you want to know?"

Blake snickered and gently dug a finger into the woman's ribs. "Everything… especially the warts… Let's start with who's the daddy?"

"Wow, you just jab right for the heart." Her head rolled over. "Roger Gertzen."

Blake leaned over and kissed her lightly on the lips. A tiny tip of tongue lingered for only a second. "If it is too painful… start somewhere else."

Chris smiled sadly. "But I know you now. It would eventually get back to the beginning anyway. So I might as well start there."

"The beginning is always a good place to start."

Chris sighed as the steward came back. The women enjoyed his attention. They had whispered at how he would fit in on the raft and wondered if his swordplay could live up to his rakish good looks. They snickered as Blake wondered aloud how Mike would look in a short tunic, leggings, and tall boots. Chris wondered if his preference ran to rapier or saber. They had stopped before their minds wandered too far into the gutter, as he seemed a diligently nice man.

As they secured their trays out of their ways and pushed back, Blake nudged the conversation. "Roberto…?"

"No, nobody so exotic. Just a nice man named Roger. I was an interpreter secretary for an American company in London. He was a nice Brit living with his mum in a large flat just north of the Heath. We both liked taking our lunches at half past one, on the west side of the Heath.

"One day, the realization struck me. If he wore, a drab old overcoat that looked like it had barely survived the bombing of London, and topped it with a mismatched beaten-down hat—he would be the man I walked a block behind every morning on my way to work. Then one chilly day, he wore them both to the park for lunch. I realized we had a lot in common and never had even said hello in the four years."

Blake found it hard to believe the woman who had wielded molten metal in a solar smelter, and occasionally kicked her ass in combat, could be shy.

"So did you adjust the separation?"

Chris blushed. "Actually… no. The job did. One day, one of the lawyers was just coming out of a meeting with a client and asked for my interpretive skills—"

"What language?" Blake had never heard her speak a single word other than English.

"English… well, British proper to be exact." She had taken on a strong, arrogant upper London accent.

The two laughed. Mike leaned in and conspiratorially whispered, "Just so you know, there are three undercover fun police on board today. If you keep this up, they will be forced to come over and make sure you're not double punching your fun card."

Chris snapped back, "Mike, do you sail?"

"Depends, honey… What's his name, and what does he look like?"

Two sets of eyes popped large. "No, we're talking sailboats—as in on the ocean."

He waved down his hand. "Oh, heavens no. I get motion sick in a bathtub. But hot tubs are okay—as long as I have plenty of sailors to hold onto." He slid away from them laughing.

As they settled down, Blake was back at it. "So what language?"

"Seriously… British. But as soon as I stepped into his office, Roger recognized me and stood while he introduced himself in French. I smiled and answered in my best four years of high school French. The lawyer was lost, and soon, we were walking out of the office heading for lunch in the park."

"But what had the lawyer needed?"

"To introduce us. Roger had seen me in the secretary pool and asked if I ate in the park all the time. The lawyer had asked his secretary, and she snooped it out. So Roger wanted an introduction… I told you he was a good mama's boy."

Blake snuggled into Christine's arm as she poked at her ribs. "So you finally met… and…?"

"We never walked to work alone again. Their flat was in the next building, and Roger worked two floors up from me. It instantly took on a strange small world feeling. Over a few weeks, we found many things we had in common. Even our tastes in food, music, weather, the comfort of old clothes over fashion, and even much of our background and heritage."

"So how long did you date?"

"Two months…"

Blake's mouth opened and then gently closed as she whispered, "Fast…"

Chris shrugged her eyes and lower lip. "How long does it take to know when something is right?"

Blake rolled her eyebrows and nodded. "How long

were you married?"

"We weren't. We were getting ready to… He ran across the foggy street to get some milk for the morning…"

Blake's face flattened in shock.

"I'm sure the drunken twit who hit him has lived with the moment to this day."

"That's horrible." Then Blake remembered. "But you were already pregnant…"

The brunette nodded.

"But Noi isn't a British name… and neither is Guetten… whatever…"

"Gertzen. No, neither is it British. Noi is Thai for small or tiny. There was just too much everywhere I looked, walked, lived, worked. It was too much. When my supervisor told me about a position opening in the Bangkok office if I thought I could learn Thai—I swore I would learn Thai even if it killed me. We lived in Thailand for three years before moving to the office in New York. After 9-11, the company fell on hard times and never recovered. After I was let go, I worked temp jobs and anything else I could—to keep us alive and out of the projects."

Blake slid her hand in and around her friend's arm. "And then you interviewed with Manny."

"I guess sticking a knife in his ribs would be exactly his kind of interview." They snickered even harder as Mike swayed by and gave them a lecherous look and smile.

AS THEY LEFT the plane, both leaned over and lightly gave Mike a hug and a kiss on his cheek. He'd find out later they had applied fresh lipstick. The giggles came in fits on their way out to the waiting limousine.

The driver filled them in as he walked them to the baggage claim.

"Because of the late hour, the school has arranged for you to be put up in one of the residencies on campus. Your daughter can stay with you starting tomorrow, but for now, she is in her dormitory room. We arranged for a car. They delivered it this afternoon. It's fully equipped with the usual company features. The fob and keys are at the residence."

The drive was relaxing, and the two dozed in the large backseat. They arrived at the school after midnight. The man standing on the steps of the house approached as the limousine stopped.

"Good morning. Welcome to Holst Academy. My name is Edward, and I will be your host until six o'clock this morning. At that time, the duties will be taken over by Lila and Graham."

Christine looked back at Blake who shook her head. She turned back to the man. "What time is sunrise?"

"About six-fifteen, but I can check..." He started to draw out his smartphone.

Blake waved it off. "Please wake us at five-thirty, so we can be present when you do the handover."

"It's not necessary—"

Blake stepped forward and cut him off. "Not necessary—but none of us want to wake up to strangers. Even you are not a known commodity ensuring trust. We want to be present and to be introduced. Also, I would personally appreciate background folders on all staff who will have access to this building. Please."

"Yes, ma'am. Right this way, please." Blake thought

she saw a small smile as the man turned. His hand extended toward the door.

IN THE PREDAWN gloom, Blake sensed another body in the room. She waited as the person felt for the bed, lifting the covers, and slid in. The movement did not threaten, but she felt it was not Chris. A slight hesitation, before an arm slid over her side, and the body snuggled against her back.

Blake smiled. A tall female—but not Christine.

"Do we at least make introductions before we kiss?"

The young woman sat up explosively. "Oh, my God… you're not my mother."

Laughing, Blake turned on the table light. She rolled over to find a dark blonde Christine.

The young woman looked at the mane of deep red hair.

"Oh, you are definitely not my mother."

The door opened, and the topic of conversation stood in the doorway. The long gray t-shirt with the skull and crossed sabers barely reached past the matching black panties Blake knew were there.

"Did someone call for a mother?"

The blonde bound from the bed and enveloped Christine. The two rocked their way back to the bed and fell into Blake's lap.

Blake laughed. "Good thing we didn't kidnap Mike. That ninja move would have scarred him for life."

"Oh, Mom. They told me you wouldn't be here until later today… like after breakfast. But I saw the car come in and figured you arrived early, so I came over."

Blake smiled at the rat-a-tat-tat of the girl's excitement. However, she was also curious about the security. "How did you get past the guards?"

There was a soft knock at the door. The three looked over at the woman standing there.

Noi smiled. "This is Lila, but we call her Nancy. She's one of us."

The woman then stepped in. "She couldn't get past us, Miss. I knew she was on the move before she left her dorm." She held up a small stack of folders. "I believe you requested our 201 files? And your requested wake-up is in three minutes, Miss."

Blake could feel she was on the verge of blushing, and it had nothing to do with her being naked. She took the folders.

"How many people are in the house at this moment?"

"Seven, Miss—Edward and the other night security, Graham, Victoria the cook, you three and me."

"That's eight…"

"You said people, Miss. By people, you imply humans. Zeus does not come under the human heading."

"What kind of dog?"

"Rottweiler mastiff mix… and please don't talk baby talk to him. He's highly sensitive about his babyish good looks." Blake noted a hint of a smile on the woman's face.

Blake flipped open the top file and then flipped it closed. "How soon is breakfast?"

"Twenty-eight minutes." The woman knew she was still in the interview stage. To the mother and daughter, she was a known commodity, but she understood she would have to pass muster with the new redhead.

Blake held up the folders. "Do I need to review these?" The question went to honesty in reply.

"You may find them of interest. I would like it if you would at least look over mine. I have sailing experience and know my way around weapons of all kinds."

Blake raised one eyebrow. The woman obviously knew about the raft and the upcoming danger. She not only knew but also wanted in. The question was why.

Blake looked at Christine who nodded slightly. She knew about this from one of her previous visits, which would explain Noi's comment of her being one of us.

Blake spread the folders and found the proper one. "I'll look it over, and we can talk after breakfast."

"Very good, Miss. We are now at twenty-six minutes." She then turned and left.

Noi looked at Blake with large eyes. "I'm in love. You are so badass." She giggled and fell back into her mother's lap as she wiggled in for a tighter hug.

Christine winked at Blake. "Sweet pea, you have no idea."

Blake waved her hand at the tall young woman. "There is nothing Noi about this one…"

Christine smiled broadly with pride. "Honey, you have no idea."

13 Back to the Raft

THE MAN IN a white shirt, an apron, and pants placed two mugs of coffee on the table. He moved the sugar container closer.

Blake stared at the table and smiled. She looked up, and her smile grew. "Pola quaquazi." *Sorry about the work.*

"Jambo bwana." *I work for you.* The man's smile was infectious. Blake had saved him from the slave trade when he was a young boy. He had always teased her she was sweet, but even a bee can use a little more honey. She lost track of him after he had joined the Navy. When she first found out he was on the sub, she was not surprised.

"Jambo. What's special for breakfast?"

"For two pretty women, I have some ugly bugs on a bed of octopus ink black fettuccine sautéed in fresh smashed garlic and drawn butter."

Chris looked at Blake with only one eye. "For breakfast?"

The man laughed. "No Miss… that is for dinner. This morning is Dungeness crab omelet Napoleon. I have four different kinds of toast, or I can make pancakes or waffles."

"Strawberries for the waffles?"

"No fresh. Only in spring. But I have compo made from frozen Oregon flavor bombs."

Blake rolled her eyes and looked at Christine. "Split a waffle?"

"As long as I don't have to share my omelet."

The man spun on his one heel. "Two omelets and one waffle with berries, coming right up."

Christine watched the man leave the mess area as he hummed a senseless tune. She turned back to Blake who shrugged as she sipped on her coffee. The flight was late, and they arrived in Seattle after midnight. The sub pushed back and made her way out to open sea under the last bits of darkness. Three hours of sleep combined with west-bound jet lag had Blake nursing a headache.

Her eyes rose to find Chris waiting for an explanation. "What?" She glanced at the door Cookie had disappeared through. "Cookie?"

Chris shrugged in exasperation. Her eyes swelled large as her lips pursed flat.

Blake laughed at the facial expression. They had both been on the receiving end of it from Noi. A sixteen-year-old, they found out, doesn't have much patience with older women acting like sixteen-year-olds.

"Who else was just here?"

"We go back many years. He was maybe eight or ten when I raided a camp on the border of Rwanda and Tanzania. From our sources, we believed the terrorist group had a large stash of arms—including several cases of shoulder-launched rockets filled with mustard gas."

Blake took a long pull on her coffee. She could still smell the camp. The soldiers were using the boys to make bombs and rockets. They could smell the punk smell of sulfur from a mile away across the desert. They had waited until night to cross the last mile. They were going to wait until dawn, but a boy made a mistake and blew up the tent he worked in. Blake found the boy's friend just coming back into the tent from peeing in the desert. Large sections of Cookie were flash seared. He looked like a poorly cooked piece of meat or a chocolate-chunk cookie.

"When we raided the camp, there was no mustard gas… but many boys forced to make bombs and rockets. Cookie was one of the lucky ones."

"Why boys?"

"They are cheap. They eat little, they work hard when scared, and if they blow up… they are easy to replace."

Christine was sitting in stunned silence when the cook returned with the food. Her eyes wandered along the side of his face and neck. The rash fields of small keloids now made sense. Everyone had a reason to be here or involved in what they were doing. The dregs of society had found a place where they felt accepted, fit in, and could thrive.

She sat back and looked at the man. "Cookie, can I ask you a question? You can tell me to go to hell, but I'd still like to ask it."

He pushed his lower lip out and nodded.

"Are you happy here?"

He thought a moment, and his face slacked. "No, Miss, I am not happy here."

Blake's mouth pinched. She knew better than to laugh and spoil the man's fun.

"Why? I mean, then why stay?"

He sat heavily on the end of another bench. Benches and tables were all bolted securely to the floor, wall, or both. His eyes rolled dramatically as he thought about how to explain such a complicated answer to such a simple question.

"You see, Miss, it is like this. I come from the svelte land of eastern Africa. As a small child, I be captured by very bad men. So I grow up as slave. We boys forced to make bombs or die. Some, like my brother, blow up. We get single bowl of rice and nyama wafu each day if we lucky. Some days it was only rice, some days nothing."

He pulled his shirt up and ran the back of his finger along his ribs. Even today, he had never put on much meat.

"The boy's like lion with no food for many days. You count the mbavu from the front or back—it no matter. What matter is—you alive. The lion, who still hunt, is happy they alive and still hunt."

He lowered his head in sadness and let it swing. Raising his head, his face was brighter.

"After a kill, lion eats until he so heavy with meat, he only roll over and sleep in sun." His finger stabbed the air as his voice rose in joy. "That lion... he knows he in heaven." His smile grew large on his face as his arms spread wide to take in the galley, mess, and the entire submarine. "I am *that* lion. I am not happy. I am in heaven."

"But you are also a mile under water..."

The man cackled. "Do you swim, Miss?"

"Yeah... yes, sure."

"You swim in the ocean out at all the boats."

"Yes... why?"

"If you are floating on water, does it matter if it swimming pool or two miles deep?"

She shook her head.

"If we are only thirty feet under the water, someone might see us and wonder if we need be stopped. But when we deep, we hiding. Nobody see us. We are like leopard in the night." His finger lined in front of his shushing lips. "We hide in water. Submarine safe and Cookie in heaven. Do you understand?"

She smiled with a slight cock of her head. "Yes… yes, Cookie, I think I do understand. Thank you. You see things clearly for what they are… and you have helped me see it, too."

He softly slapped his hand on her knee as he stood. "Good, because Cookie now go milk angry octopus. I think maybe I choose a bad time of her month." He winked at Blake. "If I no back by lunch… you get yourselves cereal for dinner."

As their laughter settled, Blake shook her head. "I really had a great time meeting and spending time getting to know your daughter. I can see why you are so protective."

"After those days in the Kendo dojo, I'm not so sure who I should be afraid for—her or anyone who tries to attack her."

Blake rubbed her upper left arm as her eyes grew large and expressive. "Yeah, she is deadly with the shinai. I almost wanted to paddle her to make her stop hitting me."

"How about the wild cartwheel in the air thing she did? I didn't know if she were going to kick me in the head, run up my face, or just do a flip—"

Blake snorted a laugh. "That was awesome to watch her lay the blade all the way from your head to your butt."

Christine covered her mouth as she pointed. Laughing, she rolled to one side. "Until she did the same thing to you, and you squawked around the room holding your butt."

"Well, she hit me harder than she did you."

"You're just a crybaby whiner."

"Oh, yeah? Well, just wait until this crybaby whiner gets your ass back to the raft." The two couldn't hold it together anymore.

The two days of transition flew by as the two women remembered the last week with Noi. Blake was a little jealous of Chris. However, she soon realized there was plenty of *daughter* to spread between a mother and an adoptive aunt. The week in New England had been as much about mother-daughter time as it had also been a deeper bonding of the two women. What had started as friends reached a depth few would ever experience. A level of trust, which went to life itself, and Blake had only experienced with a few other Ever Kinds, such as Manny and Cole.

She didn't know where to go with this new set of feelings. This strong of a bond had never happened with her and someone outside the Ever Kind. However, as they sat in the mess room, sharing meals and reliving a great time, she allowed herself to sink into the warm bath of this friendship—even knowing, on a lower level, it would not be a long friendship.

14 Not So Silent

THE TWO SAMURAI circled warily. The electronic score-keeping pad on each chest was in the orange. The pad on the blue warrior was blinking—imminent death. The bamboo sword flashed out, the other deflected. A parry, a repost, and response, the blade swished through empty air. The red warrior turned to find they were facing the blue expanse of the other warrior's back. She hesitated—not knowing the proper etiquette for this situation.

The back and head dropped from sight in the mask. She looked down in time to watch the blue sword slip between the legs and strike a hard punch to her gut. Her pad screamed her death.

The blue fell over as her pad started to echo the scream of death. The laughter was out of place with death, but Chris had become used to Blake's uncontrollable release of laughter at a kill.

Blake rolled her padded fencing helmet from her head. "You hesitated. You had the kill, but you hesitated. Never hesitate. Today you lost—"

"You died too…"

"But if you had even struck my leg or back… I would

be dead, and you would live to kill another day."

Christine collapsed next to the woman who had become her best friend and sparring partner over the past year. "I froze. I honestly was wondering in the split second when I saw your back—what is the proper etiquette in competition." She shook her head and her sweat-matted hair. She looked south across the ocean. The sun was just starting to bulge the cutline separating the gray-blue of the sky from the green-black of the sea. "I can't believe I did that."

Blake's hand fell warmly on the other's knee. "There won't be any more competitions. Everything we do from here on out will be true life and death. If you hesitate—ever—it will mean death."

"But we're sparring. In my head, I know soon it will be for real... but for now..."

Blake sat up. "Have you ever killed someone?"

The brunette shook her head.

"Have you ever stabbed someone?"

She started to wag her head, and then she smiled coyly. "Yeah..."

Blake leaned her head forward and pinched the bridge of her nose. "I mean with a blade—so you drew blood."

Chris reeled in mock offense. "I drew blood. It was the last time I ever tried using old diapers and safety pins. Noi kept bleeding and bleeding. I almost took her to the clinic."

Blake shook with laughter. "Noi? Your daughter, Noi? You stuck her with a safety pin... Noi?" Her eyes kept getting bigger as she rose. Finally, in a horrified breath, she pointed and charged. "You brute."

THE TWO COLLAPSED in each other's arms and laughed as they watched for the sun to lighten the sky of predawn. They started their silent routine of stretching out the muscles so they wouldn't ache later.

Blake thought as she watched her friend, the year and some had rushed past like a rogue gale wind crossing the ocean.

One moment, they had been feeling out each other's strengths and weaknesses with a French Foil. The next they were bound in daily combat. Nights found them in and out of each other's bed—sometimes others, but mostly each other.

The brunette was comfortable with the flow of the Ever Kind. The millennia of lives, sex changes, and relationships had created a give and take reflected in their attitudes about death, but also sharing their beds. Blake had been drawn to Chris as another woman who not only matched her height, but also taste in boots, leggings, and loose blouses. Blake wasn't even sure who was wearing whose clothes anymore. The one constant was Christine's fondness for black boots, because it matched her backfilling dark hair.

"Swim before a shower?"

The nod flowed into them strolling to the fantail of the boat. Gangways led to the floating deck. Seconds later, the two had stripped and joined the half dozen others taking a morning swim in the deep end of the ultimate pool before breakfast and the day's work.

"How deep do you think it really is here?"

Blake looked past her friend at a baldhead with a cap of tattoos. "Gunther… what is our depth?"

The head turned, and the solid black eyes blinked. "I haven't been paying much attention to depth lately, but it should all be over…" Blake recognized the man doing the math from fathoms to meters to feet. "Umm…three thousand feet or more. Try to touch bottom… We'll wait." The small crowd of swimmers laughed in the early light.

Blake turned back to Christine. "Why?"

"When I was a kid, my mother used to warn me not to swim where I couldn't touch—bad could happen. But here, I feel so safe."

Blake closed her eyes against the sun just above the horizon. She thought about what was south and east of them.

"Until the pirates come…"

Chris hummed seriously. "There be pirates here too…"

MANFRED WANDERED INTO the mess room. His attention was on the small book open in his left hand. Blake recognized the classic book on war by the ancient, but still relevant, Sun Tzu.

Blake leaned forward and whispered to Christine. "Coffee or table first?"

The game had started with Noi. There are habits people do without thinking—like playing with one's hair, rubbing something on one's head, or even picking your nose while driving. They are all done while distracted from interfacing with the world. The game was to guess the distracted person's next move.

"Table… and the book will go face down."

Blake was certain she knew her six-time ex-spouse better than just a guess. She shook her head. "Too fussy—he'll mark his place and stick the closed book under his arm while he gets his coffee."

The two smiled, and fist bumped at the great guesses.

Manny stopped, looked up, and looked around. He blinked as if he had just woken up. Turning left, he closed the book and threw it into the recycle bin for paper products. Leaning, he plucked an apple from the counter and walked back out.

The two women mirrored each other with open mouths.

The long black curls hung from the rogue's head as it appeared back around the doorjamb.

A few others joined in the laughter. More than a few had watched the women playing their new game. Manny had been warned about the game and decided to be preemptive.

"So… who won the bet?" Manny stood and walked back around the corner. Getting his coffee, he rescued the small book and laid it on the table next to Blake. "Was there anything?"

Blake slugged him in the arm. "Ass." They all laughed. "If anything, you slipped the cover to mark your place."

He opened the book. The front flap of the dust cover was between the two pages where he had stopped.

Christine's hand dropped from pointing and onto the table. "I completely missed that. I thought he only closed the book and really threw it away."

Manny chuckled. "I remember playing variations on this game. Among certain people, such as spies, it serves the purpose to be aware of the things we do as habit, and how to create randomness to break the predictability. I'm glad you two brought this back to the raft." He stood. "And now, if you will excuse me, I need to go share my apple with a little friend."

The two women chuckled. "Give our best to Jessie."

15 A Visit

THE SPAR SNAPPED over against the dogged-off line on the port side. The sail fluttered at the top few feet and then became solid. The sun was now on their faces, and the wind mostly at their backs. The small sailboat heeled slightly, but shallow enough to be lazy.

The long black hair curled over the side as Manny eased his body down into a relaxed slump. His eyelids were relaxed as the sun warmed his face. His breathing was slow and restful.

His lips were parted by the tip of his tongue. It rested there a moment, and then he took a breath. The tip disappeared as his mouth opened.

"I was just thinking about the time you took me sailing for our honeymoon. The sun was just like this. It was chilly, but if I was still in the sunshine, it was warm."

"Fuck you, Manfred. You hated it."

His one eye opened partway as he squinted to glare at her. "The eighty flea-infested, dung-reeking, drunken warriors—those I hated. The ripping from the hearth and home to sail off the end of the world—yes, I hated it. Being dragged along to start a new colony in Iceland—that was worth hating. Being only a fourteen-year-old girl with no say in the marriage to a beastly oaf who raped me on my wedding night and most nights in front of your men—yes, I hated it too. But the sun? No. The sun on my face, the snap of the sail, the sound of the waves on the hull…"

Blake slouched into the hull of the shallow boat alongside her friend. "I wasn't an oaf. I had great taste in my boots and the furs I wore. You didn't complain about the arctic fox cape I gave you the night before."

Manny's hand fell on her hip, and he held his finger there. "The cape… I had forgotten about the cape. I loved it. But you were an asshole to think I wasn't going to grow. By the next winter, it was six inches too short. My calves damn near froze."

"It didn't get too short, you ass. You got as fat as a cow."

Manny laughed. "And whose fault was that—mister I have to have a son?"

Blake patted his hand. "Yes, and you did fine with the twins."

Thought and silence fell over them like a blanket. The warm sun and gentle sea lulled them.

"Do you ever think about them?"

Blake stirred and sat up to look at the top of the sail. She pulled the rope tighter and adjusted the rudder. "The boys? Yeah… occasionally."

"Not just the twins, but all of them. Not just ours but others we've birthed or sired."

Blake checked the compass and brought the heading around. The sail now cast a shadow on Manny, who sat up and ran his zipper to his neck. "I've been thinking about them lately. How we have children, but they are only the children of our bodies. We don't produce more Ever Kind." He looked out across the ocean. The waves were low, and he could see for many miles of green-gray. He looked up, and even the sky wasn't a real blue.

"The storm is moving down from Alaska. Neil said by tomorrow night."

Manny opened one of the small holds. He looked in and smiled as he fetched out a thermos. He passed it across as his other hand reached in and drew out a second.

The warm coffee with a slight lacing of rum felt good. Blake flipped the top closed and set the cylinder between her legs. "Have you ever known any of us to birth a new Ever Kind?"

His voice was soft as he shook his head. "No."

She watched him as he sat thinking. "So why are you wondering now? Is it because of Jun?"

He rubbed the side of his mouth as his face shrugged. His one shoulder rose slightly. "Maybe." He looked up. "You would think… sometime during the past five thousand years… one of us would have wondered."

"Or produced."

He pointed and winked.

"So now… as you are on the brink of removing one of the unremovable, you start thinking about… what? Our mortality?"

Manny sat silent for many minutes, and then he snorted softly. "It really sounds funny when you put it in such a light."

He looked up and out. His jaw nudged forward, and Blake turned.

The catamaran was large, but compared with those of the raft, the thirty-footer was small. The speed in the light wind was impressive. Even with the raw, unpolished hulls, Blake could see it was overclocking the speed of the wind. The two boats were the first to be 3-D printed from salvaged plastic. Mixed trash aluminum made up the masts and spars while they worked on a newer composite from the sea trash.

The cat turned, and for a brief moment, ran alongside. Blake waved at Christine who had a bunny in the headlights look on her face. The baldhead of Erik, one of the Navy sailors, sat next to Christine as he walked her through sailing the twitchy racer. In a slow flash, the small sailboat was bobbing in their wake. Erik looked back with a huge smile and gave Blake the thumbs up. It's somewhat hard to crash into anything when you're learning how to drive in the middle of the ocean—which made Erik's job as instructor a lot easier.

The two watched as the catamaran tacked and sailed west. The group of six students was having fun learning on the wide cat. Blake smiled as she remembered learning how to sail on the small lake in India. Her father hadn't been as patient as Erik had, but the barge also wasn't as fun. The split mast sail was more of an aid to the rowing than it was the main propulsion.

"How much do you know about Christine?"

Blake's mind returned to the man in the current boat. "What do you mean?"

Manfred shifted in an attempt to become comfortable. Blake wasn't sure if it was a physical comfort or with where his mind was. His right hand stroked at his goatee. His eyes scanned back and forth across the open ocean as if he were looking for an answer.

He turned back toward Blake. His lips curled in with a

thought. "I'm not sure. I just have a feeling there is more there than meets the eyes. It's how she carries herself, or how things don't faze her. It's as if she's an Ever Kind, but then I don't have a sense of her. But then, I don't have a sense about Brie either. Both of them are like blank spots."

Blake knew what he was stumbling around about. She had stubbed her toe on much of the same thoughts. The more irritating for her was being around Christine and her daughter Noi. They had recently treated Noi for her seventeenth birthday by meeting her in Seattle. The three had taken the coast train down through Portland, San Francisco and ended their two weeks of food and fun in Los Angeles. As it was February, they had gone to an almost deserted Disneyland. The three had ridden time after time through the Pirates of the Caribbean ride, singing themselves hoarse. The three had rented a room with two king-sized beds, and Noi never questioned Chris sharing Blake's bed instead of hers. It had been a slip—but not repeated.

Blake tacked and glanced at the GPS. There were several Ever Kind on the raft that she could home in on, but the GPS was a visual confirmation of her sense. She tugged on the line running through the dog cleat. The dogs released, and she let the sail out until it started to riffle or luff at the top. Pulling the rope snug, she settled back against the gunwale.

"As close as I've come to Christine and her daughter, I have always sensed there was something there… something never spoken." She rolled her face slightly up to look at her friend. "But I have never had a feeling it was anything malevolent or which I even needed to know… it was just there."

She snorted softly. "You hired her…"

"Hmm…" Manny mused. "Even when she probed my ribs with a dull knife, I knew she wasn't a threat." He started laughing.

"What?" Blake started chuckling at him being amused.

"I don't know if she ever told you… she looked so serious trying to stick me up. But the whole episode was so amusing to me that I leaned over like I was pulling my wallet out of my pants pocket. And then gave her a kiss on the cheek."

Blake slid down the side of the boat laughing. "What did she do?"

"She told me I'd better have more than just a peck on the cheek."

Blake laughed as she thought about her friend. "Did you pull down your pants?"

Manny squealed. "Only after I told her I had a job for her. And yes, I did."

THE DRONE HOVERED with the sun at its back—if it had one. The image was vividly clear of the two in the bottom of the small sailboat.

The small Asian woman turned and faced the tall blonde. "It looks like they are about thirty minutes out. The *Albatross* isn't built for speed, just survivability."

Brie leaned in. "There is no transom. How does it not sink?"

The woman leaned against the raised desk. "The term is self-bailing. Any water getting into the cockpit runs right out the back. There are two plastic hulls with plenty of float foam between to keep the boat on top of the water no matter what the bad weather or if it tips over from a bad sailor."

"Nice."

"It's a New England design. They have some nasty seas there."

Brie glanced at one of the other displays. The students were finished securing the small catamaran. There was one she needed to talk to, so she turned and walked off.

The Asian woman's mouth tucked in on the left. She was used to the tall blonde's taciturn nature. She resumed her usual stance as she scanned the dozen screens.

16 A Meeting

CHRISTINE GRABBED ERIK'S arm. He turned. "I just wanted to thank you." She rose onto her toes and kissed his cheek. He blushed. "I enjoyed today."

The young man shied. "Anytime you want to go out…"

Chris drew back with a puzzled look. "No, I meant the sailing…"

He laughed. "So was I." He looked at her a moment and then his eyes opened largely. "Oh… oh, no… I mean… Oh, no. I thought you knew… Darrel and I… oh, shit…" His face was almost purple.

Christine suddenly understood. She leaned in. "Sorry, a misunderstanding. Blake and I… well, um… look at you." She squeezed his bicep with both hands, which made him blush even harder.

Darrel came up carrying two large bags of gear. He cleared his throat. With a flash of insight, Chris stepped over to the man and kissed his cheek as well.

"What did I do to deserve that?" His smile was pure innocence.

Chris kissed his other cheek. "Just for being the two

guys you are. Thanks again for the sailing lesson. I will always be up for any and all I can get." She turned and walked off.

Darrel turned to his friend. "Mind telling me what just happened?"

Erik laughed as he took one of the bags. "Just roll with it, dude—otherwise, it will get very complicated very fast."

They watched as Christine opened a hatch door and stepped through. The hatch led to the stairs leading down into the living quarters.

Chris was still smiling as she got to the bottom, then turned the corner, and ran into a tall blonde.

She backed up a step and started to apologize. But as her mouth opened, her eyes opened in the realization of what she was seeing.

Brie stepped and placed her hand over Christine's mouth. "Not a word." She looked around and dragged the brunette into the storage room.

Closing the door, she kept her face close to the other. "I'm glad you still recognize me. It will make this all so much easier." Brie's eyes and face closed in a scowl for a moment and then opened again. "We need to talk. But as far as anyone else knows, we have never met. Understood?"

"What the hell happened…?"

Brie growled, "I said do you understand?"

"Yes, but you can't just show up after—"

"I said we would talk… but later. I have to go deal with Manfred and Blake right now. Where are you working?"

"The solar smelter—the new one we installed this year."

"I'll come find you tomorrow. Until then, keep your mouth shut."

"Blake and I are… well, we pretty much sleep together…"

Brie thought as she searched the dark eyes. "That's fine. Just make sure you don't share any pillow talk."

"She's friends with our daughter…" Her voice trailed off.

The electrical like shock was visible in the blonde. A hint of panic surrounded her eyes. She exhaled. "Tomorrow." And then she kissed Christine on the lips. She opened the door and was gone.

Christine fell back against the bulkhead and slid to the floor. Her mind raced as she stared at nothing. Soon the tears began to fall.

17 The Arrangement

BLAKE WONDERED WHAT had happened when Christine never came to her cabin. She knew Chris didn't have a comms unit installed in her head, but she also knew it was a simple matter to check in with anyone on the raft. Even spread over a square mile, the raft was still a small community of only five thousand souls. Anywhere in the world, this only qualifies it as a town, not a city.

It irritated her that it concerned her. She knew the woman was safe. What chafed Blake was her emotional attachment to Chris. If Christine had shared another bed, or just needed a night alone, Blake wanted to think she was enough of a big girl to be beyond any petty jealousy. But she still felt a queasy empty feeling.

Blake sorted through screen after screen of workflow and product reallocations. The numbers, which usually fell into regimented order for her, continued to run rampantly wild. She put down the scrolling stick and pushed the tablet away. Her boot came up, and she jammed it hard on the edge of the desk. She could feel the slow burn of either anger or panic. She closed her eyes. If she let it win, her stomach would give her hell for the rest of the day.

Kicking the desk one more time, she stood. Her hands were on her hips. Over the millennia, she had been in hundreds of relationships. Many having resulted in lasting marriages—but this one…

She strolled down the hall toward the main control center. Ming stood at her bank of eyes on the world. Blake looked over at the station usually filled with the muscular bulk of Erik. A slim blond sailor with a bright tattoo of rope and anchor on his right arm stood the watch in Erik's stead. His movements were sparse and confident. Blake was sure the tattoo was late coming to his enlistment in either some Navy or the raft.

Turning, she walked to the small wall of kitchen. Fruit or pastries were behind suitably sealed glass doors. Liquid dispensers were bracketed by lidded containers. Nothing held more than twelve ounces because everything was refillable. Every container sealed against leakage—if it dropped or knocked over, it would neither spill nor become a heavy projectile in a violent storm. Blake hit the espresso button six times. As she turned and looked out the panorama of windows, she noticed Ming's head rise slightly. She waited.

"You didn't drink excessively last night at dinner… so you must not have slept well."

The machine finished, sealed the cap, and cycled down. Blake snatched the container. Being called out on her foul mood was not something she tolerated. But Ming being Ming, and almost a robot in her reactions to the world, Blake could feel a streak of exception coming on.

She walked toward the short wall of twenty-seven-inch displays. Blake was convinced the woman could watch all twenty-eight monitors at the same time. Her head hardly moved, and her hands barely moved on the two floating hemispheres that made a split keyboard. Blake watched the muscles of the woman's legs and bare feet. The two slightly raised plates formed another pressure keypad sensitive to the slight pressure changes. The foot pressures combined to make the functions, controls, and alternate keys. Few could *play* the station, and only Ming held it as a relaxing form of Tai Chi.

"What makes you think I slept poorly?"

The woman's head barely moved. "From the smell of the coffee, I would guess you hit all espresso instead of your usual two espresso, two Tanzanian teaberry, and two Columbian. You wanted the hit but not the hard caffeine buzz." The woman turned her head and nodded at the container in Blake's hand. "Espresso contains the same caffeine, but the steam doesn't release the oil or hard acid. Lift with no acid for a stomach already in distress."

Her attention returned to the monitors.

"You might try a short shake this morning of ginger, papaya, mango, rot gut." She turned back to look at Blake's one lifted eyebrow. "I was kidding about the rot gut. The other settles the gut."

Out of the corner of her eye, Blake noticed something on one of the monitors. Her right hand raised and started to point to it when all twenty-eight monitors became one, and the single was zooming in. "I noticed about twenty minutes ago. The conversation seemed tense from the start…"

Blake rolled to study the screen. "What the hell is going—?"

Ming leaned back and watched the redhead. "I can give you targeted sound… but because of where they are, it won't be the best quality."

Blake put her left hand and coffee container out. She could feel the liquid slosh from the quick movement. The sealed containers were for times like this. Close to a million American dollars coursed through this small area.

Blake studied the two women on the screen. Their faces were only inches apart. Their faces were tense, the conversation not pleasant. "Tell me, Ming. When you were with the People's Army Intelligence did you eavesdrop on people who were your friends?"

"I was never with the Army Intelligence—I was in the Secret Intelligence. And of course, we did. Even the commander was within our reach. If the president thought he was beyond our view, he was a fool. There were at least ten cameras and two dozen microphones in his bedroom alone."

Blake didn't have to look at the Asian to know she was telling the truth and probably had firsthand knowledge. "Do you know where Manny is?"

"Purification station."

"Can we patch this through?"

She could feel the small woman give her a hard stare. Blake knew if she turned, she would have been rebuked. Instead, she triggered her head comm. She popped her right jaw. "Manfred one."

The sound felt to be from behind her. She now knew it resonated through the bones of her head. "Manny."

"Manny, it's Blake. Are you near a monitor?"

"Yes, Papa-one-seven-four."

"Papa-one-seven-four."

Ming flinched three fingers. The large screen shrunk to a Quad-Array and the rest of her wall returned to her normal watch.

"What am I watching, Blake?"

"It's Brie and Christine having a very intense conversation. They're on the battle wing of the smelting cat. It's as far from anyone listening in on their conversation as they can get."

"Can Ming give us acoustics?"

"It's too degraded." She could feel the short woman give her another hard look for lying.

Manny cleared his throat to let her know he also knew she was lying, but he wasn't going to call her on it. "So what do you suppose it is?"

Blake felt bad for spying, even without the sound. "I didn't even think they had ever met…"

The silence trailed. Blake started to wonder if the connection had auto disconnected. She almost missed his voice in the noise her own mind. "I don't think they ever had…"

Blake watched as Brie reached out and didn't just touch Christine's arm as a salesperson might in making a point or connection. What she watched was an insistent grip—bringing the two women together—very close. Blake knew at the close distance, the eyes would be fighting not to cross. It has a tendency to focus the mind.

BRIE GRITTED HER teeth. Her voice was as slow and strident as she could make it. "Whatever has happened in the last seventeen years is not important now. What happened—happened. You need to move on and get with the new program."

"You can't just wipe out all of our history and—"

"Damn it, Chris, I'm telling you—the world is crashing, and you want to plant petunias. Look around you. Close to three trillion pounds of sterling are floating around out here. The raft is one tiny part of the baby steps in learning how to clean up the shit we threw about using the ocean for our dustbin. The raft and probably five others will be at this for a hundred years—two if we keep on it like we do today. But the raft and cleanup is only part of the battle. The other part is this crossroads—right now, right here. We can choose purgatory or redemption. You need to get on your knees and pray you're on the side of redemption."

Brie glanced around. Her voice lowered even more. "This opportunity to rid the world of the evilest person ever has never occurred before in the history of mortals, Ever Kind, or *us*. You have no idea. The *us* have never had to deal with his kind… but I have broken bread with the devil. I have looked into the eyes of him and seen hell—and the devil and his hell are coming here. There is only one way this can happen and still have the ending this world so desperately needs."

"For me to give up my—"

"Our. No, I have not forgotten. No, I was not there… but I knew. This is not something any parent can do. But there is the difference… we are not just any parent. We are us… and we will survive… no matter what happens."

Christine took in a deep breath and let it out slow and loud. "But we don't know if Noi is us."

The powder blue eyes danced desperately from one dark orb to the other and back. Searching for the answer they both needed. "No… we don't. It is the risk we must take."

Christine's hand moved to her mouth as she turned to look as far out to sea as she could. The answer wasn't there, but she could hope.

A single tear slid down her cheek as she sighed softly. "When?"

Brie moved over beside her, hip to hip. She put her arm around the familiar shoulder from so long ago. "I don't know… this summer or next is my guess. He won't come when he has to fight the weather, as well. He's evil and greedy, but not stupid and wasteful. It will be during summer, but he will need the wind for sailing. So my guess is early summer when the trade winds still have some force in them."

Chris opened her hand and looked at the two items.

"I'll call you and tell you when it happens, and again when to trigger the beacon."

Christine leaned her head onto Brie's shoulder. "You're still a horse's arse."

Brie kissed the top of Christine's head and rested her chin there. "I can live with that. I already have before."

18 Life Goes On

BLAKE'S BOOT RESTED jammed against the edge of the desk. Manny thought about saying something. Then he remembered a commander whose entire comment on his boot being placed where it was not respectful to be. Blake had commented on how unclean it was, and thus not respectful of the knighthood, or towards either his king or god. He and Blake had gone forth into Jerusalem the next day and with three hundred other crusaders had lost their lives. Manny and Blake liked the following day because then, they were on the winning side.

In the silence of waiting, Manny couldn't let it go. "At least the boot is clean this time."

One eyebrow rose, but her eyes stayed focused on the orange she was peeling. "The day I rebuked the young hothead knight... *my* boots were like black mirrors. Your boots were covered with fung."

"I believe you died before me."

Her body tremors shook her softly as she smiled. "Who do you think put the three shafts through your neck?"

As usual, Blake got the twinge a second before

Manfred. She sat up.

"Mommy's home."

Cole turned the corner as Manny was chuckling. The black man lowered his head and growled at the two. "Laugh it up, cupcake…"

On seeing Cole's face, Manny laughed all the harder as Blake covered her mouth. The more she examined the face, the wider her eyes grew.

Manny finally gathered enough control to squeak out, "How was San Francisco?" He and Blake were back to un-controlled hysterics.

Knowing he was beaten, Cole retreated. As he passed Ming on his way to the coffee, he growled at her open face. "Shut up. I've already heard it a hundred times."

As he waited for the coffee to fill, he examined his face in the polished stainless steel. The large scar ran from his left jaw to his cheek and then split. The main scar split across his nose and divided his right eyebrow on its way to his temple. The other fork crossed his left eye and made a direct line to his hairline, creating a three-inch line of white hair in his tight curls. The other four short scars on each cheek were tribal. He had them added after his bout with the lightning bolt.

He stepped toward the wall of monitors and stopped. His eyes scanned the monitors as he sipped on the coffee. He found himself rushing to get through at least half of the monitors before Ming changed the cameras. He guessed she was good enough and fast enough to scan all of them before wiping the wall for the new feeds.

Ming's head only flinched slightly as she took in the tall black man with fresh pinkish scars. Her eyes were al-ready scanning the fresh feeds as she thought about the man standing near her.

"With your skin tone and those scars, I would think a two-inch heavy-beaten gold hoop would be in order instead of the cheesy CZ crystal stud."

He almost shot coffee through his nose. "What makes you think it's not real?" His voice was a squeaking crock.

"The light refraction is too pure. It's playing hell with my back scanner. Please turn your head a little more toward me… Yes, that's got it." She smiled at his buying into what she was saying. "Obviously, you have thought about the hoop. So the stud is just the placeholder until the new piercing heals. If you were going to be serious about a diamond, you would be more of a two-carat tops kind of guy. My guess is you looked at closer to a karat and a half."

Cole took another smaller sip. He liked this woman, but he never knew what she might say. He took another sip as he thought about what it would be like to hang out with her for the next few hundred years or so.

Cole moved toward the office. "I was looking at a one-point-three. It had seven inclusions, and was definitely blue."

Ming nodded. "The claw marks are a nice touch. But sorry about the lightning strike."

"It blew the game… tenth hole and I was already seven under par."

Ming refreshed the screens twice before she sighed. "Well, must have been major suckage."

Cole stepped into the office for a second try, growling at Blake to shut up and glaring at Manny the entire way to a chair. He sat down and took a pull from the container. He missed the steam in his face from a regular mug.

"Fuck you two."

Manny leaned back in his chair and stacked his boots on the corner of the desk. "I heard about the lightning strike. Sorry about the game. Is it true you were six under par?"

"Seven." The man leaned back with his eyes closed.

Blake gave a low whistle. She remembered Cole was the man who made huge efforts to go to Scotland during the Great War to shag balls down the fairways.

His left eye opened as he rolled his head over to look at Blake. "It wasn't as bad as if it was Galway or anything. Not to finish the round there—I would have been pissed. Pebble…" He waffled his open hand in the air. "Eeh. But it was a spectacular round."

Blake raked at her cheek. "And the…?"

Manny groaned. "He's getting ready to go get drafted."

She frowned at Manfred. He was silent and looked like he was ready to drift off to sleep. And then she got it, and a smile washed across her face. "You'll be commanding what kind of ship?"

Cole chuckled. "I'm old school. She's a Corsair. She's two hundred eighty feet at the waterline with a forty-two beam. She sports five masts and carries a push at twenty percent over. She's in Curacao getting fitted right now with a flying and racing spinnaker."

"Impressive numbers?"

"She held sixteen knots over a twenty-mile beam reach, but she was under standard sail. I think we can squeeze twenty with the fly or twenty-two on the racing. We'll see on her shakedown to Bombay."

Manny stopped fussing with the set of calipers and frowned out of the left side of his face. "What's in Bombay?"

"A pair of mini Gatling guns—thirty-two hundred rounds a minute."

Blake and Manny both pushed out their lower lips as they nodded. "Which mounting system?"

Cole looked back at Blake, the weapons nerd of the three. "Roll out wing mounts. They're building them in Bombay. Supposedly, the cycle time is under five seconds."

Blake frowned in thought. "Garlands?"

Cole nodded. "Rebuilds for the most part. I think originally, they were New Old Stock, mothballed near the end of the Vietnam War as part of the bribe support programs."

"Where did you get them?"

"One of the drug cartels had them in the bay doors of a Huey slick. They were using it for indigenous species suppression in the back valleys of Columbia."

Blake's eyelids turned to burning slits. "Killing the Indians to make room for the farmers."

Manny toyed with the ceramic mug on his desk. "And the Huey?"

Cole shook his head and snarled his lip. "Rusted piece of shit—wasn't worth the effort to salvage… not even for a suicide mission. But I've got a line on a couple of early Hawks we can have delivered out here. We might even talk the captain into hanging around long enough, or at least be available, for the big party."

Manny pursed his smile as he played with the hair on his bottom lip. "What is the ship?"

Cole smiled. "Remember the hospital ship the International Red Cross was running off the west coast of Africa during the Ebola crisis in the eighties?"

Manny's lower lip pushed out with a smile. "The one with a helipad on each end?"

Cole's head bounced a nod. "The same."

"A floating hospital would be nice…"

"Hawks are nice too." Blake's eyes sparkled.

Cole chuckled at the playful little girl look on the redhead. "One is just the standard NATO 7.62 mm system, but the other is coming with a full thirty cannon both sides with a forty grenade launcher. If you're a good little girl, Daddy might let little Blakey have the keys some Saturday night. You can go terrorize some black market tuna fishermen off Hawaii."

Blake growled with a laugh. "This is a business meeting… don't start teasing me sexually. I'd have to slap Manny around and talk to him about sexual harassment. What kind of round loads come with them?"

Manny's head hit the desk. Cole ignored the laughing man and continued with the real conversation, which was degrading fast. "The light NATO Hawk will have about a dozen full loads, but the heavy only had just shy of six. I'll see if I can scare up some more this week."

"Especially the thirty caliber rounds… and if you can, armor piercing with tracer would be nice. Makes it easier to target at sea—"

Manny's head rose. "Speaking of which… when are you heading for Singapore?"

"Next month—we have a deal to do in Venezuela first. I have a meeting with this fat guy in a few months. I heard Brie was on the raft right now, so I want to get her update before I talk to this guy."

Manny and Blake exchanged looks. Cole read the

sudden chill.

"What?"

The large mustache flared as Manny rolled his lips in hard on his teeth. "We're not sure." He swung the monitor around so they could all see it. He popped his jaw. "Ming?"

"Would you feed the video here into the office please?"

The monitor flickered. "Thanks."

Cole leaned in. "No sound?"

Blake let Manny respond.

"Who is the brunette?"

"Christine. She is the lead on the metal smelters. We've been…" Blake wasn't sure where to go from there. She wasn't sure where to go with any of this as she watched the video for the third time.

Cole kept watching. "Can we slow this down?"

Manny pushed the mouse around and restarted the video at half speed.

"There…" Cole pointed at the arm grab. "They have some serious history. Does this Christine have any protective training?"

Blake rubbed at her right shoulder. "Yeah… she's good."

Cole sat back. He didn't need to see the rest of the video. "Whatever is going on, they have a past, and it's not just a hook-up for coffee on some Wednesday instead of work. The arm grab was more a protective and intimate securing. If you don't want to back her into a corner, I'll sound her out this afternoon when I have her brief me."

Manfred watched his finger draw random lines on the desk. His eyes rose to meet the solid black of his friend's eyes. "Do you think Brie would seriously team up with

Jun?"

Cole rubbed his long fingers over his fresh scars as his mind raced. Manny could see the eyeballs twitching back and forth as the reflections on the deep black orbs changed.

"Normally, I would say it would never happen…" He waved loosely at the monitor. "But after watching this… something is up… or has changed."

Manny sat back as he stroked his mustache and goatee. "Find out what. We can't afford to have her as a wild card. She's the critical key, and we need to know we can count on her completely."

19 Intentions

COLE HAD EVERY intention of easing into the meat of the conversation. He knew the recent additions to his face were unnerving. But Brie seemed especially affected by the new look. Her answers were less than direct, and at times, evasive. For all the solid information he was getting out of her, he might as well be interviewing a street hooker in Shanghai.

Cole leafed through notes and then looked over the forms he would need to moor off Singapore. Some of the information Brie had already entered to ease the entry set off alarms in Cole's head.

He riffled back through the papers and then looked up at the map on the wall. Absentmindedly, he picked up the dirk on the desk, and as he stared at the map, bounced the tip off the paperwork. He frowned as he rose. His focus was on the map.

"We generally sail at fourteen to fifteen knots. We should be able to make a run from Singapore to Port Klang in a day, shouldn't we?" He rounded the desk and stood in front of the map. His left knee pushed against Brie's left thigh. She moved her leg slightly, but also, torqued her body around to look at the map.

Cole dropped onto her lap. His legs straddled hers. Pushing in one great thrust, he buried the dirk through her thigh to the hilt. His left hand slapped down on her mouth as she screamed—slamming her back to the wall. Death is no threat to an Ever Kind, but serious injury or maiming will get their attention. From the wild flare in her eyes, he knew he had her full attention.

His face was only a few inches from hers. His voice dripped with threats of venom. "If I sail my ship anywhere near Singapore with this paperwork, they would blow me out of the water before I could reef a single sail. You come on this raft, threaten one of the workers... and now you pull this shit?" He eased body mass forward as he prepared to do more damage. The movement was not lost on her. Her head started to move back and forth as the wild in her eyes turned to fear. She saw the second, smaller knife, in his hand.

Cole's words were more breath than voice. "I'm going to take my hand away. You have three seconds to start telling me the truth before I start probing critical tendons. Do you understand?"

The tip of his knife pinked at the dent above the knee-cap. She nodded.

The knife stayed, but his other hand slid to her throat. She swallowed.

Brie gritted her teeth. "Do you have a comm unit in your head?"

Cole nodded.

"Get Manfred in here. If I'm going to go through this... I only want to do it once."

His black orbs reflected her face as he growled for

Manny. "He's on his way."

She watched his face. "You don't have to keep threatening me. I'm not going anywhere. Think what you want now… but I am all in on this side. Always was, and no matter what it might look like down the road—you can bet the bank I still am."

"Then why are you threatening the dark-haired woman?"

Brie's eyes stuttered between his two. "There are some things which go beyond what we are doing here. Things which are beyond even the Ever Kind…"

"What could be beyond the Kind?" Manny strolled through the door and took the seat across the desk. Blake, followed closely by Christine, eased around the corner, and leaned against the wall. The small office was small—and now packed.

Cole stood and filled the door. Manny leaned the chair back and rested his left boot on the corner of the desk. "Go ahead. We're listening. What could be beyond the scope and understanding of the Ever Kind?" His left hand floated in the air with the palm up.

Brie glanced at Christine. The split second was a full communication.

Christine tensed. Her hand almost reached out. Her mouth formed, but only her breath said, "No…" Blake could feel the tension.

Brie turned to Manny. "There is a lot going on before next summer." She turned back toward the door and Cole. "You need to stop screwing around in South America. The few million you would get for running those drugs—I'll give you. We don't have time for the petty things. Pack the mini-guns in the hold, make the racks on board, or order them in Singapore. But you need to be through the Suez before Christmas. If you can do it—do it by mid-November. The crescent is going to be a choke point for many nasty people this winter. A fine, fast sailing vessel like yours will be easy pickings for the fleets of Zodiac maniacs."

She turned back around. "Jun is moving people, arms, and ships from all over the world. We need to be part of the movement." She leaned forward. "But you have to trust me. Right now—I get it—you don't. So I'm going to show you one thing and one time only. I will not explain it. Not now. It has nothing to do with the raft, Jun, or the Ever Kind. And yet... it has everything to do with the Ever Kind. After we get rid of Jun, I will explain. But for now... I trust you with my life, Christine's life, and the biggest secret you have never even thought of."

She lurched up. Her left hand shot out, grabbed Christine's hand, and pulled it to the desk. She slammed the hand down with her hand on top—trapping the other. Her right hand pulled the dagger out of her thigh and smashed the tip down through the two hands and burying the end in the desk.

Both women winced, but neither cried out.

The two watched Manny. Christine's eyes slid closed, and the tension in her shoulders slumped.

Holding Manfred's intense stare, Brie jerked the dagger out of the hands and laid it handle first in front of the man. She slid her hand off Christine's hand. Everyone watched as the two wounds gently closed and stopped bleeding. In minutes, Brie grabbed a tissue, spit on it, and cleaned first Christine's hand and then hers. The two scars were pink.

Manny looked up at Christine. "So you're Ever Kind also?"

She shook her head. Brie cleared her throat. "All you need to know for now, is neither of us are Ever Kind. Well, not as you know them."

Cole was now standing more at attention. Manny recognized the man was uncharacteristically unnerved. "So what are you… aliens from outer space?"

Brie turned and smiled. She stepped to the man in the door, and as her palm cradled his jaw, her thumb traced the lightning scar. "We are every bit as human as you. Just not as old or scarred." She leaned in, kissed the light pink line, and whispered, "Did I ever tell you how sexy I find a good scar?"

Turning, she rested both hands back on the desk. "Playtime is over. Chris needs to get back to work because I need the gold she's working on. We need to go over what is moving about in the world, and what you will need by May." Her face was intense.

Manny waved his finger at the two hands. "And so this…?"

"This is for another time."

Manny looked at Blake who shrugged and pushed Chris into Cole and both through the doorway. Her growl was low and threatening. "We are so going to have a talk."

Brie whipped around. "No. That is not going to happen. I don't care what your relationship is with Chris, but you will continue as before. Nothing has changed, but you must be as if this here never happened. Trust us on this."

The two held the other's gaze, and then Blake broke it with a nod. History had proved over and over—appearance was not the reality. The vision of the blade standing through both of their hands held some powerful meaning, and Blake knew it would require her waiting. She also guessed it involved the silent conversation she had watched on the bank of monitors.

As they listened to the boots retreating, Manny stood. His eyes gently drifted closed as he slowed his breathing. On the fourth breath, he opened his eyes. There was still no spark of the Manny joviality.

"I was just getting ready to feed Jessie… and my office is more comfortable,"—glancing down at the chair she had been sitting in and at the desktop—"…and less bloody."

20 Curacao and the *Stern Mistress*

THE EARLY EVENING set the scattered clouds on fire. The lights on the swinging bridge, across the mouth of the river, twinkled as it slowly opened for the giant cruise ship, still a mile out to sea. Two sailors stood against the rail on the fantail of the large yacht. Their eyes sparkled with the sunset and the streetlights from the bridge. Their conversation was far from the tranquility of the bucolic scene or the multicolored buildings of Willemstad.

The darker sailor with dreadlocks stopped talking as a small electric boat glided by in the channel. The blond man leaned heavily on the railing as he switched to an eastern dialect of Mongolian.

"Will they move it by water?"

"The closest they be to an airport is four days at sea or more. The man say we know when we know. I say he maybe know before he tell us. I no trust him."

The German looked out to the large cruise ship as it nosed over the breakwater. Tourists lined the decks. Many knew little or nothing about taking photos in the evening, as witnessed by the sparkling flashes about the ship's railings. Both snorted with knowledge of the flashes only being useful within thirty feet, which would leave the images of the town as dark with dots of lights.

The blond snorted as he turned to look up at the tall ship. The two sailors missed the small flash from the tiny electric boat now sitting quietly near the end of the movable bridge. A hole appeared on his shirt where the green dot had been a second before. His body took an involuntary short breath.

The Rastafarian looked at the man in surprise. A green dot appeared on the side of his head for a split second. A hole replaced the light. Both bodies collapsed to the deck as a blonde woman stepped aboard the boat.

Brie listened as she glanced toward the aft. The lipstick flashlight blinked twice as the electric boat moved off. It would follow the cruise ship from the other side.

There were only two voices coming from the salon of the yacht. She knew there would be three other crewmembers—probably on the bridge. She walked silently along the deck, her silenced pistol held at the ready. As she passed a porthole, she looked into the cook's galley. A single man with ear buds hummed to a tune only he could hear. His focus was on the confection he was decorating—probably a late evening snack which wouldn't be needed.

Brie slipped through the door. The man looked up with lazy eyes. The person he saw was not the person he had expected. The hole in his forehead mirrored the hole of his surprised mouth. Brie quickly checked the purser's office and stepped back out onto the deck. The soft clatter of the man's dropped icing spatula had gone unnoticed.

She stood looking in toward the lights of the inner city and port. Her gun was at her leg—hidden from the young couple walking holding hands along the quay. In a city invaded daily with shiploads of tourists, one had to be more cautious about being seen by the nervous traveler than by anyone in authority.

The couple waved gently. A soft good evening floated up to Brie. She turned with her spoiled pillow princess look. Her wave was only slightly friendly towards the peasantry. The two never stopped. They knew their place. They had been dismissed.

Brie continued toward the bridge. She had been onboard already more than twenty seconds.

The captain and first officer were looking over paperwork. The first officer was in shorts and a sleeveless t-shirt. The small Beretta rested in a holster clipped at the small of his back. His head snapped and struck the captain's as his left ear canal became deeper.

As the captain stood erect, his left eyeball exploded. The 7.21 slug flattened inside his skull. Both bodies slumped to the carpet. Brie checked the office. It was empty.

As she stepped back out onto the deck, she hit the light on her phone. She passed the illumination down to the dock. A similar light flared in the shadow of the warehouse.

Her inner clock was now past thirty seconds.

She slipped through the open door to the salon. The large redheaded man frowned as he turned. His body corkscrewed to the floor with an extra hole in his head.

Brie smiled at the woman lounging with a drink in her hand. "Hello, Mavis. Or should I say, Leonidas?"

The woman's eyes sparkled under her dark hair. A small streak of gray hair crested over her left eye—a nod to her almost three-hundred-years of age. She languidly moved the glass to her lips and sipped. The ice cubes softly clinked in the heavy crystal.

"It always irritated me how you could mask your presence, my dear." She nodded gently at the body barely showing behind the end of the bar. "Do you have any idea how hard it is to find good help these days?"

Brie sat. The butt of the gun rested on the arm of the overstuffed chair. "You'll get over it in your next life."

"And what do I owe the end of this life to?"

Brie shrugged her face as she rolled her head. "I could say it was because you decided to throw your lot in with the nasty side of the Kind. I could say it was because you were plotting to kill many innocent people. I could also include several thousand Indians deep in the jungles of Columbia—but then, you only supplied the helicopters and ammo."

The pistol spat once. The older woman's right knee exploded. Her face contorted but she remained silent. Her mouth set with her gritted teeth. "Just fucking finish it. You're boring me to tears."

The pistol spat three more times. The other knee, as well as both elbows, joined the condition of the first.

Brie rose with a sadistic smile. She reached into her pocket for the next clip. There were still a few left in the original, but she didn't want to be caught with an empty if anything went wrong.

A small face peeked in the door. The bleach-tipped hair and freckles would be more fitting of a surf rat than that of a paid assassin.

The young Eurasian woman smiled and saluted with two fingers and tossed a dark object. Brie caught the weight belt in midair. The face disappeared. Brie knew she now had less than ninety seconds to finish and be clear of the yacht.

Brie holstered her pistol in her deep pocket. She bent and grabbed the older woman by the shirt. Pulling her forward, she strapped the heavy diving weight belt around her chest. She clicked the buckle shut over the woman's spine. Pulling on the one end, she cinched the belt so it wouldn't move.

She smiled at the woman. "Mostly, my dear." She pulled the woman to her feet and caught her with her shoulder. Carrying her toward the channel side of the yacht, she continued. "I'm doing this because I simply enjoy killing you. I've always enjoyed it, every time."

She sat the woman on the railing as she looked up and down the channel. There were no boats, and the tourists across the way would only notice the yacht as the lights went out.

She drew the woman close. "You see… I never will forgive you for killing my brother. He was a gentle soul who loved everyone, especially his older sister. But you see, he wasn't one of us—he was mortal. But you, I get to keep killing every chance I get."

"I've killed many people…"

"Yes, I suppose you have. But my brother you turned your charger, and with all the weight of the armor on you and your Friesian, you laughed as my brother was ground under the hooves. You laughed… and for that, you will die every time."

The lights on the yacht flickered and died. Brie pushed, and the woman made a small splash. Brie hoped she would transfer into a small fish—who would be eaten by a larger and torn apart by a shark and then spend a few decades among the fish. She also knew most Ever Kind made a habit of beaching themselves so they could get back to a human form as quickly as possible. But there was always hope.

As the young woman and Brie climbed into the black Saab, they felt more than heard the deep crumpling sound of the burning yacht's fuel tanks exploding. "Did you have fun tonight, Cherie?" They smiled as they drove off. At the blinking yellow light, the car turned left toward the residential part of the city. Their laughter, much like the stars above and the city lights around them, sparkled in the night.

THE CARIBBEAN SUN rose to sear the island once again. The small birds took to the air over the inner port. The two women flanked the powerful black man with patterns of small bumps of scars decorating his body. Only the small area under his running shorts remained covered. They stood at the rail on a veranda overlooking a Chandler's dock. The sleek black hull of the Corsair glowed in the morning light. The few lights in the cabins would wink out as the day took over.

Never much for sailing, the young assassin's eyes took in all the rigging on the multi-masted sailing ship. "Do people actually climb all the way up to the little cage up there?"

Brie smiled a half smile. "It's called a crow's nest. In the old days, there was a person there night and day. Even in a storm. It was a shitty job, but we didn't know any better, so it was just as much a part of the job as drawing up the sails on the square-rigged ships. You either paid attention to your footing, or you were lost at sea."

"So what is it used for now?"

Cole sipped his coffee as he hummed. "Electronics mostly. The white blister holds the base electronics for the short- and long-range antennas as well as other monitors. Our radar is the big gray ball on the back, but we also triangulate with nodes in the four nests as well as on the outriggers."

Brie chuckled at the fresh paint and gold leaf on the back of the ship. "So the old name of *Sangue Ruim* didn't work for you anymore? So who is she named for now?"

"Bad blood? Nah. We may be pirates, but the blood is by no means bad." He sipped to hide the small chuckle.

"And the *Stern Mistress* would be who… Blake?" She started to laugh.

Cole joined in softly laughing, which also drew in the young assassin. "What? You can't see her with a matching red leather whip and dominatrix rig to go with those boots?"

Brie's laugh died off as she focused on the stern of the ship. She grew quiet.

Cole frowned with concern as his focus flipped back and forth from ship to blonde. "What…?"

Brie's face smoothed into gentle as she looked at Cole. "I don't know… I just never thought of her in those terms. But then, I've only known her since the court of Louie XIII, and there she was a dandy married to the child bride Manfred." The small Eurasian woman squinted as she looked out across the inner bay. "That was long ago."

She turned and leaned the small of her back against the rail. Bending backward, she molded over the rail. Several of her spinal joints crackled.

She stood erect and smirked at Cole's smile. "The joys of a youthful body." Turning, she watched down the quay. "I guess they can move the gold and other on to the ship today, ya?"

Cole nudged his chin. "They want two more days to contaminate the containers. It is six or seven weeks to Singapore, and we don't want them to degrade."

Brie continued from his other side. "It needs to appear as if you stopped and left the plutonium somewhere in Somalia or Yemen. I think with Fat, the better is Yemen. Someone mentioned he may have interests there." Brie rolled her hip against the railing. "If he thinks he can get at it after you have forfeited your life and ship, the more he will like it."

The young woman whined softly, "So, we don't sail for another three days?"

Cole and Brie both chuckled. "Poor little Nina. For one who has never sailed, you sure are acting like a pirate at heart."

The young assassin protested, "Hey, it's a new adventure."

Cole raised one eyebrow and nodded. "And in the end, you get to kill many people…"

She snorted softly with a smirk. "Promises, promises."

21 Raft Drill

THE TORTOISE STOOD on the desk. His neck stretched out as he reached the leaf of bib lettuce in the center of the plate. Blake stood bent over with her chin on her hands. Her face was only a couple of hand spreads from the reptile. Her focus moved from one square of the shell to the next.

"I can see why we prized the shells of turtles for so many years. It's just a shame we killed them to enjoy their beauty."

"I haven't killed Jessie…"

Blake sat up, still focused on the tortoise. "That isn't what I meant." She looked over at Manfred as he studied and made notes on some paperwork. She found it a riddle for paper to be used in the twenty-first century. Even worse, it existed on the raft—which existed solely to clean up the environment. She mentally grumped to think they might still be pushing physical paper in the twenty-second century.

Manny lowered his pen and looked at her. "Then what did you mean?"

Blake was distracted in her thoughts. "I'm not sure of

the answer, but we killed Jessie's cousins for this look here." She reached out and ran her finger along the shiny shell. "I remember hair combs in Spain, and even back in Russia and China, made from the shells of giant land tortoises. The mottled brown and yellows were the beauty, but it was the translucent part making them the most prized and valuable."

"You can't see through Jessie's shell."

"No, but because you give him a daily bath and have sanded smooth his shell, you can clearly see the true beauty of the concentric squares of the modeled colors."

"And yet… here he sits… eating us out of house and home."

Blake chuckled. "Oh, you poor baby. The other four thousand plants of lettuce in the hydroponic gardens aren't enough?"

They watched the tortoise move slowly around the plate until he could reach the next leaf. There was a distinct Zen-ness about watching the animal.

"I figure you're going to trap Jun in Jessie somehow… but then what…? How long do they live anyway?"

Manny distractedly put down his pen. It was obvious he wasn't going to get any real work done while Blake was in this mode.

He leaned back in his chair as he stroked his beard. "Some of those large ones have records going a couple of hundred years—"

Blake cut him off as she looked up at the ceiling. "Ming?"

Manny knew by her looking at him that she had connected with the only other person who knew his endgame plans. He echoed the connection.

"What do you two want? My hands are kind of full right now."

Manny clicked on a change of the monitor. The woman wasn't at her station. He clicked on the breakroom. The woman was holding a large sandwich. He pointed it out to Blake who silently chuckled.

"I'll keep this brief so you can go back to molesting Cole."

The Asian woman carefully put down her sandwich and glared up at the tiny camera she knew to be in the corner of the room. "He's in the Atlantic and just passed the Canaries. We expect him to pass through the Straits this evening."

Manny and Blake fist bumped. "We were wondering how much longer Jessie could be expected to live."

Then woman sighed and then growled, "Long enough."

Manny interceded. "She means years. I know some of the big ones have been known to hit two hundred, but they aren't California desert tortoises."

"Best we can tell Jessie is about six to eight years old. Fed regularly and with a good balanced diet, he's good for about forty or more years. In a forced hibernation he—"

Manny rolled his eyes and cut her off. "Thank you, Ming. End all connections."

Manny was rigid as he waited for Blake to blink. His wife, husband, commander, underling, and partner of many lives well knew the game. A grandfather clock could have unwound if the two ever carried their nonverbal battle to a natural conclusion. Blake blinked.

"And with a chilled chamber to force hibernation…?"

"Two hundred or more…"

"Which is long enough for...?" Blake started to get edgy.

Manny stood. His hand rested on picking up the tortoise—now finished eating, but nosing around the edge of the plate. "Just be happy with the world having no Jun for the first time. Imagine how the world can be from just a couple of hundred years without an Attila the Hun, without a Genghis Khan, without a Vlad the Impaler, no Caligula, no Hitler, no Idi Amin, no Jack the Ripper, or no evil focus of any sort..."

"But—"

"Just focus on that. It's enough for now." He picked up the tortoise and walked out.

Blake started to work through the dynamics of a hundred-year-old cryogenic chamber. She wondered if an Ever Kind could perceive a body in stasis to be dead enough to transmigrate. She thought about the many hundreds of moves she had made. Not one had been a conscious move—they just happened.

Her hand flopped to the paperwork as she thought about Manny. Surely he had worked out preventing Jun from shifting out of Jessie's body.

She sat up and pulled one of the short forms toward her. It was a notice of movement from the raft to San Francisco. She hadn't been told about the vacation time.

She stood and turned to leave as the monitor pulsed with the outer inch of the screen in bright red. Four pulses and then there was an urgent barking horn. Three electric barks followed by a three-second silence. The emergency alarm sounded over and over five times.

Rushing into the bridge area, Blake noted Ming's combat brace bar had risen from the deck. She knew Ming preferred to stand, but during battle or a heavy storm, she would need support. The bar and wide belt ring gripping her hips and lower torso provided as much support as Blake's combat chair.

As the final alarm sounded, Blake slapped the two triggers on the side of her short chair. The back extended, and she let it grow into her armpits as she let her head fall back the few inches to be embraced by the headrest. The monitors in front of her lit up as her chair linked to the communication node in her head. Her subvocal commands were a rapid-fire checklist. The scene from the many outward cameras flowed through the cascading displays as they changed from white to yellow to combat ready red.

The last cascade of yellow turned red. Blake locked the weapons into full search and respond mode.

"Sections seven through twelve, ready and showing clear."

Ming passed her hand through the air. She had long replaced any manual system with one that read her Thai Chi movements. As she had proven many times, her system was faster than four people with joysticks, mice, or combat gaming consoles.

"Southern quadrant is fully red and ready to engage."

On the sides of their monitors, they could see the status bars of the battle zones to the sides of them. Across the boards, the raft was ready. The battle clock passed through the nineteenth second since the first alarm.

Blake's attention jerked to the right monitor. "I have two rail guns going hot—self-acquiring."

Ming echoed at the same time. "I have two rails, and a pulse now live… searching."

Blake could feel the large railguns above them vibrate.

The servomotors were large enough to push the two tons of gun and their shells around as easily as a child turns their head. The monitor tracking froze. Three targeting circles with incremented crosshairs lit up.

"I have three targets."

Ming echoed. "I have four targets, and one bogie just went airborne. Three mini-guns are now live. Three more bogies airborne."

Blake watched the targeting circles turn from thin red to orange with green rims. "Three targets just breached the water and are now airborne." She kicked at the floor pedal. "Mini-guns are all hot. Range to fire in three, two… engaging now."

The hair on the top of their heads stood on end as the electromagnetic railguns charged the area around them. The separation from the rails with their blue cloud of electrical charge to their heads was less than ten feet. Blake just hoped the sound insulation was better.

The two pounds of dense cast garbage steel, acquired from ocean carried junk, ejected onto the rail silently. At the very nanosecond the taper-ended slug was within a quarter-inch of touching the rail, it was already traveling at over six thousand miles an hour and covered half the distance of the twelve-foot rail. It was still speeding up when it left the end of the rail and broke the sound barrier five times.

Blake called for the battle helmet. She hated the confining pressure on her head, but the thunder above her head was deafening, and it would take its toll. The heads-up displays transferred to the shield covering her face as she adjusted the helmet on her head.

"I have seven more bogies in the air."

A muted horn sounded and five paths were outlined on the water in front of Ming. "Incoming torpedoes, I have five… make it ten. They are closing at ninety-three knots. Switching rails."

The railguns controlled by Ming switched from hardened steel slugs to two-foot long bundles of quarter-inch thick rods. The bundles would stay together until they were within a quarter mile of the oncoming torpedo running less than twenty feet below the surface. The rods would create a cluster area thirty-foot across. Nothing would explode, but the torpedo would be torn apart by the almost molten hot steel rods.

"Hornets away. Contact in four, three, two…" The ocean on her screen boiled and then was calm. Every bundle had found its target.

She started to turn her head, but the left monitor flashed red and started long-range zooming. The visual flickered, and she knew it had automatically gone from twenty-five-mile lookout to one hundred. She was seeing over the edge of the horizon. Three ballistic missiles had breached the surface and were still heading straight up. She held down the button on the side of her helmet—connecting her to all launch control stations on the raft.

"We have ballistic launch. I repeat. We have ballistic launch. Three bogies at one-niner-six degrees and range is eighty-seven miles. I repeat. Three bogies—ballistic launch. Target one-niner-six degrees. Bogies cresting and are now at seven-niner range. Altitude is five-two-hundred feet, crest expected six thousand.

Both women watched the modified SAM missiles leap away from the raft. Only one was trailing a white cloud of smoke.

Blake turned toward Ming with a frown. "We're burning a real SAM?"

Ming nodded. "We're burning a real ballistic missile too. This exercise is not cheap, but we have to know if we are good to go."

The two continued watching the screens as the exercise played out. The SAM missile's white trail became a white blot and then exploded into a larger ball of orange and black. Even with the computer magnification, the debris of the two missiles falling into the ocean was not something they could see.

The banks of display screens became scenic windows to the ocean. The attack drill was over. A small yellow square patch in one of the upper corners remained pulsing. Blake leaned back into the combat chair. She thought about how real and unreal the last few minutes had seemed. She understood why these chairs, and even more complex chairs, were prized by the nerds who lived in their mommy's basement and played video games. She had heard about one guy wearing diapers and survived on slamming caffeine drinks and gnawing on Pop Tarts and jerky until he passed out in the seventy-third hour. The guy was over three hundred pounds and covered with zits—but in the gaming world, he was a god.

"How much of what we saw was real?" Her head rolled toward the Asian woman chewing on her one thumbnail as she stared into the last screen—frozen at the moment of the two missiles exploding.

"Ming?"

The woman nodded slightly. Blake guessed she was listening to a private communication. Her guess was Manny.

"Ming out." She turned her head to take in Blake as her battle chair collapsed back to the original low-back swivel. The armor initiator pedals reseated in the flooring. "Your number seven mini-gun is jammed, but it went the distance. You will want to tear down the auto feed of your center rail. The feed was slow and was backing up the supply thrower."

Blake acknowledged the report. "Was anything graphic on mine?"

"Only your threats." The woman's face clamped down as she spun out of the now retreating brace. She stopped and took an extended breath. For her, it was a deep breath. "Manny wants to see you in the Ops Center on seventeen."

Blake turned to see only the back of the woman striding down the open hallway. Blake had never seen her get so out-of-control emotional. Something was up, and she didn't like it.

"Blake?" The communication node in her head opened.

She turned toward the hatch leading to the outside and the fastest way to get to the other Operational Center. "Manny," she completed the link, "I'm just leaving now—"

He cut her off. "Grab your go bag and meet me at moon pool three. Pack for Hawaii."

She burst through the hatch and jogged the length of the catamaran. At the nexus, she crossed diagonally as she headed for her quarters. She thought about the weather in Hawaii and what she might want to wear. She laughed as she leaped from one catamaran to the other. Her thigh-high boots gripped the deck. There wasn't even a smidge of slip. The special deck and boot soles made for the most dynamic connection she had ever experienced aboard a deck. Even her two hundred years as a barefoot pirate didn't provide this connection.

She hesitated in front of the mirror. With a smile and a toss of her long red hair, she pulled open the closet door. She pulled three loose tops from the hangers. She could buy more if she needed. She reached into the top drawer and grabbed a large handful of rolled black leggings, three sports bras, and a small wad of thongs.

Her hand reached into her small sock drawer, and she froze. She threw one pair at the small bag and cleaned the drawer into the wastebasket. The nylon would become some kind of usable item within the week. There was no such thing as waste on the raft. She needed to go shopping anyway.

She zipped three more t-shirts into the bag that for someone else would be a shoulder purse. Looking around, she spotted her phone, still on the charger. She slid the phone into the holster inside the top of her right boot and shoved the charger into the outside pocket of her bag.

The door clicked closed when she was already twenty feet down the hallway. Her long stride enhanced by the heels of her boots gave her a territory eating walk. Once on dry land, there were few who could truly keep up with her. She wondered how many days it would take her to walk from San Francisco to her other favorite city of San Diego.

She swung open the large hatch to the largest of moon pools on the raft. Originally built for research with access for divers or small submarines, it was lengthened to allow unseen access to the top of a nuclear submarine's sail. The whole sail was too tall, but they could suck out the water in the flying bridge enough to open the hatch.

Manny stood on top of the sail. His legs were spread,

and above his white tank top shirt, he was wearing a floppy hat with red ostrich feathers. Blake almost laughed, but instead, she called out their war cry from the early 1700s. "Give them hell, and may barnacles never know your backside."

"Well met, my dear scoundrel. May your jibs never droop, and your poop deck never leak."

Blake walked across the plank to the sail. Manny dropped down into the flying bridge and met her.

"Care to explain why I get the ultimate hundred-forty-million-dollar limousine to Hawaii," she moved her face close, "or why I'm even going?"

Manny silently moved to the back wall. Resting his arms on the top, he leaned into the wall and looked at the wall of hanging dive gear. His stance was the one he always took when he was looking at the horizon but talking about important personal stuff, which may include feelings.

"I want you in Kona, Hawaii before Christine arrives. She's meeting her daughter at SFO. They have reservations at the St. Frances for one night and then off to Kona for eight days. I want to know why." He turned and looked at Blake. "I want you two to kiss and make up if that's what it takes—but I want to know why, and more importantly, why now."

"May is a nice month in Hawaii, but Noi's birthday isn't until September. Do we know when Chris's birthday is?"

"Thanksgiving."

Blake snorted. "Which always moves around except Thursday. No, I mean the date."

"That's what she put on the forms—Thanksgiving."

Blake hung her head as she looked sideways with enlarged eyes. "Do we know the year?"

Manny growled. "Mid-twentieth century."

The two started low rumbling laughs. The date was so very Ever Kind. "I love a woman of mystery." Blake guessed her birthdate to be closer to 1980.

Manny leaned, laughing against the wall. "Then you shouldn't have killed me, kind sir."

"Fuck you, Manny. The horse only had a small limp before you took over. You were the pansy who couldn't walk out of Mongolia on all four."

"And surprise, surprise. Who would have ever thought a eunuch would be hiding under a chadri?"

Blake flattened and buzzed her lips as she rolled her eyes. "It wasn't so bad… once we got past which one of us had the larger, more glorious mustache."

Manny whipped off his hat and fanned it at Blake. "Go have fun. Get laid. Bring me back information." They embraced and kissed each on both cheeks and then on the lips. His voice lowered as he heard the crew returning. "Look after yourself."

Her lips tightened. "All of us."

She stepped through the round hatch in the floor and slid down the ladder into what was once a Russian sub. She could feel the pulse of power as the large turbines rumbled making electricity. Hawaii was only two days away.

"Pirate on the bridge."

She turned to find three friends standing at attention and saluting. She smiled. *Maybe two days wasn't enough.*

"Permission to come aboard." *Some traditions never change.*

22 Hawaii

BLAKE SAT FORWARD in the large zodiac. She closed her eyes and leaned her head back with the sun fully on her face.

"So how did you pull this rough duty, Kewika?" She had to remember to pronounce the Hawaiian 'w' as a 'v'—the same as German.

The diminutive Hawaiian rolled his head as he stretched out his arms and cracked his knuckles backward. "I grew up here."

Blake opened one eye. She studied the tribal tattoos on the stringy muscled arms and legs. "When?"

Kewika snorted softly. "Which life?"

Blake rolled onto her side. "When did you come to Hawaii?"

The brown face cracked into a large toothy smile. "I was on the first wave from Polynesia, about a thousand years ago. I don't remember the months at sea, because I was born about halfway here. The wa'a kaulua, or catamaran, had about sixty people on it. Two of us were born on the trip; only I can talk about it now."

"What were you before?"

"I was a boat builder. I was Hai'lia's uncle. She was in the work shed when I suffered a massive heart attack. I loved my niece and didn't want to take over her body. So, instead, I took the baby. Something was wrong with the baby's heart."

Blake smiled. "But as the body of an Ever Kind…"

He nodded and waved behind him at the island. "I was here from the beginning." He winked and rolled over to look at the island getting closer.

He pointed at the lighter point. "We landed there. We didn't have a name for it, but today, it is South Point." He pointed at a tiny light square of a building. "See the little white building? That is the southernmost radar station in the United States. Over there, the black line on the beach to the right was where I lived for most of eight hundred years."

Blake could hear it in his voice. "You love it here, don't you?"

The man laughed. "Everything but getting the tattoos—those hurt."

"But now, you're out on the raft or on the subs."

He shrugged with a smile. "Eh, what's a couple of hundred years among friends?" He snuggled back into the warmth of the boat. "If we don't clean up the Pacific Patch, the ocean will die. Too many fishermen find tuna who should weigh a quarter-ton, and yet they are only a couple of hundred or smaller. They open them up and their guts are full of plastic. In a hundred years of making plastic, we are killing the planet."

"Brah?"

Kewika looked at the pilot and then where the other Hawaiian was looking. The white prow of the Coast Guard cutter floated above the white of the bow-wave. The large boat was moving fast.

"Ita kine brah. You pull out." He waved at the large bundles under the tarp. "It jus' trash we bring home."

The man opened his rolling eyes wide as he throttled back to a stop. The boat bucked as the wake caught up with them. The two men clambered to remove the tarps. Blake laughed as she recognized the packaging of iced fish.

The cutter wallowed as one of the coasties threw a line. The Captain stepped out of the bridge. "Ey! You tie it good this time, Kewika. We don't you kolohe garbage makai like last time."

Kewika flipped the man his finger. "Speaking of stink eye. You skank sister still burning slippas on the streets of Punalu'u?"

The man laughed as a coastie swung out the boom crane. The first frozen block of fish rose into the air. "Brah, you be makai too long. She pushing ono malasada and rubbing the baby bump you left the last time."

"Think she have time for a long lunch?"

"She's off on Wednesday. You know she be kine to see you."

The last of the fish swung over the rail and onto the deck of the cutter. Kewika waggled both hands in the air. "Pau hana brudda. Tomorrow, jalike lesgo bust da kine dive, Brah. We grind ono onoliscious luau."

"You lolo buggah. I work fo da man."

"Shaka brah, I dive, we eat."

"Mo bettah. Mahalo." He pointed at the large pile of now covered fish. "Kewika, brah you bring malihini wahini." The man waved as the cutter side crabbed away from the pontoon boat already making headway toward South

Point.

As Kewika settled back into the prow, the driver opened the throttles. Soon, the light boat was slapping along the top of the small swells.

Blake stared at the Hawaiian. "Care to explain all this?"

The man's eyelids floated down as his eyes rolled up. His lips flattened as his face and shoulders shrugged. "They get a ton of the best tuna in the world, and in six days, they will look the other way while a Russian submarine surfaces to take on seventeen tons of green coffee and other supplies."

"How sure are you about the security?"

"My little brother?"

Blake smirked as she rolled her eyes. "So the skank is?"

"Our sister. And the mother of our four adoring nieces and nephews."

"And the skank part?"

"A moke at school said my little sister was a skank who walked the streets of Punalu'u. The next morning, they found him tied to a Kehavi tree facing Pele's wrath."

"Pele's wrath?"

"The slow-moving lava was about a hundred feet away. It was moving about a foot an hour, but by dinner, his skin would have started to scorch off."

"You are brutal."

He snorted. "Not me—them. Actually, it was her. He just went along for the fun. The kid was a jerk, and Danny was only in the fourth grade."

"I bet he never called her a skank again."

Kewika laughed as he grabbed the line at his feet and

prepared to jump to the dock. "All the time. She says the day he stops is the day she will file for a Hawaiian divorce." He took a second glance at the question on Blake's face. "She'll throw him directly into the lava."

"They got married?"

The man nimbly jumped to the dock and flipped the rope around the tie-off. "They've been bumping uglies for going on fifty years. They almost make you believe in love."

He caught the other rope and tied it off. "You like donuts?"

"Sure."

"Then let's go grind an onoliscious malasada or two." He waved his thumb at the thick muscled Samoan driver. "Paulie here is wasting away to nothing, and we have to fight hunger. Eh, brah?"

The man grunted with a large toothy smile. Blake could tell by his eyes that he was ready for a half dozen of whatever was being served.

23 Making Up

BLAKE STOOD LEANING on the rail. She watched the two women below. Christine and Brie reclined in the morning sun by the pool. Even from a distance, Blake could tell they had the relaxed continence only coming from a longtime close relationship.

Their conversation wasn't steady. It was the short snips of comments only happening with knowledge to fill in the gaps. Blake wished she had a parabolic microphone to hear what they were saying.

"They're talking about what to do with me."

Blake spun around.

Noi walked to the rail and pushed her hips against it as she leaned and stretched.

"You do know they can sense you are here." She turned toward Blake. "I mean seriously, who is the child and who are acting like children? You sneak around spying on Mom. Mom thinking she is being so smart by meeting me in San Francisco and then coming here to talk to Brie. It's all so tedious."

"There is a lot going on you wouldn't understand." Blake started to reach out but drew her hand back.

Blake watched the rise in the young woman's eyebrows, telegraphing the roll of her eyes behind the mirrored aviator glasses. Her face was bored disgust.

"Stop. Please, just stop. You treat me like I'm just a kid. You don't even know the first thing about…"

She whipped out her cell phone and thumbed it on.

Blake frowned. "What?"

Noi held up her index finger as she put the phone to her ear. "Mom, Blake, and I are going over to a beach she knows… yeah… okay. We'll see you back here around eight for a late dinner. Love you too." She shoved the phone into her back pocket as she stood with a look of defiance. "What? You don't like the beach?"

"We're on an island. What are you up to?"

"We get to go to some beach while Brie and Mom get time to talk. I hope they act like adults." She hip-slouched in teen boredom. "You do know where a beach is, don't you?"

Blake leaned in and growled. "It's a fucking island. And, just remember, you're not too old or too big to turn over my knee."

"Which means you have to call a friend about a beach?" Noi tipped her hip further out with her hand drumming her fingers. She raised her sunglasses onto the top of her head. Her eyes locked on Blake's, her face as blank as the mirrored glasses.

Blake waited and then stood up. "Be a good child and shut up while I talk to a friend."

Noi turned back toward the rail and waved at her mother. She kept her smile pulled up on the side Blake couldn't see. Adults were so easy to manipulate.

Blake turned and leaned her butt against the railing.

"Kewika? Blake. Yeah, I know we're here for five more days. I wanted to know if you or your skank sister wanted to show two girls around your beaches."

Noi's head tilted and cranked around in disbelief. Blake had actually called someone about going to a beach. She listened raptly.

"Okay, we'll meet you at the bakery in a couple of hours." She laughed. "Of course, we brought bathing suits. What do you think this is—the eleventh century?"

Putting the phone away, she turned to Noi. She took in the sundress and sandals and figured a bikini was underneath. "We need to go buy me a swimsuit."

Noi held up two fingers.

Blake threw her arm around the young woman, hugged her neck, and laughed as they walked away.

Who comes to Hawai'i and doesn't bring a swimsuit?

Evidently… a lot of people. The gift shop had a full range of great swimsuits, and thirty minutes later, they were pulling out of the Sheraton, heading south.

Noi laid her head back to take in the sun and the wind. When Blake rented the car, there had been no choice. The bright red convertible all but screamed at the two women. The low growl of the large engine in the Charger matched Blake's mood.

They turned right onto Highway 11. Noi pointed her finger at the rapidly approaching McDonalds. Blake waited for the girl's head to turn with her mouth open.

Blake stuck her finger in the girl's mouth—pointing. "Don't you dare start with the crap, young lady. We are headed for the southernmost bakery in America and pigging out on fattening Portuguese stuffed donuts. And I don't want to hear one word of back talk today. Not about the donuts, not about the beaches, and not about what I want to have cleared up. It's been like an armed camp for over a month, and I'm sick and tired of it. This shit is stopping right here and right now in this fucking car. You have a little over an hour to get clean with me, or I'm throwing your ass into a volcano."

Noi closed her mouth on the finger and started sucking.

Blake fought to keep a straight face. "Are we clear?"

Noi continued to suck.

"Are we?" The edge was sneaking back into her voice.

Noi blew the finger out of her mouth. Crossing her arms over her chest, she leaned back in the seat—pouting. "Crystal."

Her voice sounded grumpy, but Blake knew better. She reached over and wiped her finger under the girl's armpit. The giggle was quick to start.

The wind fluffed and pulled at the young woman's hair as she wound her head in the open air of the convertible. Finally, she slumped down into the seat and away from the wind.

"About a month or so ago, Mom changed. It was little things in what she talked about on Skype or the length of texting. I didn't know Brie before, but I guess they go back to before I was born."

She looked out, catching glimpses of the ocean through the zoetrope of trees along the highway. Blake knew the distracted look—she had caught herself over the lives having the same look when she had been away from great water for too long.

Noi looked back in the car. "There is something about Brie I'm attracted to." She pursed her lips in thought.

"Maybe that came out wrong. More like drawn to like a magnet, instead of a sexual thing."

Blake nodded. "I got that." She lightly touched the young women's arm. "But if you ever need to talk to someone about the other—"

"Oh, no… Mom and I are good. We had *the talk* a few years ago. It was a little late, but it was good to have Mom in my corner." She looked over. "Boys… I like boys. I'm cool with you and mom and all… but I like boys."

Blake wiped her brow dramatically. "Whew. Well, that made the whole drive worthwhile." She expected the glare she got.

"You and Mom are so weird sometimes." She turned the seat and leaned against the door. "So I guess you two haven't been sleeping together lately?"

"What makes you think…?"

Noi pulled out her phone and scanned through pages of texting. "Because I've just gone back about three weeks, and she doesn't mention you once." The click of the phone sounded so final to Blake.

"I didn't realize she talked about us so much."

"She used to… more. I used to get a kick out of her talking about you two fighting every morning. She would show me the bruises and rattle on about the swords and other stuff." Her head hung back into the wind passing the car. Her hair whipped around as she rolled it in the air. "I miss those days."

"When did it change?"

Noi thought as she snuggled back into the less windy corner. She squirmed and finally landed with her head on Blake's shoulder.

"I think it was when Brie showed up. She started getting serious. I mean she has always been serious, but now it's like intense."

"Have you asked her about it?"

She rolled her head and leaned back against Blake. It seemed like they were talking with a certain ease, but Blake sensed Noi was having a hard time putting into words what she had only been feeling.

"I feel like I'm only ten again. She said it was just serious stuff, but she couldn't talk about it yet. She was saying I was too young to understand." She chewed on the side of her thumb. "I hate being a kid."

Blake hated being in the middle. "It is serious stuff. I shouldn't tell you, and you have to swear to keep this secret—but you're not a kid anymore, and what's coming will affect you one way or another."

"Okay…?"

"There's a big battle coming—a battle which could destroy the raft and everyone on it. Everyone knew this was coming when they signed on. There is a very real chance of only the Ever Kind surviving."

"But it's important?"

"Very. It's hard to explain, and it sounds like so much over-the-top sensationalism—but the wellbeing of all humankind and the world is at stake. Which makes it worth the risk." Blake glanced over. "Your mom knows we will always look out for you, but she… well, she is in the middle of it."

They rode in silence for a while. The road had curves, but the slower speed limit turned them into just curves—no leaning or fun in a red sports car.

Blake thought Noi had maybe drifted off to sleep with the warm sun and slow winding road, but as Noi rolled over, Blake could feel the wet on the young woman's cheek.

"I really hate being a kid. I wouldn't want to ever do it again."

Blake leaned her head on the other. "You only get one shot at it."

"Yeah, but you don't."

Blake glanced in the rearview mirror. *Point taken.*

"Sweetie, everything had its pluses and minuses. Yeah, I've been a kid more times than I want to think… and a goat, a shark, a cockroach, a snake, a man, a camel and the list goes on. Everything is up and down."

Noi looked up. "Ever been a queen or king?"

Blake laughed. "Is this the game of 'in a past life I was Cleopatra'? Because if everyone who thought they were, had been, they would have been her for maybe twenty seconds tops. She only lived to be about thirty-eight or nine."

"Never… nothing?"

"Eh, a princess here, and a potentate there, but nothing famous. I was a Viking queen for a while, but then died when I was about twenty."

Noi rolled back into leaning on Blake's arm. "Cool."

"What do you really want to be when you grow up?"

"I want to work on the raft with Mom. I don't care what I do, but I want to be there with her."

"What about college?"

"Whatever the raft could use… marine biology, microbiology, whatever. Mom said they would pay my way, so I figure they get to choose what they need."

Blake's phone rang through as the stereo turned off. "This is Blake."

A male with a thick accent answered. "Nefu? This

Mali."

Blake stiffened and almost ran off the road. Nefu, her name for many centuries in Mongolia. A name she hadn't heard in almost two millennia.

"Mga pangomosta, Mali"

The man laughed heartily. "Busaya works Nefu. Han and I are making our way to you. We sense many moving to middle of Pacific Ocean. Whatever happening, we want in."

"Come to the big island of Hawaii. We're in Kona for a few more days. How did you get my phone number?"

"We sold the Black Sheep some gold. She said to talk to you. How fairs the limping camel we gave you?"

"He made it to the middle of the Silk Road. I had to kill him to get a caravan I could work with."

The man laughed. "We talk in few days. I need to find someone with a passport and visa."

"Make sure they're good for a battle."

"Oh, now you just talk sexy like always."

"Behave. I have a virgin in the car. Give Han a hug for me, and we'll talk soon." The radio clicked twice, and the music resumed.

"Virgin?"

"You behave also."

"Okay, we'll shelve it for now… but battle? The battle you were talking about? Who was the dude?"

Blake sighed as she noted the GPS and turned on her blinker. "An old friend I haven't spoken to for over a thousand years."

BLAKE LAUGHED LATER as they stood on the black sand beach. She licked her thumb and wiped the lemon frosting from the side of Noi's mouth. She pointed at the drop of papaya-strawberry on the new red bikini. "We can't take you anywhere dressed up nice."

Kewika laughed. "Ah, little one's first malasada?"

"Oh, my God, Kiki, these are so good." Some of the donut sprayed from Noi's mouth.

Karin snickered. "She called you Kiki."

The man blushed. "She can call me Kiki. She's young and cute. *She…* can call me Kiki." He glared at his sister until they all started laughing.

Noi wiped her face. "What's wrong with Kiki?"

"Nothing," the man growled.

The sister took Noi aside and whispered. "Keiki means small child, but Kiki is north island slang for a man's parts." She pointed at Noi's crotch. They laughed.

"Don't be a nasty old skank."

"But I am a nasty old skank. Just not your nasty old skank."

Blake cleared her throat. Holding up an empty quart jar, she asked. "You started to tell me about this?"

"Is it empty?"

"Yes."

"Did you open it and look inside?"

Blake leaned in with a growl. "It's a clear jar."

Kewika shucked out of his long shorts and shirt. He took the jar and handed it to Noi. "You examine the jar." He stood there in just his Speedo trunks.

Noi opened it and sniffed. "Smells like old sardines and kimchi."

Karin laughed and took the jar from her. "It does not. I washed it this…" She sniffed and looked wide-eyed at her brother. "It does."

The man snapped the jar away and took the lid from Noi. "Stop. No kine be that way. Go sit on beach like turtle and tell story."

He closed the jar and walked out into the water. Soon, he was out far enough and dove under the water.

Karin patted her hand on the rough volcanic black sand as she sat. "We sit here so we can see Mauna Loa, home to our goddess Pele." Her hand swept back to behind them. "And we can see the home of Kanaloa, god of the ocean."

She picked up a handful of the coarse sand. "This is all lava. If I have a block of lava and I pour water on it, the water will run into the lava because it is porous. Ya? This means the water can enter all the tiny holes. But also, it is permeable. This means water can also run through the lava. Ya?"

She wiggled her fingers down through the sand in her other hand until they came out through the other fingers. "It fills with water because it is porous but moves the water downhill because it permeates."

She waved her arm indicating the top of the volcano and the crown of clouds gathered there. "One or two hundred years ago, a cloud like the white one, spend the day doing what the white one is doing today."

Noi chuckled as she wiggled her hanging fingers in the air. "Raining."

Karin pointed at Noi's hand. "Very good. You must be part Hawaiian. Yes, they rain—it is what clouds do on volcano. It is their job."

She hung her hands in front of her with the fingers hanging. "They rain, and the rain comes to the top of the lava. Then what do you think it does?"

"It goes in because it is porous."

"Yes, but it is also permeable, so the rain becomes a stream which becomes a river. But Goddess Pele, she likes the water to feed the trees and plants growing on the side of her home. So she make it take long time to once again reach the ocean. For you see, Kanaloa gives us the rain from his home the ocean."

Blake leaned back on her elbows. Hearing ancient stories to explain nature was one of her favorite things. "It is the cycle of life or water."

The woman pointed at her. "Exactly, little one, but our story doesn't end there. The village I live in named Puna-lu'u. In Hawaiian, this means spring water diver. The spring comes from Pele, but to get to the water, the divers must ask passage from Kanaloa. Many centuries ago, young men like Kewika, would take large jars made of tightly woven seagrass that they could seal back up. They would dive down to the bottom of the warm water until they could feel the cold water coming from Pele."

Blake sat up frowning as she looked out to sea. "Where is Kewika?"

Karin patted her on the leg. "Relax. He is doing what he did then. He is bringing you old water from Pele."

Noi looked over her glasses. "Rainwater? Freshwater... from the ocean?"

"Have you been listening, child? I have been telling you how he is doing this. But back from before King Kamehameha the First, they would take the sea grass bags rolled up tight. Then, in the rush of the cold freshwater, racing to become one with the ocean again, they let the water unroll the bag and fill it with fresh spring water. Then the diver rolls the long snout of the jar back up to seal it and swim back to shore. Just like Kewika has done just now. Ya?"

They all looked to see the man walking out of the ocean and across the black sands. He held out the wet jar. "Here, feel."

Noi took the jar. "It's ice cold." She held it to Blake, who also felt it.

Kewika rolled his hand in the air. "Go on. Open it and drink. I brought enough for all of us."

Noi tasted the water and then guzzled a large drink. Wiping the back of her hand across her mouth, she handed it to Blake. "So it really came all the way from the rain?"

Kewika raised the jar toward the volcano. "We thank you, Pele, for your life-bearing gift." He took a sip and then raised it to the ocean. "And to you, Kanaloa, for the water." He took a fuller drink and passed it to his sister.

SEVERAL NIGHTS LATER on the raft, Blake and Christine lay on the webbed deck. The moon was only a sliver, but both knew it didn't matter. There were plenty of cameras designed to see in much dimmer light.

"Was it salty or did it taste good?"

"Have you ever had mountain spring water so cold it made your teeth hurt?"

"Sure…"

Blake smiled at the sliver of a moon. "Just like it."

The webbing moved. Blake looked at Christine and

smiled. "Good evening, Manny."

Christine mouthed the words, "That's creepy."

Manny sat down next to them and stretched out. "So good to see the boys again after all this time."

Blake rolled her head. "And you were wondering why they came out of Mongolia?"

"No. I understand why. Under Khan, Jun kept killing Han over and over every day. He laid him on top of children and old women. Then he would repeat it the next day. He wanted to see if we had only so many lives—and he was willing to go through half of the population of Mongolia to find out."

Christine frowned. "But the two are brothers?"

Blake nodded as she rolled her head. "They're the only twins we know of among the Ever Kind."

"There couldn't be others?"

Manny sat up and looked out across the shimmering ocean. "There're only about a thousand of us." He turned to lean on his elbow. "Over the thousands of years, we have pretty much met each other. We also have a sense of where everyone is. It's not as exact as a GPS, but it's worked all of our existence."

"Except for Brie…"

Manny smirked. "Except for the black sheep, yes. She's also an anomaly."

Blake laughed. "Don't forget Rek the Red."

Chris rolled up onto her elbow. "Rek?"

Manny chuckled. "Rek was old before Gilgamesh. He's never changed his name. He's always a he, and he always has a red beard. He's what we call a standout guy."

"Because of his red beard…"

Blake snorted as she sat up. "And because he always

stood about seven-foot tall. But, for us, it's because we see him as three people." Blake held her hand just above their heads. "But his auroras are all a wee bit over his knee in height."

"But every time? I mean how does he find new men built big with red hair?"

Manny snorted. "It's his anomaly—he doesn't. We saw him killed at the battle of Crecy. He had his head taken off by a battle-ax—very impressive. Well, actually, it was the pike and two swords in him being impressive. But I digress. So he dies and standing next to him, and almost crushed by the giant, was a small squire or something for the Frog."

Blake took over with a chortle. "By morning, he is six-foot tall, naked as a red-bearded jaybird, and has already slaughtered a hundred Frogs as they slept in their camp."

"He killed a dozen more getting past their picket. He strides into our camp, with a battle-ax in one hand and a maul in the other, asking when breakfast is to be ready."

Blake smiled at the memory. "I sure hope he tunes in and makes it here."

"He'll be pissed for centuries if he misses this."

The brunette finally reclined. "You guys are so weird. Nice, but in a really weird way."

The chuckles were soft in the air.

The three souls lay in the night air, stewing in their thoughts as the sliver of silver slid into the sea.

24 Confusion & Clearing the Air

AS THE CRACK between the small curtains grew brighter, Blake knew the dawn workout of martial arts and swordplay wouldn't happen. The exercise had lasted most of the night.

Rolling onto her side, she folded into the other naked body in the bed.

"Oh, gawd, woman. You're insatiable."

Christine adjusted to become the outer spoon. Her chuckle was soft and silent as she planted her nose into Blake's back and kissed it halfway as her head became heavy.

The two lay unmoving for many minutes. Blake thought Chris had fallen back to sleep. Some of the things Noi had said stumbled around in her head.

Probably looking for coffee.

"I can hear a question coming" Chris's voice was slurred with sleep and muffled by Blake's back, but it cut through the morning like a knife.

Blake didn't move. The seconds slid sideways—there was no traction for what she needed to know. "Do you want to start now or after we have coffee?"

"Oh, good gracious. After last night, coffee precedes even peeing—and don't move or I might have to pee."

"Not in my bed, you don't."

"My cabin."

Blake opened her eyes. True enough. The curtains were short and the wrong color. Blake closed her eyes. "Ming?" The pause was less than a second. "Yeah, good afternoon to you too. Who is near Christine's cabin with two fists of coffee?"

A second connection broke in Blake's head. "Fifteen meters away including scones."

"Thank you, Manny."

"Now I've gotta pee." Chris jumped out of bed and opened the door on the way to the head.

MANNY NEVER EVEN turned his head. "Good afternoon, Chris." He placed the tray on the bed. Blake frowned at the stack of scones, jellies, and three large mugs of coffee. Manny picked up a scone and mug. "They were for somewhere else." He bit into the still-warm scone and took a sip of coffee.

"Thanks." Blake embraced a mug with both hands and sipped with her eyes closed.

"Any answers?"

Christine poked him in the back as she slid around. "Actually, we were just getting to the interrogation part. The three or four hours of beating and torturing the captive softened her up. Care to stick around and make sure she misses nothing?"

Manny stared blankly at the woman now in a small

blue satin robe. The words were disrespectful and spoken in a playful manner, but he sensed the overtone was not so light and cheery.

He grabbed one more scone and turned. "I have others to beat." The door clicked shut softly.

Blake watched with one eye over the mug as she slowly sipped. The brunette held her gaze. Blake put her mug on the small nightstand and took a nibble of her scone.

"There goes the man who dreamed up all of this. He makes sure the lights are on, the food is here, and we are all taken care of like nobody has ever taken care of you or any of us before. And when I mean us, I mean mortals and Ever Kind alike. There is nobody on the raft who cares as much about yours and my well-being—nobody. When it comes to you, you're here—but he makes sure Noi is looked after even more. She's the one who is not here under his direct protection. I don't know how he ever finds time to sleep or even be a nice person to be around because he has a small city worth of people to look after. Being a First Commander under Napoleon must have been a walk in the park compared with this."

Christine tried to break in, but Blake held up her hand. "Before you ever even think about treating him like that again, just pack your bags. I will untie your lanyard and cast you adrift. He took you in from the street, gave your daughter the chance of a lifetime. Gave you a place to call home for the rest of your life doing something with meaning—a purpose which brings healing to this planet and to the family on this raft. If the job is too much, just say the word. He will give you a severance which will probably outlast even Noi."

They sat glaring.

Chris looked down into her mug. "Is it my turn yet?"

"Yes."

Christine looked up with tear tracks down her face, but she licked her lips, and they were firm. "I deserved that. I knew the second I even said it to Manny. Everything you said is true. Since my husband died, nobody has made me feel safe, secure, and." She choked.

"Loved?"

The brunette bit her lip and nodded. Blake waited her out. "I… I never loved a woman before." She looked up. "I never knew anyone who accepted me just the way I was. You never asked about yesterday, last year, or even my life before. You took your time and figured out what I knew about the martial arts and swords. Then we moved forward."

She took a sip of coffee to clear the phlegm in her throat. "Manny was the same. I had a knife of desperation stuck in his side. He didn't flinch or strike out. The waiter walked up, and Manny ordered us some desert. When we were alone, he offered me a job. He took out his wallet and told me to take all the money from it. There was over three thousand dollars. He promised he would get me as much as I needed, whether I took the job or not. I hadn't even told him about Noi yet."

"And you said yes."

She shook her head. "No. He gave me his card and told me where he was staying. I told him I needed time to think. He said it was fine, but if I needed more money, to please call instead of trying to hold up an old man with a spoon."

Blake chuckled. She had seen Manny do the trick before.

"You're laughing. He's done this shit before?"

Blake nodded. "Manny is a speeder. In short burst, he can move a bit faster than you can see. So at first, he probably took your knife while he was ordering the desert. He knew you would be mentally short-circuited by him doing something so non sequitur. When you took the wallet, he slipped the spoon into your other hand. He probably moved slowly with the wallet, knowing you would be watching at things developing at the same speed. And, by the way, don't gamble with him at cards or dice. I'm not saying he cheats. I'm just saying you won't win."

"When I finally went to find him at the hotel, he was gone, but there was a package at the desk for me."

"Package?"

"There was fifty thousand dollars in a large envelope, a set of car keys, and a valet ticket. When I got the car, there was an address out in the country, already plugged into the GPS. The note taped to the screen said, go here. I went. There was an old woman living there. She was sweet, made us tea, and told me a crazy story about immortal people."

Blake rolled over laughing. "Yeah, she was a fun woman."

"We went for a drive to the school. They enrolled Noi without any other information than her name. There is an endowment in her name. It is there to pay for any other girls Noi finds in her lifetime or has a daughter."

"A bit overwhelming, was it?"

"There's an understatement. But I needed you to know my whole story… because what you are going to ask me next goes against everything I want. I owe you and Manny so much."

Blake got up and kissed Chris on the top of the head. "Let's give this a whirl and see what we come up with. But, right now, I need to tinkle."

Christine had the bed made up when Blake came out. She answered Blake's eyebrow question by showing the bottom of her empty mug. "Let's go over to the smelter. I heard we just got a fresh batch of Kona coffee beans, and if I know Squint, he has already roasted up some sweet French light."

As they walked down the alleyway, Blake glanced down at the black boots. "What made you choose those over the knee boots? I would think they would get in the way at times."

"I had never had tall boots. I didn't even know if they were comfortable. In New York, I had watched the hookers and women on the streets, and one item stood out. The working office girl bought tan or brown mid-calf boots she hoped were warm. The street girls wore theirs up to the knees to attract attention, but also, they could take the extra cuff and flip it up when they had to kneel in the snow to give a blowjob. Only the confident, bold, and daring wore them up over their knees.

"When Manny told me about the interaction of the deck with whatever shoes we wore, I thought about where I was going to be living. A woman alone better show the most confidence to be bold enough to dare change their address to the ninety-fourth wave and just north of no-where."

Blake laughed. "And the black?"

"Same reason you wear red. It matches my hair."

"Nope."

"What do you mean nope? It does so."

"Oh, the matching is true—for you. Even when I was a blonde, I wore red boots. They don't show the blood as much."

The aroma of fresh roasted coffee overwhelmed them as they opened the door to the smelter room. As they came around the corner, they could see the one person in the reflective heat suit tending the giant smelter. They turned right into the small galley to find the lanky Australian leaning back against the counter with his nose buried in his mug.

"Any good this time, Squint?"

He just smiled and kept smelling his mug. Blake reached over and tipped the large mug outward so she could see what was going on. There were only beans.

Christine laughed. "He doesn't drink the stuff—he only roasts it for the smell. The wet stuff is over here."

They sat on the upper deck about the solar consolidator. The position provided them with seclusion as well as privacy. Both knew there weren't any of Ming's little cameras watching this small service deck.

"Brie."

Chris nodded and looked east and into the breeze. "We have old history together. Well, about twenty or so years. We met in London where I worked for an American company. And before you ask, yes, I knew. She had explained things. Manny didn't need to work hard to explain the Ever Kind."

Blake snorted softly. "But he does like his teaching moments."

"I didn't know she was involved with this. We had lost touch, and then, one day, she just shows up in the middle of the ocean. Things hadn't gone well right before we lost touch, and well, it spilled out. We've since gotten past it and moved on."

"She explained what her connection is to all of this?"

"Not all of it, but enough. I know she is a key pivot in the whole event."

"No, I would say she's the pivot point it all hinges on. In the world, she has the most important job, and probably, the most dangerous. It's not her life hanging in the balance, but all the mortals involved. The number is enormous and all that could go wrong, mammoth. That's a lot of pressure."

"In Hawaii, while you and Noi were off swimming, we hashed our issues out. We're good now, and I'll do my part. However, here's the rub. You and Manny need to trust my loyalty to the raft, my new family, and to Noi. There are going to be… things." She hung her head and then looked at Blake. "You have to trust in my love. It is all I have. It is everything within me. As a mom, you don't let your five-year-old daughter go to the park alone at night. You hold them close, and you wait until you can explain to them about how you love them and have to do mom stuff, which, at the time, doesn't make much sense." She looked down at her mug. "It is what I'm asking of you now. Afterward, we all need to go sit on a beach and talk. But until then, I need to do what's required of me, and I need your trust and your love. Without those, I might as well just jump in there." She nodded over her shoulder at the giant opening they both knew led to over two-thousand degrees of concentrated solar power.

25 Let's Get This Party Started

THE COMMUNICATION LINK opened in Blake's head, but there was nobody there. The deep sleep was certainly over. Blake looked back at the lump in the bed as she padded her way in the dark to the head.

"Manny?"

She felt the second link open. "Yes?"

"I have another link open, but nobody is there. I thought it was you."

"I have one also. Ming?"

The first link went active. "Shh. I'm working here."

Even in their minds, they could tell she had spoken in a whisper or barely subvocal. The system was designed to pick up either so a person who needed to remain quiet could still communicate.

Blake felt Manny's connection. "Command center."

She slid into her leggings and grabbed a boot. Feeling with her whole hand, she felt the three-inch collar she knew would have gone above her knee. Her boots landed on the bed beside her. "You threw your boots on this side... and I believe you are in my pants."

Blake smirked in the dark. "Feels good too." She

kissed near the face in the dark, and two hands shot out to grab her head.

"Geez, you really do suck at being in the dark." The kiss was wet and almost long enough.

Blake grabbed the boots and jumped to the door bare-footed. As the open door spilled light on her naked breasts, the tank top hit her in the head. She pulled the top on as a night duty personnel walked by. She gave the man credit for not glancing, but she smiled when he looked back from the end of the hall.

Pulling on her boots as she hopped down the hall, she turned the corner as she saw Cole coming out of another quarter she knew wasn't his. The two barely nodded as they hit the outer deck and sprinted across three catamarans. Blake noticed the man was barefoot and wearing a distinctive pair of running shorts. The word BOSTON in an arch across the butt was in pink on the black shorts. Blake smirked knowing she wasn't the only one with some age related night blindness.

As the three walked into the command center, they found Ming's station empty. The large screens were almost black. On one screen, a small red glow seemed to shimmer or dance. If the tactical graphs weren't posting down the sides of every monitor, the three would have thought Ming simply turned them off and went home for the night.

Manny bent over and squinted at the dark red blob no larger than a small fingerprint. "What the…"

"The screen is looking seventy-five miles away. The object is moving at sixteen knots, which is a bit faster than the ocean swells, and would account for its movement, except it is moving against the tide current."

The three turned to find Ming sitting relaxed with her

legs crossed on top of the table. She was sipping tea from a delicate bone China cup and saucer. On the table was a small plate of what appeared to be petit fours or cucumber sandwiches with the crusts cut off. "I watched it for three solid hours. I gave up and figured I had lost my mind, so I made supper. Tea, anyone?"

Manny looked back at the screen. "What kind of boat?"

"There isn't one." Ming sipped her tea.

Manny's head whipped around and looked back at the dark screen. "Then what are we looking at?"

Cole grumped and walked to the table. "Why am I awake at this hour?" He took a sandwich and shoved the whole into his mouth. Ming's eyebrow rose. Cole nodded, took another, and headed for the coffee.

Blake was still squinting at the blob. "The resonator starts compiling the image about—"

"It will make its first crude guess image around sixty-two miles, but the first one that will make any sense will take until it is inside the fifty-five-mile ring. Then we can scale up the Doppler and wash out the background noise."

Manny sat with a mug of coffee in his hand. "But no boat."

"There is some metal, which set off the alarm at the one-hundred-mile ring. It's about the same size as a radar ball on a sailboat. But FADA took a second jump around eighty miles. It appears to be two objects the size of radar balls but about forty-three kilograms combined. The density return was of high-density steel with a solid carbon trace."

"Warrior class weapons grade. Those are some damn heavy balls." Cole took another sandwich.

Ming smirked. "You would know, Cole."

Blake plopped down into the last chair. "So we won't have anything until…" glancing toward the top of the doorway where the local time was always displayed, "shortly before sunup."

Manny smiled. "Workout or breakfast?"

Blake glared at him as if he had just said something vulgar. "Workout, and when I left, the mat was still warm." She stood as she looked to Ming. "Let me know when you get an image from fifty-three." Ming nodded.

She flipped Manny off and stuck her tongue out at Cole as she left. The three were still laughing as the outside hatch banged shut.

DAWN ON THE ocean is flaky. With the slight rise in temperature, an occasional fog lifts off the surface. Blake stood grumpily just outside the hatch. The damp air hung. As she looked down the giant raft of catamarans, she could only see halfway to the end. The last several cats were totally lost in the gray. Looking straight up, even the blue wasn't pure. She had spent the last two hours forcing the computer to weave an image that might make sense.

The hatch opened, and a small Asian woman stepped out. "Ming say she got image you might can work with."

Blake turned toward the door. "Thanks, Tink." The woman nodded in a short head bow and walked along the deck.

The redhead watched the woman who she always thought was secretly a pixie or fairy. Blake wasn't sure she'd be surprised if one day the woman sprouted wings and flew off.

"What did you get, Ming?"

"I slaved the radar, FADA, and the photo together. The radar can see through this shit, and hopefully, you can make the photo figure it all out."

"What about the FADA?" *Find, Assess, Decide, and Attack.*

"Crazy piece of shit. It found the target all right because it's been watching it since midnight local. The assess evaluation is more like ejaculate. Decide has somehow looped into junk because it now thinks there are three objects. As for the attack, you might do better just going out there and throwing a harpoon at it."

"Speaking of harpoons, are we sure this isn't some rogue sperm whale migrating on the surface in the moonlight?"

Ming shook her head. "A whale would have blinked off and on. They never stay on the surface this long."

"What about sending out a drone?"

"We'd lose it in the fog. Go play with what the metal midget built for you."

Blake sat down at her station and pulled up the file. Ming was right. The raw data was beyond wrong and useless. But she looked for the grapple holds and pulled it back together. As she developed the image, she found it to make no sense.

She pulled up the images she had compiled through the morning. Finally, she set points and overlaid the images. Turning them all to transparencies, she stacked them and flattened the whole.

Drawing samples from the surrounding image area, she built a crude manual Doppler separator. Slowly bringing it in behind the merged transparency, she submerged the background noise. She stared at the final image. It wasn't great, but it did make sense.

"Manny?"

The connection *plinked* in her head but had a hollow sound like a tin can on a string. She could feel Ming connect as well. "Blake?"

"Manny, you will never guess who is coming to dinner and how he is getting here."

Manny laughed. "We're on a remote patch for the comm link. I got tired of waiting. I'm in the Growler sub. The first mate is Nordic. He grew up on his grandfather's fairy tales and Norse legends. I can't get him off the periscope."

"I built an image, but it has all three of him. Is there anyone else?"

"Sure, and about a half hour ago, I figured out who the other two are."

Blake slumped back as she looked at the giant of a man standing with his arms folded. On one side of him was a giant battle-ax, and on the other was a great hammer with a short handle. They were standing on what appeared to be a shelf of water. Blake now knew it was one of his boats he could call from the water. The boat could hold as many or few as needed. She studied the three objects.

The smile was slow to come—Mjolnir, Thor's hammer. Jarnbjorn, his battle-ax—originally made from a great white bear. The stories would have come from somewhere.

"Just offhand, I would say we are looking at the origin of Thor, his hammer, and his battle-ax."

Manny's chuckle rattled in her head. "Smart girl. I think he is here to get the party going. Ming, you need to dust off the disco ball and put on some music."

Blake could hear Ming's connection close just before she heard the mutter from six-feet away.

"Crazy gaijin."

Blake chuckled at the woman who had never left Asia, even when Asia hadn't treated women nicely. As she stared at the still blurry image of three men standing on a rogue wave of water, she thought about how selective many of them had been about the regions they roamed.

Blake and Manny had both come from the great crescent known as the greater Middle East. They were both drawn toward the seductive centers of Mesopotamia, and then Egypt. Their lives had flowed back and forth across, as well as to and fro, along the Mediterranean Sea. Occasionally, they guided their destinies, but for the most part, lives were taken as they came. Mongolia, the freezing north, and England had only been side trips out of boredom.

A small thought made her chuckle quietly. She remembered the sunny day on the side of the hill of what would eventually become the Atlas Mountains. The young boy was tasked with watching over the small herd of goats. In the shade of a small tree, the boy discovered what was to become his favorite toy.

His father was happy he no longer complained about his long days alone. His mother's only silent complaint was his soiled kaftan—always in the same spot. But for a year—he was a happy boy.

The jackal Blake became after the pack had killed the boy was her start on the nature of being a pirate.

She glanced over at Ming and wondered at the start of her solitary nature. The woman became one of the first

Night Smokes or a form of female Ninja predating Japan by over a thousand years.

A video appeared on one of her monitors. "The fog suddenly cleared."

Blake looked at the distance on the display. She also noticed the speed. "Looks like Rek is getting hungry." She looked over at Ming. "I hope we have more than just those cute little sandwiches."

The woman dressed in the black bodysuit stuck her finger up. They both laughed.

"Looks like his target will be Cat-12, and at this speed, I would say in about twenty minutes." Blake could tell by Ming's stance that she was comm-linked to Manny. She looked again at the prow of what had become known as a Viking ship. She could see through the water form to the man behind. More amazing, the ship had an unchanging prow wave. It was as if the ship was unaffected by the water it was passing over or through.

Ming nodded as Blake rose. She knew Blake probably had history with this Ever Kind and understood a greeting of friends is better than none.

Blake walked into the gray noise of the blast furnace room. She stood next to the silver-suited figure and yelled. "Can you get away for a short while?"

The man stepped back and pulled off the soft helmet. "Manfred came and got Christine a few minutes ago. I think they are somewhere on the southeast deck. I don't know which cat, though."

Blake rested her hand on his shoulder. "Thanks, Tosh, I think I know where." She squinted back at the pit of molten metal. "Pulling gold?"

"Tin right now. We'll get the gold this afternoon with

the higher heat."

"Thanks. I'll let you get back to it." She understood he was at a critical temperature that separated four different metals within only one hundred degrees.

She found Manny standing with nine others along the blue-water cable railing. His long black curls were ruffling in the wind. Standing next to Christine and her long wavy black hair, they could pass for twins. She had never thought about Manny's taste for his boots to come just to the top of his calf but had a hand-width of leather cuff turned back over the tops. his taste in clothes and boots For as long as she had known him, his taste in clothes and boots ran toward the same deep cordovan color of a Roman legionnaire's skirting with black sandals or boots.

She thought about the two and about the hundreds of relationships that she'd had through her lives. Only a few were fair or with straight or even short hair. She smiled. *Good to know about myself.*

As the ship of water approached, it sped up and got taller. Rek was either making an entrance for the crowd or simply raising his deck to match the catamaran.

The two boats almost touched as he stepped from the water deck towering six feet above. The water held its form until his feet landed. The form collapsed and became the ocean twelve feet below. With a huge smile and spread of his arms, he took a step. His smile turned to confusion just before his butt landed on the deck with his boots in the air.

"What the hell?" His roar quickly turned to laughter. "Manny... what *majik* is this?"

Manny leaned over and tugged at the man's boot. "Go barefooted until we can adapt these." He looked at what he was holding. "Cristos, Rek, how long has this poor wolf been dead? Is this still congealing blood?”

The man reached out and snatched the boot. “Don’t make fun of my animals.”

Blake joined in the game. “I think the left one just moved. Let me shoot it.”

The man roared. “Bloody hell, it still has my foot in it. Of course, it moved you, silly little girl.”

She leaned over and slapped the man across the face. “No husband of mine will ever call me silly.” She grabbed his beard with both hands and pulled his face to her lips. The kiss was full of affection and heat. Everyone was stunned except Manny.

“Hold him down, Blake, while I get this other bloody carcass off his pinkies.” He slipped off the other boot and threw it next to the other. The pair looked like a couple of large hairy dogs lying by the hearth.

Blake pulled back an inch and rubbed her nose on his as they laughed. Rek’s voice was soft as honey and warm as the hearth. “Ah, Nessie, I have missed you all these millennia. You were taken from me far too young. We could have ruled for hundreds of years.”

Blake kissed him on the forehead and helped him up. “I heard you were lost at sea only a few years later.”

“Aye and I lived a grand life with the cows from the Arctic circle to the southern sea. In those days, a whale’s life wasn’t so bad. It was when men started killing them by the pod it stopped being grand.”

He tenderly tried his footing. Manny chuckled. “Barefoot works just fine. It’s when you have dead hides or other footwear, and then the secret of the deck takes over. I’ll explain later.” He stuck his hand out, and they shook by grabbing up on the forearm. “Good to have you aboard.”

Each Ever Kind stepped forward to make a touch connection. Only Christine was standing alone. Blake reached out and dragged her forward. "Rek, this is my partner, Christine."

The man reached out and quietly took her hand. His one eyebrow rose enough for Christine to notice. He shook her hand up and down slowly. "A strong grip on this one, Nessie. You've done well."

"Back off, big guy, she's mine, and she's not a cow at the village fair." The two laughed, but Chris was quick to remove her hand.

Rek held his hands down, and his weapons jumped up into his grip. "I don't know about anyone else, but I'm starving. It was a long ride from Japan."

Manny took him by the arm and walked him away. "Japan, you say? Did you happen to see any gatherings of ships on your way here?"

The man nodded. "Two nights ago… It wasn't like when the Americans and English attacked Normandy a while back—but close. But it had the same feel, a lot of shit, but trying to keep it all a secret. As I came through, I got the feeling of two dogs fucking on your front porch, but these were elephants."

THE PLATES HAD been pushed away as they looked at a quickly printed set of maps. Rek could look at a monitor but only saw the red pixels. His thick finger pointed to a section about eight hundred miles southwest by south of them. "Most of the larger ships seemed to be converted cargo ships like we used in Africa. Push them up on the shore, crack open the prow, unload your cargo, and float it back off with the high tide."

"Do you think they could do it at sea?"

"What… and have baby boats inside? It's possible."

"How many sailboats?"

"About half their fleet. Most of them were about thirty to fifty meters, small trader ketch rigs, as well as old cargo sloops. They felt heavy with souls. Many angry and evil men."

Manny nodded in thought. His fingers combed through his hair as he leaned on his elbow, looking at the map. He lifted the map and stood. Musing, he moved toward the door. Rek scrambled to follow. His footsteps were cautious, as he still didn't trust the deck.

Manny peeked back and smiled. "We'll get your boots adapted tomorrow."

As they walked out into the command center, Manny looked for Ming. A slender blonde turned. "She finally went to bed. It's her bad habit of sleeping about once a week. What can I do for you?"

Manny looked at the map and up to the monitor. He pushed the image around on the monitor until he had the right area of the ocean. Studying the monitor, he pulled in the movable coordinates bars. The GPS notations now read on the left side.

"Sloan, can we send Captain Mike, on the Huntress submarine, this screen?"

"I'll hook him in live to it." Her fingers danced around the keyboard, and a small box appeared on Manny's monitor. The box displayed in red tones. The bridge on the sub bathed in night light.

Rek's face lit up as he pointed at the small square of

reds. "Hey, dat's Toof." Rek liked Mike from the moment he met him years before and had called him by the ancient word for friend ever since. "Hi, Toof." He waved.

The man looked up, smiled, and waved. "Hey, Rek. How's the Goof Da of the north?"

"I'm great. We're down in Kyoto. You should come down and meet my mama-san Kiamichi."

Manny cleared his throat. The submariner looked over. "Sorry, Manfred." He scanned the map and looked at the coordinates. "This is about a day away and only slightly off our racetrack."

"Rek came through a large mixed cluster of ships just sitting station there. I think this is them getting ready."

"We'll goose the engines and give you a sitrep by lunch tomorrow." The sub's captain gave Manny a two finger salute.

Mike turned to his executive officer and pointed at the screen. "Give us double revolutions until about here, and then we'll go silent." He looked back at Manny and Rek. "Boys—I've got to go to work. Great seeing ya, Rek, and I'll plan to come see you and meet the little woman."

The screen closed. Rek frowned. "How did he know she was little?"

Manny reached up and patted the man on the massive shoulder. "It's just a saying, Rek. I'm sure she's not so small."

26 Movements in the Dark

28° 42'25.75°N, 177°42'40.62°W – 800 miles northeast of Wake Island, Pacific Ocean.

"SONAR TO BRIDGE."

"Bridge."

"Sir, I have multiple bogies making revolutions."

Mike looked through the periscope. The fairly dark fleet sitting station in the middle of the ocean was turning on lights. "Keep me posted, son. When most or all of them are making revolutions, give me a holler."

"Aye, sir."

Mike turned to his executive officer. "Warm up the bays. As soon as they move off fifty miles, I want a clean launch."

The short bald woman saluted him.

The captain stepped through the hatch and turned right into his room. As he sat down at his tiny desk, he thought about the letter he needed to write. The man was a half-world away, but never further than his heart. Mike knew his executive officer and daughter-in-law would probably never see her husband again. The least he could do for the two of them was detail her final days and weeks for his son. Cancer sucked, but the jobs they had all chosen went far beyond a single person or a single lifetime. Their lives became about the single planet and the seven billion others on the planet the minute they stole the nuclear submarine.

Dear son,

I cannot begin to put into words the admiration, pride, and blessing it has been serving with Suzanne. Hands down, she has been the best executive officer I have ever had the pleasure of serving with. I have spoken with many of the crew, and they feel the same way. I'm sorry you two never got the chance to live a normal life where her skills of motherhood could have continued with a next generation.

Tonight, we are preparing to start what we have been preparing for. My guess now is the fleet we have been stalking for a while will make their final move. When you have read this, you will already know about a nuclear device going off in the northern Pacific. The device is a sub-ton EMP. Its complete job is to turn a fleet of pirate ships into floating hunks of metal. I'd like to believe it would be called end of game, but I know it won't be the end.

I understand you had some dealings in arranging the self-destruction of certain large weapons. If we are lucky, they will never get the chance to use them—but, if they do, I pray providence guided your hand.

I will sign off now, as I need a few hours of rack time.
Take care of yourself.
Your loving father,
Mike.

27 Aboard the Raft

THE CELL PHONE on the carpet vibrated softly in the dark. Christine studied the unmoving body sharing the bed. She softly rolled over to look at the screen on her phone.

Using the light of the screen, she grabbed her leggings and boots. Silently, she slipped out of bed and into the hallway. She pulled on her boots and walked off.

The door opened a crack and widened. Blake stepped out of the room in her bare feet as she watched the head of black hair exit the outward hatch. The hatch led to the back of the catamaran and onto the smelter cat. Blake followed.

As she softly opened the outside hatch to the smelter, Blake could sense the mixed odors of the molten metals. Without the sun, the smelter was silent, but there would still be a heat kept from the thermal mass and electric backup from the other forms of generation.

She held the door with her small finger and then slid it out. The door snuggled to the ring with a dull silence. Blake eased to the end of the cabinets.

Christine stood with her hands at her side. Her head was back as she looked through the large opening in the ceiling. Blake could see something in her right hand. The left held her phone.

Deliberately, she raised her right hand. She held a small device to her phone. Her left hand scrolled through something and then stopped. She thumbed something on the screen. A small red light glowed on the cube in her right hand. Blake had seen them before. It was a beacon. It would pulse out three cycles of coordinates in less than a second. She watched Christine thumb the switch on the activated beacon. The small black fob pulsed red three times and went dark.

The small black dead cube fell off the tips of Christine's fingers into the molten mass below. There was only a small flare, and it was gone. The brunette slipped to her knees holding herself.

Blake slipped out of the hatch.

"Manny."

The connection fluttered in her head. "Blake?"

"They're coming. Chris just triggered a beacon."

"Thanks. We'll talk in the morning, um, later." The link went cold like a lead balloon of nothing in her head. She started to walk back to Cat-7, but instead, turned and went back to her own cabin. Sleep or confrontation was the last thing she wanted right now.

800 miles northwest of Wake Island.

THE KNUCKLE ON the door rapped softly.

Mike rolled over, hanging his legs over the edge of his bunk. He checked his glowing watch. "Come."

The door opened. "Sir, they're on the move."

"Come in, Suzanne, please."

The officer opened the door wider and stood in the opening. She had two mugs in her one hand. "I figured you might want some coffee, sir."

"Thanks. Close the door, please. I want to have a moment with my daughter-in-law."

The woman closed the door and handed him his mug. Unlike the usual white mugs, his was black with a skull and crossed sabers trimmed with red. The irony of his being a die-hard Buccaneer's fan didn't escape anyone. The man was sixty-eight, and the Navy didn't want him anymore. He had taken his severance package in the form of a nuclear submarine. His last crew consisted only of volunteers—two were Ever Kind. The cook and bosun's mate he had known most of his life. And the only ones who also knew of his enlarged prostate.

He pulled the letter out of the folder. "I want you to know this is the last voyage for both of us. I've known for three years. Well, let's just say… I want to die with my prostate just the way it is."

Her lips rolled in as she sighed. She nodded. "Boats told me. I know you have been best mates your entire career, but he thought I needed to know." Her head drooped to one side.

Mike's head bobbed gently. "That you weren't alone."
She nodded.

He reached out and took her hand. "Everyone on here has their own reason to be here. For us mortals, it is about our kids and grandkids. For others, it's about a better place going forward. Some, it is the last hurrah. Others will carry this time in their hearts going forward. Two of them will remember us in the telling of great stories and legends."

She snorted softly and took his hand. "Somehow, the names Mike and Suzanne don't inspire great legends of heroic deeds."

He smiled as his eyes sparkled wetly. "Don't laugh. They just need writing and being sung drunkenly by the right Vikings and pirates. But take heart, mate, there is much to be sung at our wake."

Her smile pulled up on one side. "Did I ever tell you I have a lovable goofball for a father-in-law?"

He stood. "Give this old goofball a hug, and then we have work to do today."

27 Call the Ball

THE COMM BUZZED.

"Yes?"

The comm buzzed.

"Manny." He realized the comm wasn't in his head but on the desk. He rolled over and slapped it. "Yes."

"Sloan, sir. The sub is calling."

"What time is it?"

"Three-ten, local, sir."

"Tell Mike to hold his breaches. I'm coming up." He slapped the comm and rolled onto his back. Looking into the black of the room, he wondered aloud if he was getting too old for these young man games. He rolled over onto the floor and did fifty fast pushups.

Jumping up, he smiled. "Nope… still got it."

Ming's head appeared from under the comforter. "You are so weird."

He smirked back. "It's why you love us, Ming. Crazy gaijin, we're kinky like octopus sex but sweet as honey in your kimchee."

A growl came from the floor on the other side of the bed. "Shut up, unless you're bringing back food."

Manny paused at the door. "Get some sleep, kids. I'll bring back food when I know more."

A pillow hit the closing door.

Manny almost wanted to whistle a happy tune as he walked down the hall. He hadn't felt this alive in decades. Rek, Ming, and he had played a violent old card game until past midnight. Sometimes swapping old stories or tales can be more rewarding than a heavy romp through the sheets. Even though, Ming occasionally could come close.

He headed for the coffee station. "Sloan, get Mike on the horn."

"I'm right here, you old carrion bait. Oh, you look like shit. How many were playing Kill the Saxon?"

Manny didn't even turn around. He smiled about Mike knowing him so well. "Only three last night, Mike, but I'm hoping for a lot more." He turned with his mug of coffee and strode toward the communication station. Sloan only gave the shirtless man a glance.

"About seventy percent of the fleet is in the strike zone."

Manny paused. "And… the others?"

"Some of the boys got a little bored, so they went for a stroll around the neighborhood last night. Some of the ships are having, um, issues." His smile was large and toothy. "I'm just waiting on you for final launch."

"Are you far enough away?"

"We will be. We have three thousand under us for a crash dive. It takes ten minutes to make the arch and bring it in from the top. By then, we will be sixty miles away, and over two thousand deep. There are thermal layers here, and we should be under at least four of them. We're fine." He turned to look at a pad. "Back on observation projected for dawn or five-forty local."

"Thanks, Mike." Manny nodded. "Let's knock out some bastards. Give me good news to go with my frosted flakes in the morning."

The man saluted with two fingers. "Aye, aye, sir." The display went black.

Sloan looked to Manny.

"Thanks, Sloan. We can expect them to take at least two or three days before they get back together. And then they'll still have a hard seven-hundred-mile sail." He thought a moment. "Take some time today to Skype home. I'm sure your mother will enjoy talking to you."

"Will do, sir. And, sir… thank you for all of this."

Manny nodded but remained watching the monitors. He remembered Sloan's recruitment. They extradited her just before an arrest for ecoterrorism. Her father had been a NOAH officer. He discovered the end of a six-mile-long pipe dumping toxic waste off the coast of China. Jun's company hunted him down and cut him up for fish bait.

They caught Sloan four miles off the Chinese coast with five others, and two hundred pounds of Semtex explosives. Their game plan also included twenty pounds of Hexavalent Chromium atomized into an airborne nature. The game plan consisted of dumping it into the air intakes of Jun's office tower. On any given day, the population in the single large tower was twice the population that was in the New York twin towers.

Manny's stomach growled. He nodded to the young woman and quietly went to wash out his mug. As he hung the mug on the rack, he ran his hands over the twenty-some mugs. Everyone was different. Everyone represented what each person held precious. Soon, some would hang untouched—as a tribute to fallen friends. It had always been this way, but for some reason, this time it hit him in the gut.

THE FOUR HUNG their legs over the edge of the web-bing and watched west as the sun rose. The calm sea was molten lead with tips of gold. Nobody spoke, all were aware of the moment. Nobody understood it, but sunrise was an Ever Kind phenomenon. It wasn't about a party or joyous nature. It was always a quiet coming together. Not one of them had ever spoken to another about why it meant so much to them.

The web moved. Manny and Blake looked back. Cole walked barefoot across the web deck suspended twenty feet above the water below. He sat down next to Blake and gave her a hug. His hand reached out and rubbed Rek's giant shoulder. The touch was all the communication.

The sea was calm, and the winds held steady between ten and fifteen knots blowing up from the Sea of Japan. The air was clear, and the early sun felt good on their faces. All seemed right with the world. It was July 31, 06:23 lo-cal.

28 From the Gates of Hell

FIVE COMM LINKS clicked open.

"We have multiple bogies incoming. They just crossed the seventy-mile ring. ETA is two hours fourteen minutes."

The links closed.

Four people in four separate cabins moaned in unison.

Blake rolled over onto Christine. She wanted to say it was her fault. However, she knew it had started a long time before the woman's family tree was even a glimmer in the eye of a reptile on the edge of the original pond of scum. Hell, for all Blake knew, she had been that reptile with the original gills.

Christine rolled over and pulled her arm around Blake's shoulders. She plucked sleepily at the red hair. "Are you okay?"

Blake thought about the question. There were so many ways it could apply. The simple and straightforward was the most honest. She sighed. "No. No, I'm not. This is where I want to spend the next day. Right here. This bed. This woman."

"But…?"

"In two hours, we will be at war."

Christine rolled over and kissed Blake on the forehead. Her lips held there. Her eyes stung, and the tears fell silent on her shoulder. Nothing could make it all right or better. The day would be whatever happened.

The two lay quiet until they drifted into an unsettled slumber.

THE SUBMARINE BRIDGE remained in battle-station red light. Mike had put on his last clean uniform shirt. Unseen below the camera he wore on his favorite lucky sweats. The word Buccaneers in bold red letters trimmed in white ran down the outside of each black leg. The skull and crossed sabers stretched across his butt.

"The best we can guess is the six large containerships were heavily shielded. The EMP did stop them, but they were back up on some other reserve power within the day. In the evening, we lost them in a freak fog. Later, we figured it was manufactured. We only saw the last of the surface effect boats in the distance. We have no way of knowing how many you guys will be facing, Manny."

"Thanks, Mike. You made our job a lot easier no matter what. It's my personal feeling to let you go ahead and drop what you can. I'm sure there's nothing but skeleton crews left on the hulks. That crew can always take to life rafts. Maybe someone will take pity on their souls."

Mike's face pulled up on one side as he looked to the right. "Ming, you might want to fill him in on what a modified fifty-three really does to a ship."

Ming took a large calm breath and rolled her face toward Manny. She shook her head as her eyes blinked lazily. "There won't be any life rafts… or people needing them. The depleted uranium is superheated by passing through the armored hulls. Once inside, all the oxygen is burned off at a temperature approximate to summer on Mercury or closer to the sun. Anything capable of exploding—will."

"What about those above decks?"

Mike cleared his throat. "They call them Hellfire for a reason. As the deck superheats, it doesn't melt, it vaporizes… and everyone with it."

Manny was acutely aware of what the man was saying. "Mike, they chose which side of the great divide they wanted to be on. You decide what you think is best. You're the quarterback, and I'll back your play no matter what."

The man saluted and turned. "Ex Oh."

"Sir."

"Get out the mop."

"Yes, sir."

Mike turned back. "Manny, we'll catch you on the flip side."

"Make it so, my friend. Make it so." He saluted him back, and the comm went black.

He turned. "How far out?"

Ming scanned across the six monitors. "Front wave just crossed the forty."

Manny sighed as he rested his hands on his hips and looked at his feet. "Let's get the kids up and fed. It's going to be a long day."

In every crew quarter, the soft lulling sound of crickets became a thunderstorm at a distance, and finally, the groaning of a klaxon horn sounding general quarters. As the sound subsided into silence, the click was audible.

Ming's voice pervaded every corner of the raft. "We are now on countdown—war minus forty-eight minutes. Please eat a good solid breakfast and make sure your war packs have enough supplies. Check your water bottles. I don't want any of you kids dehydrating. Forget playing fair today—this is for all the marbles. For all of you mortals, we the Ever Kind salute you for being here and for doing what you will do today. We will write songs and poems about the heroes of today. You will never be forgotten. This is our most solemn oath to you. You honor us by your presence, we revere you, and we cherish you. Thank you, one and all. Now get a good meal. You're going to need it. All door clocks are now set on countdown to estimated time of contact."

THE BATTLE RACK slid up and embraced Blake's hips. The upper apparatus spread out around her shoulders but did not restrict her movements. The targeting helmet would come later.

"Range?"

"Ten miles… baring two-three-one."

Blake passed her hand through the air and rolled it down. The helmet rotated from atop the rack and settled onto her head. The tinted shield across her face lit up.

"Going starlight."

The ocean swells were black as death. Blake knew the real death was the green foam of boats cresting the rolls of tide. As the sea undulated, Blake could see the carpet of soft glowing neon green. It extended for miles.

She kicked the plate at her feet. The command pedals

separated from the floor. A small roller shelf issued from the rack to support her weight and allow her to use her feet. She could feel as much as hear the railguns above the center go active.

"Live and targeted."

The targeting computers would now track the movement of targets as they rose and fell on the waves. The distance for a bullet to cross from weapon to target could mean the difference between a hit and a miss. The computer made the adjustment—the shooter only needed to select the target.

Ming's comm opened to all the command centers and the general raft. Here voice was soft and cold. "Ladies and gentlemen, let the games begin. Smoke 'em as you find 'em."

Blake and Ming exchanged a fleeting look as they smiled. Blake shook her head. "You are so weird, Ming."

The first twenty-pound slug raced out of the railguns, followed by five more—Blake had the units set on bursts of three. She watched for effect. Two foam blobs flared green to white in the first traces of light. The golden line of dawn slit the throat between the dark gray sky and the black of the sea. The sea was running three-to-five with a steady six-knot wind. The sky was cloudless. The first pillars of smoke began to end the calm and beauty.

"Air, I'm showing two slow albatross in the south. Neither are squawking turtle."

"On them, Ming. One is squawking US Navy, and we warned them off. The other is getting the standard Seahawk greeting… now."

In the corner of their upper left display, they watched the fire trail as the SAM leaped into the air. In seconds, it was only a dull red tracking square. Moments later, it winked out. Four more red squares appeared with targeting crosshairs.

Blake kicked at the pedals and the railgun chuffed. As the sun rose, the sea became a mix of targets, as well as incoming fire.

MANNY SAT ON a high deck with Rek, his right hand warmed by the black mug of coffee. A small cabinet set in the wall was just large enough to hold a few mugs and a thermos.

"They're close enough for small arms fire." Rek looked over and smiled. He pulled the lever back on the Barrett XM109. The 25mm shell sounded like a small car wreck as it seated into the chamber.

Manny nodded with his jaw. "Sorry we couldn't find a larger rifle for you." The heavy-duty rifle almost looked normal in the large man's hands.

Rek snorted a small laugh. "Let's see if your boys did their job right. What's the scope sighted for?"

"One mile, just like you asked."

"I still think looking through glass is somehow cheating."

Manny rolled his eyebrows and flattened his lower lip. "We can always take it off."

"I'll suffer through… but just this one time." He nodded at the oversized ear protectors on Manny's head as he pulled his down. He slipped on a wraparound pair of shooting goggles and pulled the rifle up to his knee. He had learned to sharpshoot in the First World War and never changed his stance unless he was shooting farther than a mile.

He sighted toward one of the surface effect boats as it started to crest a swell. Manny watched as dust and water droplets appeared in the air and the small alcove recoiled from the sonic boom. Even with the double suppressors, and the small twin rows of pressure relief slots in the barrel, the noise tortured the surrounding metal walls and deck.

The pilot station on the boat had sucked into itself before the back half blew apart. The bullet of depleted uranium, when it hit, had the mass of a small Cadillac passing through the boat.

Rek turned to Manny with a smile. He counted on his fingers and then drew a question mark in the air. Manny showed him his hands four times. The large redhead grinned like a child in a candy store and looked back out to sea. Forty would make a dent... but only a dent. He shrugged and positioned again. The alcove shook.

COLE HELD THE snubbed automatic out to Christine. She shook her head. "I fired it a few times, but never got comfortable enough to be much good."

"Anything you are comfortable with besides a sword?"

"I'll take the Sig with a belt of clips. I used to also be good with a squirrel rifle."

"A twenty-two or two-twenty-three?"

She shook her head. "My uncle had an old 30-30 from his grandfather, and he came home with his M1 carbine.

We were just getting rid of the fuzzy tailed tree rats. We didn't need any parts left."

Cole thought about the old guns and grabbed one of the AR-15s and three belts of ammo clips. "You'll love this one. It's just as good, but doesn't kick like those other two." He smirked. "There are plenty of fuzzy tailed rats out there today."

Chris snarled as she started to leave. "I was a lot younger then." She hefted the light rifle.

She looked back. Cole looked on the small map. "How about up there in the pocket, over the smelter?"

She nodded with her chin and left. She would be comfortable there. And when she ran out of ammo, it was an easy slide down to the main deck to use her sword.

MANNY TIRED OF watching Rek have all the fun. The fast boats were close enough for his .30 caliber sniper rifle. He swapped out his spotting binoculars for the rifle. He sighted for the boat drivers until it became obvious the windscreens were armored against anything smaller than the cannon Rek was using. He resorted to his old saying about a man with a bad gut—in a shit storm, any head will do.

The head was dark-haired but exploded all the same. The pirate knew a head exploding all over his shipmates' faces and bodies causes panic and faintness of resolve. The next head to pop up above a rail was blond… and then red.

Manny watched as the pilot station of the boat he was aiming at imploded. He looked over at Rek. The Viking looked over and said something with a huge smile. Manny didn't know what the giant was saying, but he knew the man hadn't been this happy in many decades. Manny shifted and started working on a small wave of boats working their way east to come at the end of the raft. The side movement exposed the drivers.

As his finger was easing into a pull, the pilot and station disappeared. He frowned and looked back at Rek. The man, still focused on the main assault, had not been the shooter. Manny rose above the shield and looked down two catamarans. The twin railguns were actively taking apart the small wave. He smiled and went back to helping the giant Viking. There would still be plenty of bodies and targets for everyone.

Blake had noticed the small group of a couple dozen boats break off from the main body. She had kept throwing slugs at the furthest reaches of the invading mass. As the pincer group swung sideways to the raft to make their final run, she took advantage of the larger targets.

She reached out with her left hand and drew a circle in the air. The pulsing red target formed on the upper left monitor. She waived it over to Ming.

"Got them. You knock out the boats, and I'll shred the water."

Ming's fingers massaged her large command balls as she switched from solid bullets to rounds that broke-up in the air and became tiny three winged darts called *flechettes*. The edges of the winged darts were serrated razors. Thousands hit the water and air around the exploding boats. Nothing short of an Ever Kind could survive the onslaught as the shells filled the air.

The ocean around the raft was rapidly becoming a sea of blood. If there were sharks within several hundred miles, they would be homing in and swimming at top speed. They would be gathering and feeding by the next dawn. The noise and turbulence would keep the usual shy feeders at bay for now.

Manny looked up as five fighter jets flew past with less than a hundred feet to spare over the tops of the tall turbine masts. Even with the sound suppressing headgear, he could hear their jets. As they lowered, he watched their sonic trail cut troughs in the ocean, kicking up hundred-foot rooster tails. The small boats in the direct path were struck and slewed to a stop. Manny didn't have to look in his scope to know the sonic wave had shattered the eyes and eardrums of the crews. Some would die outright with burst lungs or caved-in chests. The others would die in agony as they slowly bled out through their eyes, ears, nose, throat, as well as massive bruising to the struck area. He wasn't sure where they had come from, but he was happy for their help. The boats would soon be slamming into the raft and vomiting their crews of crazed mercenaries.

CHRISTINE SAT BACK and sipped on her bottle of water laced with potassium, several vitamins, and a mild lacing of methadrine. She had only one belt left of clips. Even on only triple-shot bursts, she knew the two thousand rounds wouldn't last for long. The wave to her right was shifting. Soon they would be in her optimal range.

She took one last sip and repositioned herself and her rifle. Her finger barely moved. Three pieces of lead leaped out toward the ocean and a figure in a boat. She never saw the man collapse. Already three more slugs were on their way toward a crewmate. Her shots were mechanical. Breathe for three seconds, hold for two as she targeted, and gently squeeze the trigger. Breathe. Repeat.

She didn't have to search for targets. They were a constant assembly line of live bodies to dead. As one dropped out of her sight, the next took its place. The rifle clicked. Her thumb automatically depressed the button, the clip fell as her hand grabbed the next—ripping it from the Velcro strap. She slammed the new clip home and cycled the bolt. Thirty-three shots later, she would repeat it.

"WE HAVE INCOMING." Ming swung the right command ball out of her way and draped her hand over the replacement. Her right screens changed.

"And the ones we have been dealing with were outgoing?"

"These are air… coming in from northwest by west." She nodded as the targeting helmet re-extended from above. As the screen locked in place on her head, the heads-up-display lit up. "We have slow movers… under two hundred… probably helicopters."

"Sam Station… how many Sidewinders do we have?"

A small hand-sized image appeared. The man had a silver brush cut. He looked like an actor in a fifties movie. "Ming, I've got only twenty Sidewinders, but thirty Hellfires. What do you have?"

"I'm guessing Hinds coming out of North Korea or off the straight. They are maintaining one-fifty constant."

The man rubbed his face. "Flying slowly… means they're loaded down with arms and manpower. They might have figured it's a one-way ticket. Let's start with the Hell-fires and work down from there."

"Load 'em out, Tiger. I'll need them in about twenty."

The man turned. "Hell-fires it is, and she needs them in fifteen seconds." He held his one thumb up and turned back. "Launch pod three. Ready when you are." The image winked out.

Using the HUD, Ming selected six of the slow movers. The targeting marked each uniquely and paired it with one of the twelve missiles in the launcher. She went on to select the next six. The launch and tracking would be automatic from then on. She noticed the second launch pod was now armed and ready.

The first pod went from a box of twelve green dots to six and then twelve black squares. She knew the pod would now stand on its rump while twelve new missiles auto loaded. She continued her selection of the slow movers to create the most havoc and psychological effect. The high fliers would rain burning hell out and over those lower and behind them. Two flying in a tight tandem can also cause damage as the one blows possibly sideways. It may not cause an immediate secondary kill, but damage to a heli-copter over open water can be tantamount to the same end-game.

Twelve green lights went black.

Ming and Blake felt the hit as much as heard it. Blake noted the square in her one display as the automatic fire-suppression unit winked on. The sign for the main railgun went black. She signaled the secondary and kicked the feed into auto. She knew it would burn itself out, but there would be a few more tons of slugs spewed across the ocean before it did. The railgun never overheated, but the feeder slowly built heat in the moving parts. She swept the targeting across the oncoming flotilla. A pair of twenty-pound rods left the rail every second. Whether it was a direct hit, a glancing blow, or a hole through the flimsy hull of a surface effect boat, all took their toll.

REK HELD UP the giant rifle, kissed it, and threw it like a thirty-pound javelin at a boat coming alongside. Two pirates about to board the raft were the recipients. He picked up his two favorite weapons as he stood.

"Manny, I'm finished with the woman's work. Play until you're done and then come join me. Be a man." He laughed as he jumped the thirty feet to the main deck. His feet crushed two boarders as his hammer splattered another. His giant battle-ax cleaved yet another man down the center. The man roared in glee—he was home. The great ax scythed over the shoulders of four as they stood from boarding. Four heads flipped back into the boat.

Blake kicked at the rotator. The railgun's feed had jammed. She looked at the armor weight left. She shrugged at the last three hundred pounds of rods. Ninety seconds of spewing death can be a long and productive time. She thumbed through the alternatives left to her. Three SAM missiles still sat in their launchers. She looked at the long-range targeting and scrolled out as far as she could. A large sailboat headed their way, but without enough metal, she could not get a positive lock. She looked north just as the mast of a submarine surfaced. She knew the next to surface the deck and doors would open. What nasty present the new box would contain didn't make her happy. The sub's mast was painted all black. No number, no country designation, not even a respectable skull and crossed swords like their fleet.

She locked onto the mast, and two SAMs jumped off their rack. She waited for the deck to appear and a deck door to swing open. Waiting… It was the one virtue she was never good at—especially in the heat of battle, but as warfare became more electronic and longer range, waiting became the more valuable commodity.

The deck cleared. The captain was like Blake. Even with the sheet of water still on the deck, the long doors started to open. Blake recognized the doors and knew they covered the Russian version of the gift she was sending. The last SAM leaped from the launcher, and the control patch on her monitor went dark.

Blake kicked out of the battle restraints. "Ming, I'm out. Where do you want me?"

"Take the Uzis and belts by the head door. Leave the MK-15s for me. Happy hunting."

Blake stopped at the door and pulled on her back scabbard and saber. The ammo belts went over as bandoliers. She noticed a tech belt with twin .50 caliber handguns and strapped it on. She jumped up and down to check the weight and balance. A little top heavy… but well set for a busy day. The final string sling for the twin Uzis and their 100-shot clips was last. It was designed to incorporate with the bandoliers.

She smiled as she heard noise just outside the door. Eyeing the small security screen, she saw two friendlies. Everyone wore the same red or gray t-shirt with the skull and crossed sabers front and back. She swung the door out quietly.

"Hello, boys. Have you been finding any fun today?"

They both chuckled. One held up his finger to his lips. The other pointed at the crew of a boat about to board the raft. He mouthed the words *'Just watch.'*

As Blake watched, she remembered her first experience with the amazing deck. Her embarrassment at slipping onto her butt lasted much longer than the actual pain. The three erupted in laughter as a dozen boarders ended in a tangled mass.

The large Hispanic smiled back at Blake. "Now, we just take out the trash." The three washed the heap with lead and continued down into the boat they had come from. The shorter pulled a grenade and pitched it in behind the pilot's station. Soon, the boat was awash with blood, bodies, and sea. The three ringed the pontoons with holes. The boat would sink, but it would take a while. As a unit, they moved toward the next set of boarders. Some had figured out to take their shoes off and were offering resistance.

29 Holst Academy, Belgrade, PA

THE LARGE PUGILIST-faced man watched the television. The series was highlights of the previous season's march to the Super Bowl. The Seahawks were tearing New England apart. Brady looked as underinflated as his reported balls. The large man groaned as the Seattle front four tore through the line and two-ironed number twelve to the turf with the soft ball pinned to his chest between the one and the two. It was the seventh sack of the game with eleven seconds left before halftime.

The young girl looked up at the television and then at the man. "Maybe you need a new sport to bet on… like knitting, or sailing, or something exciting like Pop Warner."

The man ground his head around and glared at her with one eye. His hand joined his face and ran his middle finger up along his bulbous nose. "Little girls should be seen not heard."

Noi put her pen down. "Great. Let's go for a walk about the quad and be seen. I'll even keep my mouth shut so as not to be heard."

The man moved his finger away from his nose.

There was a light tapping on the door. Two taps, a wait, followed by three. The door swung open a few seconds later. The man with the thinning red hair sloughed off his coat. He held out his cell phone to his partner. "It started four hours ago. Glad I'm here instead of there. Evidently, they figured we were coming."

"So what does he think?"

The man walked to the small utility kitchen. "It's not the walk in the park they had been led to believe. It may take a few days."

The ex-boxer shifted forward to turn around. Even being tall, the hundred pounds over his boxing days slowed him down. "What about your classes?"

"I'll still have to teach them. If I don't show, they will send someone around."

"What about her?"

The teacher put down the cup of tea he was making. "Speaking of her, what is she still doing up?"

Noi leaned back in her chair. "She is right here. And if I don't have to go to classes, what does it matter?"

The heavy man looked over his shoulder. Turning back to his partner, he asked. "Was she always this much of a smartass in class?"

The man thought as he probed the tea bag up and down. "Hmm, somewhat." He turned. "It's after ten, head to bed."

Noi leaned back in her chair. "And if I don't? What are you going to do, Mr. Stevens... give me a failing grade? That would be as meaningless as the 'A' you gave to Tiffany Roberson because she stayed late after classes a couple of times in your office. You do know she posted the videos online in the pervert chat room."

The man turned with a horrified look on his face. "She told me she wiped them off her phone. I watched her."

Noi rolled her eyes. "The GoPro in the air vent was streaming constant. You are such an ass. And do you think I really believe you plan to let me go after this? Mugs here already spilled the beans."

The redhead turned almost purple as he slapped his partner on the back of the head. "What the fu—"

The big guy jumped up. "I didn't tell her nuthin'. She's just making this shit up."

The teacher stopped and looked at the smiling Noi. "Go to bed. Now." He turned on the man who was almost twice his size. "And you shut the fuck up."

Noi stood as she closed her laptop. "My work is done here. Good night. Sleep tight. Don't let your conscience bite tonight." As she picked up the laptop, she heard the tiny ping confirming the file upload. *The teacher was so screwed.* She smiled and turned down the hallway.

"Leave the laptop."

Noi's shoulders sagged as she froze. Grinding on her right heel, she reluctantly returned the laptop to the table. The teacher was smart enough to know it could also be as deadly to his plans as a phone.

The two men watched with folded arms and disapproving faces as the electronic weapon was deposited back into their care. Neither man was smart enough to realize the damage was already done. Both were only watching the contrite face of the little girl.

At the bedroom, she closed the door and sat on the bed. She held her hands between her knees and waited. The clock on the small desk slowly passed through twenty minutes. Noi stood and undressed. In her leggings and long red t-shirt, she opened the door and crossed into the bathroom. She brushed her teeth and brushed out her long hair. She flushed the toilet and removed the lid from the toilet during the noise. Lying in the bottom of the tank was a burner phone sealed in two zippered plastic bags. *You would think by now they would come up with a waterproof phone.*

She slipped the phone into the waistband of her leggings and draped the plastic bags over the back of the toilet tank. She flushed again and replaced the lid. Everyone knows young girls have strange toilet habits.

Taking out the phone, she sent two text messages and then put it back in her leggings. Thinking better, she moved it to the crotch of her panties. She didn't think they would grope her so intimately if they searched her.

There was a soft but parental knock on the door. "What's taking so long?"

Noi opened the door. "You've been teaching for enough years to know that girls aren't boys. We don't come into a toilet and spray our piss all over the walls and seat. We are ladies." She slid past him with a look of disgust.

As she snuggled down into the bed, she felt the vibration of the silenced text. She pulled the phone out and checked the text.

"Soon, sweetie. Daddy." The phone lit up her smile. She returned it to its hiding place and smiled as she drifted to sleep.

30 Raft… or What's Left of It

BLAKE HEAVED HER left shoulder back around as she dragged the heavy saber through the air. The weight shifted in the sword to create enough energy to slice the entire neck of the boarder. His head hinged back on the spine and disconnected. The tearing of the last patch of skin was a wet sucking sound. Blake flipped the blade in her hand and jabbed it down between her spread legs as she bent over. The blade buried halfway into the man's crotch. She pulled it out and bumped him with her butt as she stood.

Twisting, she side-kicked the bearded oaf in the chest as his eyes finished rolling up into his head. The body flipped over the railing into the open cavity above the smelter. The temperature was barely over twelve hundred degrees, but enough to vaporize most of the man's mass on contact. She wrinkled her nose at the stench. *I wish they would take a bath before they attack.*

She turned around. The overlook was empty except for her. Bodies lay strewn about, but none were moving or moaning. She looked at the most light in the gray-black sky. She guessed at early afternoon. Not a long battle by any exaggeration, but a very deadly and destructive conflict.

To the south, the nuclear submarine still spewed black smoke. She knew it was from mostly hydraulic oil, bedding, and bodies barbecuing in the large cylinder.

A red veil of blood blocked the view to the east. She squinted and wiped the blood away. Her vision was better but not perfect. Several of the catamarans drifted loose from the raft. She knew the one burning had no living soul on board. The composites, when burned, created a cyanide-like fume invisible and killed on contact.

She thought about the wooden ships burning to the waterline. Five thousand years to create a ship more deadly burning than sinking. Technology was a blessing and a curse. She could talk to someone on the other side of the world, but the hulls of the ship would kill their sailors.

She thought about the glorious rockets in China, used for the celebration of life. All too soon, the black powder turned to killing others.

She tried to roll her right shoulder. It was numb and dead.

She looked down at the large hole weeping blood. Laying the sword on the top of the capstan, she probed her left middle finger in the hole—it was loose. She exchanged it for her thumb. She knew the large bore bullet had left a similar hole on her back after shattering her shoulder blade.

She looked across the disheveled landscape of the raft. "Manny?"

The link opened. "Blake, how are you doing?"

"She was a good ship, and it was a good fight, but I think I'll be looking for a new body."

"Now… or soon?"

"I was looking forward to cracking open that bottle of hundred-year-old scotch you have in the bottom drawer, but it will have to wait for another day."

"I can't tell where you are…"

She looked over at the large opening. "I'm on the overlook of the new smelter."

"On my way."

Blake could feel her boot slip on the cat's deck. The blood and whatever else caused the special connection to fail. But it wasn't the connection Blake wanted. She wanted to feel her bare feet on the deck. She wanted to be looking at the deep ocean. She wanted to die like a pirate.

The hatch to the control area howled as the bent metal protested in the damaged hinges. Blake knew it wasn't Manny. By the footsteps, she knew it wasn't a boarder, but she didn't want to look at the woman who had betrayed them.

The hand slid up the top of her shoulder and then out across to her left side. The head hugged onto her shoulder. "You're bleeding… a lot."

A tear traced its way down Blake's face, cleaning the dirt and blood as it went. "What's a quart or three… more or less?"

Christine looked back over Blake's shoulder at the other side of her back. "Would it help if I pulled the spear out?"

Blake chuffed and then coughed wetly. The blood frothed on her lip. She coughed and spat the large wad of half-clotted blood. Shaking her head weakly, "The spear, the knife hole, the sword cuts, the small bullets, the large holes…" Her head rolled over to look into the eyes of her lover and friend. "Eventually, it all adds up. No one thing will help anymore.”

Christine snuggled her head down on the bloody shoulder. Her voice was husky and small. “I’m sorry.”

“That you weren’t here?” Blake looked at the greater carnage. “What part?”

The woman hugged the dead arm tighter. “All of it. I’m sorry… but I had to do it. I had no choice.”

Blake leaned forward. Her thumb kissed out of her shoulder. She reached for the boot, but the leg wouldn’t come up. She thought about the other boot but realized her left hand was already numb. She leaned back.

“I need my boots off…” Her face turned. As Chris looked up, their eyes were mirrors of pain and wet. “I need… to feel… the deck.”

Christine squatted and slipped off the red boots. She noted the small gold toe ring she knew Noi had bought for Blake in Hawaii. The toes curled on the deck.

Christine gently folded the soft leather boots and placed them beside the woman’s feet. She stood and reached around for the short heavy saber.

She leaned the point against Blake’s breastbone. “They are holding Noi. I didn’t have a choice.”

Blake nodded with her eyelids. “I figured as much.” She looked into the eyes of the woman she loved. “We’ll find her. It’ll be okay.”

Christine shook out her long hair. It hadn’t been lost on either of them, how much they could pass for sisters, except for the color of their hair. “In my head, I know it’s true, but in my heart…” She swallowed the stone in her throat. The gravel was still there. “She’s my only baby…”

Blake ran her left hand through the dark hair and pulled the face closer. Their foreheads touched. “I know…

but it will be over soon."

Their wet eyes met as Chris looked up. Her nod was small as she bit her upper lip and then licked them wet. She took a deep breath and sighed long.

"You know what will happen when you kill this body."

Chris blinked and nodded. A small smile tugged at the one side of her mouth. "But not what you think will happen."

Blake's brow furrowed.

"When was the best moment you had with Noi?"

Blake slightly shrugged her left shoulder. Her face cleared.

"We were sitting on the black sand beach in Hawaii. She was sitting between my legs and leaning back into me. We were watching the sea turtle sunning herself on the beach. Noi said it was how the world should always be—peaceful."

Christine moved the blade tip down just below the bottom rib and leaned in. "Focus on Noi and that moment." She leaned forward and kissed Blake wetly as she slid the blade up, and split the heart in two.

Blake's body trembled and then stood fast like a masthead. The body shuddered with the last bit of life and Christine eased her friend to the deck. Her mind roared and then calmed as all the memories and identity shuffled. The searing storm hissed and then became calm.

With luck, she knew Blake was now in the body of a sixteen-year-old brunette—young, healthy, and in great shape.

Christine gently swung the saber around in the air. She had always favored a lighter sword, but she could feel the power of the shorter, heavier, and more deadly blade Blake now favored.

She looked out at the long-range helicopter approaching. The unmarked black looked sinister and ugly. As it turned to find a spot to land, she saw the light spot in the one window. She knew who the blonde was and a small smile tugged at her mouth.

The hatch door screeched shortly as Manny stepped onto the deck. He wiggled his boots as he tested the connection to the deck.

Chris nodded. "It's the blood and oil."

Manny walked over and looked down at the body of the redhead. His sigh was short but no less heartfelt. "She had a great run with that one."

Christine hummed as the helicopter touched down. "She would have been two hundred and forty-seven next month. It would have been one hell of a cake." She looked over at Manny. "Ready to finish this?"

Manny shrugged and smiled pure mischievousness.

"Well, then, let's go kill us an immortal."

As they reached the lower deck, Chris pulled the cell phone from the back pouch in her leggings. She looked at the text, smiled, and showed it to Manny.

"Here. Bad guys dead. Love you. Blake & Noi"

31 Jun

THE TALL BLONDE and Jun stood near the helicopter. The squat but powerful Chinese man stood with his legs spread slightly.

The light breeze tugged at his black silk suit. The black tie was a study of shine against the dull surface of the black end-on-end shirt.

"You look more like an undertaker than a business-man, Jun."

The Asian turned his head to the voice. He watched the man in red leather knee-high swashbuckler boots, red velvet pantaloons, and a red t-shirt with a skull and crossed sabers approach. The woman next to him was more of a study in black, except for the matching t-shirt.

"Manfred, I presume."

"Oh, please. Let's at least be more friendly—as we were as Khan and Dahl."

The Asian smiled. "As I remember, you and the other left with your tails between your legs." He pointed at Christine. "But this isn't that one. This is a mortal."

Manny smiled softly. "Blake went on ahead. She had pressing matters to attend. I'm sure she would have loved to be here… but she went to Pennsylvania to kill your stooges."

The man startled only slightly before he caught himself and smiled. "Well, then, what now? I don't see a three-legged blind goat for you to kill me over."

"Kill you? Jun, Jun, Jun… what, and let you get away? Please. I have much better fun prepared for you."

Jun spun around, and in a blink, stood behind Brie. His right hand held a small knife to her jugular vein. "If you kill me, I'll just flow into our friend here. If you shoot through her to get me, I'll take the brunette. You can't win here, Manny."

Manny shrugged his face as he raised his arms with his hand outstretched. He slowly turned a complete circle to show he was unarmed. Stopping, he dropped his hands and casually clasped them in front of his crotch. "You've misjudged the show here, Jun. I never intended to kill you. In fact, this was all about you being alive. If you are alive, then we know where you are."

The man jerked his hand at Brie's throat. A tiny drop of blood showed on her skin. Her face was impassive. "Explain yourself."

Manny stepped a few steps closer. His voice lowered. "For millennia, we have killed you, and you have killed us. The big difference is you have enjoyed killing millions of people. You have done it for no other reason than it gave you pleasure to watch others suffer and die. You blanketed the steppes of Mongolia with the bodies of men, women, and children. The rivers ran red as you impaled thousands as Vlad. As Caligula, thousands were killed in the sun to add blood lust to your orgies. The world will never forget your concentration camps to kill millions as Hitler.

Jonestown was very personal to thousands of families. No, we have all killed in war, or small murders in private, but you… you, Jun, have done it on a scale no other has come close to." Manny grew his smile slowly. "And that is what we invited you here to end."

The man laughed. "But to end it, you would have to kill me. How do you propose to kill an Ever Kind? You and I both know it is impossible."

Manny watched Brie's right hand. He waited for her to wink. "Well, maybe so, but at least, we can do the waltz with the devil and see who ends in hell before the other."

Brie winked. Her right hand moved back as she stepped left. The Taser hit the Asian's leg near his genitals. The connection was instant. She spun and followed him to the deck as his body dropped, convulsing.

Manny stepped over. "That's enough, Brie."

The blonde looked up. "I just wanted to make sure." She pushed her hand and Taser down into the man's groin as she stood. She smiled like a little girl at Manny.

"Knocking him out was sufficient."

"But extracting my share of revenge. Let's just call it dessert for all the crap he put me through."

Christine stepped over beside Brie. "And let's not forget our daughter."

Brie leaned in and kissed Christine on the cheek. "Speaking of daughters…" She pulled her cell phone out of her pocket. She thumbed it and put it to her ear. "Where are you?"

A small Eurasian woman waved from around the end of the catamaran. "Just wrapping up here… I'll be there in a moment." She disappeared behind the structure, and they heard two shots from a handgun. The slight delay was followed by a splash. The small strident voice was distinct. "When I tell you to stay down, stay down."

The pixie like woman popped up into view. The frosted tips of her hair were now tinted with red. Grease and grime smeared her face and arms. As she walked toward them, she dropped the clip out of her pistol and then threw both into the ocean. "Russians make such crap these days." As she neared, her voice turned childishly cheery. "Hello, everyone."

As she walked up, she stepped in Jun's crotch, and then stepped over to the tall blonde and kissed her on both cheeks Euro style. Turning, she looked at the other brunette. Putting out her hand, she smiled. "You must be Christine. Mommy has told me so much about you and your daughter."

Christine didn't raise her hand. She stood with a deadpan face. She looked at Brie and then back at the woman. "Seven hundred years and all you expect is a handshake? Boy, are you easy."

The small woman laughed as she stepped over for a hug.

Manny cleared his throat. "Um, am I the only one feeling lost here?"

The three women looked at him. "Shut up, Manny. You're a man."

Brie laughed at his frozen open mouth and pleading face. "Manny, this is Nina... one of my daughters."

Manny put out his hand but frowned. "But you're not..." He looked at Brie. "One of...?"

Nina nodded for Brie. "Ever Kind? No, I'm... well, let's take care of the business at hand and wait for the whole family before we explain. Shall we?" With the side of her boot, she kicked the groaning man on the deck. She had aimed for his crotch, but it was close enough.

"Whole family…?"

Chris stepped over and took his arm. She pushed her chin out at the now rousing Jun. Brie snorted and handed the Taser to Nina, who smiled and jammed the unit in the guy's neck. "Whole family. Now, where did you want this trash?"

Manny bent and produced a wad of long milky colored zip-ties from his boot. He smiled at Christine. "Wasn't it you who questioned my sanity when we started stamping out these zip-ties from the smelted plastic we gathered?"

"No… it was when you were talking about putting some kind of wire in them."

He held the one tie up to the light. She brought his hand closer. "I have younger eyes. I don't have to read large type at arm's length." She examined the tie. "Holy evil machinations… Is this the microwire I've been drawing?"

"Two are the titanium, the black ones are the polycarbonate, and the other two are just the waste steel. Between the three and the tough plastic, they are nearly unbreakable."

She handed the tie to Brie as Manny began wrapping the man about the knees and ankles. He passed another fistfull to Nina. "Bind his hands and arms to the body at the wrist and just above the elbows."

With the body bound, they looped more to make handholds. As they lifted Jun, he moaned. Nina snickered and zapped his neck again.

Manny grumbled. "That much juice to the neck causes massive neck spasms later."

Nina looked back and smiled evilly. "I'm counting on it."

Christine's pocket buzzed. She fished the phone out and thumbed it on. She read the text and reached forward to show Brie. The blonde laughed.

Manny frowned.

Chris stowed the phone. "Blake and Noi will be tied up for a little while. Evidently, they need to go find a red head in great shape. The body Blake landed in is out of shape, ugly, and a dude. Then they have to go boot shopping." The three women laughed as Manny shook his head.

32 Bodywork

NOI ROLLED HER eyes. This was the sixth yoga studio this day. It wasn't even lunchtime in New York yet.

The man next to her folded his massive arms across his large chest—which is to say the crossed arms rested on top of his bloated belly. Blake had been aghast when she was sitting in the bathroom and noticed the tag inside his pants. He had called Noi in to show her the numbers. He hadn't thought about the girl having never seen a man with his pants around his ankles. The two had giggled about it for the last two days.

"Jesus in a flatbed truck, Blake. This is such a waste of time."

"Where do you think we should look?" The man growled or just farted his words. Both were a possibility from the sound of the voice.

Noi pointed at the class in session. "Take the front row. The red unitard—Clairol G2, with HE77 highlights and the silicone… or maybe her real butt?" She turned to look at the mashed and bloated ex-fighter's face. She shuddered. "Then there is the, oh so proud vegan, who's got to be sucking blood from something to stay alive. Then the bulimic, the cookie sneaker, the one who thinks salads are the answer, the one with silicone everywhere except her face—which is either concrete or way too much Botox. Out of the forty or so in the class, only the instructor has ever held a job where sweat was in the job description." She jabbed her finger up to the second knuckle into the man's belly. "This mook worked harder to finish breakfast."

"So where should we be looking?"

Noi sighed back into her chair and mirrored the crossed arms. Blake noticed it pushed the breasts up to form a small cleavage at the scooped top. A striking young man walked past as Blake snorted and farted.

"Nice try, kid, but I saw him come in holding hands with the big jarhead over there." He fanned his hand toward a muscle-bound bodybuilder in bright magenta posing Speedos. Blake noticed the arms drop and the cleavage disappear.

"Maybe we should go look in farm country. Where do all those big breasted strapping blonde Hilda types come from?"

"I liked my red hair."

Noi stood and walked over to the instructor who was taking a break. Blake let her go flirt as he went back to watching the one body move under and around the slabs of silicone.

"I have an address." Noi held up a piece of paper.

In the taxi, Blake looked at the name on the paper. "Is this a porn studio? ExEx, it sounds like porn lite or something."

Noi stifled a snort. "He said it was extreme cross-training for ultimate martial arts. It sounded like your kind of place." Blake looked down at the large belly pushing the buttons on the shirt. "Yeah, well, maybe in a former life."

"Hopefully, in a future life as well."

The two fist bumped as the taxi stopped and started in uptown traffic on the way to the Bronx. Blake didn't even want to look out the window. He was thinking of the raft as he had last seen it. The pain in his chest wasn't from the meatball sandwich the mook had eaten the week before.

"Where did you get your last body?" They were sitting in a grinder shop in the Bronx, two blocks from the last fiasco. Scarily, the females had looked more masculine than the males. It was no fly from the first glance.

Blake had toyed with just getting a salad, but broke down and had the Ruben. She chewed as she thought. "The French Revolution was a while off, so the crown was still burning witches and such. The invention of the guillotine brought out the crowds. I was number three on the dance card for the morning… she was standing close in the crowd. It wasn't uncommon for the women to flirt with the dandies who were losing their heads. She blew me a kiss. She was only twelve and already turning tricks on the backstreets of Paris."

"So she was just standing there?"

Blake shook his head and smirked. His eyebrows arched in a shrug. "At least she wasn't a three-legged blind goat."

"Nor was she ugly…" Noi's voice tapered off as she frowned and cocked her head. She pulled out her cell phone. She thumbed the phone a few times and then watched a video. She turned it for Blake to see. "Is she pretty enough?"

Blake watched. "She's a brunette."

"That's not what I asked."

He shrugged. "What's your point?"

Noi looked at the man's hip. "Is there enough in that wallet to get us to Los Angeles?"

"Sure. He has three platinum credit cards and one black. Why?"

"One stop and then the airport."

Blake stood on the sidewalk while Noi worked her charms. The gym owner gave her four names and addresses in Los Angeles. He also gave her a name and address a few blocks away, still in the Bronx. She hugged him and promised she wouldn't forget him if she hit the big time.

An hour later, they were back in a taxi headed for the airport. Blake looked at the new ID. It said they were producers of a new show about the glamor women of extreme martial arts. Noi was scouring YouTube on her phone for videos. The women kicking, hitting, and wrestling across the mat were not the same look of women they had seen in the gym. All the fighters looked fit—but from central casting, for the pretty jobs. Blake was smiling or leering with each new video.

As they were about to board the red-eye to Los Angeles, Blake spoke with Manny. The conversation was short and to the point. Manny kept laughing at the voice, which was deeper and throatier than his was. Blake signed off by telling Manny if he kept it up, Blake would not get a new body but return and kick Manny's ass from one end of the Bay Area to the next. Manny closed with an *Adios, cupcake*.

Blake pushed back into the first-class lounge seat. He sipped on a scotch in a bucket with no ice. The flight attendant must have taken a liking to the large teddy bear look. He brought him the glass half-full.

Blake looked up at the smiling bearded man. "Thanks, James. You're a champ."

James's eyes twinkled behind is horn-rimmed glasses. "Any bear in a storm. I didn't think you wanted to have the dinner kill the buzz. The chicken Kiev looks really yummy tonight. He looked at the few empty seats and the others who were already asleep before the silver bird sliced its way to a cruising altitude of thirty-six thousand feet. He leaned over. "I can probably slide a second chicken onto the plate if you want."

Blake thought about his body and then considered the warm brown eyes. "I'm trying to get back to my fighting day's weight. So if anything, slide some extra veggies over."

James smiled and winked in commiseration. "You've got it, big guy." He looked at Noi who was checking things on her phone. "What about your...?"

Blake squinted at Noi and smiled. "Niece. Don't worry. She eats like her uncle did in his fighting days. I just want to know where the hell she hides it. I know the five hours a day in the martial arts gym doesn't burn *that* much."

James's eyes opened almost as large as his thick Clark Kent glasses. "What kind of fighting?"

"She does all around extreme like her mother."

"What does she do?"

Blake smiled. He had set the man up. "Judo, kickboxing, knives, swords, small arms up to .50 caliber automatics, and other fun weapons of war. She just had a very successful tour in the Pacific. I think she walked away with the trophy sword with at least a few dozen kills." He held the man's gaze.

James stood with a slight choke and cough. "I'll go see about dinner."

Blake couldn't help himself. "Thanks, Teddy Bear."

The man looked over his shoulder with a large smile and fluttered his index finger in the air as his lower body gave a subtle dance. Blake chuckled. Flirting is flirting, no matter who you or they are. It always feels good to make someone's day.

"You are so evil. You know he'll never see you again."

The big man ground his massive head around and leaned over to the much smaller redhead. "That wasn't the point… and don't make me take your redheaded body."

Noi snorted. "Clairol 7.43, copper blond highlights, and you can't anyway."

"All right, you're off the hook on the red, but when your…" Blake stopped as James walked by. With a lowered growl, Blake started again. "When your mother killed me, I should have flowed into her body. But she had me focus on you… or us on the beach."

Noi smiled and leaned against the large shoulder. "When we watched the turtle on the beach. I would have chosen the same moment."

"I've never traveled far to flow into another body, but I also didn't flow into you. So what gives, and don't make me beat it out of you. I haven't been on a blood-splattered plane since…" He waffled his hand in the air. "Just don't make me beat you. Now talk."

"Mom, Dad, and I have already talked about this. So, you either get it here or in San Francisco."

Blake's growl was a rumble deep enough to shake the seats. "Now."

Noi moved her seat up a bit. "Let's start with you. How old are you? Not this body… but you?"

He frowned. "What do you mean?"

Noi rolled onto her side as she drew her legs up into the seat. "What I mean is, put it all together. What is your first memory of a lifetime? Rome? Egypt? Mesopotamia? Neanderthal? How old do you think you are?" Her eyes watched the flight attendant approach.

"How's that drink doing, Mr. Baer?"

Blake looked at the quarter full glass and then up at the man. "I think I'm good for now, James. Thanks for asking."

The man patted him on the shoulder. "It's no problem. It's not often I get a real bear onboard. Besides, I think my grandfather watched your father and Battling Hays go at it."

Blake thought about what the man was talking about and then remembered. "It may not have been the true fight of the century, but it was until Ali came along."

"Good to have you and your niece on board." He continued toward the galley.

Blake rolled his head and frowned at Noi. "I'm not sure."

"But you remember at least four or five?"

"Hundred?"

"Thousands."

Blake leaned his head back. An Ever Kind remembers much of the past because they lived it. They reminisce with others about the events and things they did together— including whom they killed or who killed them, but he had never thought about where he or the others started. It was an intriguing idea.

He rolled his head back. "Yeah, maybe five or six thousand. Why?"

"How many children have you had?"

He pursed his lips to think. Having children for Ever Kind is a touchy subject. The length of the relationship is one-way—you will outlive your children, their children, and even their great-grandchildren. "Maybe one or two in a century—if that."

The young woman rested her hand on the large plate-sized paw. "This is the tough one, but it is important for you to understand it completely."

Blake nodded. "Okay…" He took a sip of the drink.

"So you had a kid, say, two hundred years ago."

"We were in the court of Louis the Sixteenth. Manny was a winsome young daughter of a courtier, and I was a dashing rogue. I swept her off her feet… and we had two children. A boy and a girl. They, as we, were killed in the revolution."

"Okay, so they died at an early age."

Blake nodded.

"I want you to think and here comes dinner. So after we eat, I want you to tell me about one child you remember who lived to be old and died of natural causes."

Blake opened his mouth, thought a moment, and closed it. They ate in silence.

"Gwelfith. He was already old and feeble when they recruited him to go on the second Crusade with Richard. He was fifty-six when they returned. He had an arrow pierce his lung, but it never healed right. He returned to Raylees in Northumberland on a stretcher. He lingered for the rest of the summer, but the cold gripped him and took him before Twelfth Night."

"Were you the father or mother?"

"Father."

"And the mother wasn't Ever Kind."

"No, she wasn't. How would you know that?"

"I'll explain later, but for now, were there any other children by you and a mortal?"

James came and took the trays. Blake declined any more alcohol. He realized he needed every bit of his wits about him. "A few... and I think they lived full lives too."

"But the offspring of a union of say you and Manny..."

"I had never thought about it... but I don't remember any of them living very long. Usually, they took up the family business and then were killed. After a while, you become jaded to losing your children, expected even."

Noi nodded with her upper lip between thumb and fingers. "Um hum. How old do you think Mom is?"

"She's thirty..." He was so sure of the answer, but when point blank, it was an answer he didn't have. "About thirty-three...?"

"Okay, this is where you need to grip the armrest." She dropped her head at the mentioned seat. Blake gripped the seat to humor the girl.

"Next March, she will be one hundred twelve years old."

Blake studied the young face and then growled. "Shut the front door." And then he had the follow-up question. "How old are you?"

The girl laughed. "Silly old Blake. That day on the beach, I turned eighteen."

"But your mother isn't Ever Kind."

"Neither is my father or me."

"But I thought your father died in an accident."

"He did. He flowed into a young woman on the bus. She was tall and blond. You know her as Brie."

Blake paused. He felt the slippery ice he skating on. "But Brie is—"

"Ever Kind? No. Close but no cigar. She's one of Us. We're the children of Ever Kind, but not Ever Kind."

"Children…"

"You can sense Manny and others, right?" He nodded. "But you can't sense Brie."

"We call her the Black Hole or Black Sheep."

"Right and then she shows up and announces herself. Otherwise, you wouldn't even know she was immortal."

"But…"

Noi rested her hand on his sleeve. "During the Civil War… excuse me… The War Between the States, you had a sergeant under you. His name was Jack Dewater."

"He was killed by a jealous lover of the prostitute he was seeing. But how could you know?"

Noi shook her head. "The prostitute was young, no more than fourteen. Jack liked her and had asked her to marry him. She loved another but knew Jack would persist, so she shoved a blade between his ribs when he was… um… distracted. You might say, he came and went in the same short breath."

Blake did the math. "But that would have made your mother…"

"Her daughter. But only until she died in childbirth many years later."

"And she flowed into her own child."

Noi patted him on the arm. "Now you're getting up to speed."

Blake growled as he unsnapped the seat belt. "I've gotta go use the head."

NOI GOT A little concerned it was taking so long when the light went out, and the door opened.

Blake leaned into the galley for a moment.

As he adjusted back into the seat, James showed up with a smaller glass.

Blake took a sip and set the glass down. "Okay, so we have two Ever Kind, but they don't produce Ever Kind progeny."

"Correct. Their children are also immortal just like the Kind, but the Kind can't see them for whom they are. We call ourselves Us, with a capital U."

"Us…?"

"As in—not them."

Blake closed one eye and took another sip. "So if two Us, or is it Usens?"

Noi punched the large arm. "Us, just Us. And yes, they breed true."

"So you are…?"

"We don't know until we start to mature. My first period, I was fourteen, so we were sure my biological clock was slowing down. But when we were on the beach, I stepped on a piece of glass about the size of your thumb. It pushed in quite deep, and when I pulled it out, I bled for a few moments. But within a minute, it was a pink scar. When we got back to the hotel, I told Mom and Brie, but there was no scar to show them."

Blake was running the math in her head. If she had

even twenty kids still running around, it would make for a large population. In addition, if they were breeding even more…

He mused to himself. "That is a lot of immortals."

Noi patted his hand. "Actually, it isn't so bad. A long time ago, many of them did the math and stopped searching each other out as mates. The vast majority of them only have sex with mortals, and some choose to live away from humans, altogether."

"But they never told us… their parents."

"No, only Brie lived among you openly. In addition, she never took an Ever Kind as a mate. In fact, none of the Us has ever bred with an Ever Kind."

Blake sat thinking about Christine. She had joined in some of the casual group activities, but only to a point. Blake had thought it was her being true to Blake, but there was only some occasional oral activity.

"As long as you were a woman, Mom and you couldn't breed."

Blake winced at her mind being read. He rolled his head toward Noi to try to explain.

Noi beat him to it. "It's a lot to take in. As the days go by, you will have more questions. But let's not rush it. As you now know… we have plenty of time."

"And your mom and Brie are explaining this to the others?"

Noi nodded as they both laughed at saying the same thing. *Oh, to be a fly on the wall.*

33 Bye-Bye, Jun. Hello, Jessie.

JUN LAY STRAPPED to the bed. The bed was little more than a cot made from printed plastic reclaimed from the ocean. The same style existed in every military barracks. The only difference—no padding on the springs.

Jun could feel the cool springs pinching the flesh of his naked body. The restraints only allowed him to turn his head. His head was still aching from the neural shocks to his neck and groin. He looked around the darkened room. It looked like a warehouse, but he knew they couldn't have gotten to land this fast. He struggled at the restraints. His body was bound every six inches from the arch of his feet to his shoulders.

"Relax, Jun. There is nowhere else you will ever go."

"What the fuck, Manfred?"

Manny stepped through the open wire mesh doorway. "It's very interesting, Jun. We've been doing some experiments lately. What we have found is there actually is a way to kill an Ever Kind."

Manny pulled up the wooden chair and sat. He could tell he had the other man's attention.

"You would probably remember Jin Sha. I believe

back then, she was one of your favorite concubines. Well, she was turning pretty evil as of late, and so we experimented on her and her sister."

"You're lying."

Manny pushed his lower lip out. "Sadly for you, I'm not."

"How?"

"Well, we discovered a very interesting thing. Just before she flowed, her nervous system opened and resembled a mortal. However, to make it all work, the threat is close, but not lethal. Once the toxins in the nervous system become hyperactive, we introduce an agent to cause the whole system to overheat. The internal core burned itself up. Trust me when I say, it was not a pretty sight."

"So you're going to burn me up? I've been through it before." He scoffed and spat.

"Oh, no. We aren't going to burn you, Jun. We are only going to heat you until your skin starts to sear. The burn will come from your own body. Well, actually, it comes from the part that is Ever Kind. For some reason, we don't like the heat, so we burn ourselves up."

The man squirmed on the bed.

"Squirm all you want, Jun, but the bed is designed for it. Soon, you will feel heat start to sear your veins, and then the process takes over, and you simply wink out."

Jun seemed to focus and then looked around in the dim light. "What's with the chicken cage?"

Manny smiled as he stood. "That, my friend, is the insurance. You see, we're in a Faraday cage. The electricity running through the cage stops any electromagnetic transmission from getting through. It also stops us from moving through." Manny panned his hand slowly around the cage.

"Quite the amazing invention little Michael Faraday created. Who would have ever guessed it would be an Ever Kind's undoing." He turned and looked down. "Well, actually, only the three of you. After you, I don't think we'll need to put any more to a true death."

Manny noticed the color of Jun's skin. The flush had become a darker red. "Ah, it appears the bed is doing its work."

The man was beyond talking, and he was beyond mad—he was fighting for the one given he always had— his life. The harder he struggled against the restraints, the redder his skin got.

Jun could not see the figure behind his head in the dark, just outside the cage. Nina sat at a small desk—the control of what they were doing. The first injection was a dangerously high dose of niacin. The dose was organic B3 and harmless in small doses. The dosing wouldn't kill Jun, but it would expand his capillaries to a point where he felt a heat coming from inside his body. His mind would do the worst.

Some of the restraints were biological sensors. They allowed Nina to watch his blood pressure, pulse, and capillary expansion. She nodded to Manny as she started the next drug—ultra fast-acting insulin. Every day, millions of people take the drug in small doses. It saves their lives. But this version, in the dose she was pushing into his system, would first put him to sleep, and then kill him. The dark of an induced sleep to an immortal should result in a change of perspective from a new body. For about eight to ten minutes, the lizard part of the brain will sense it isn't happening. None of the people standing in the cavernous warehouse knew what would happen afterward.

Manny didn't mind experimenting on Jun. The minimum of what they knew was the body would die while the experience would be at least terrifying. Manny would settle for that.

The naked body, under the intense light, stopped struggling. The drugged sleep had taken over. Manny looked at Nina. She palmed her hands to the side of her tipped head. He was in the sleep part of the process. Manny closed the wire mesh door and noticed the small LED light near the handle turned from red to green. The meaning was the entire cage was now working and blocking electromagnetic transmissions. As far as they knew, the cage would now stop Jun's spirit from escaping. He had only one avenue in which to go. The cardboard box under the bunk was quiet.

It was now a waiting game.

34 Do You Want To Die?

THE MAN STOOD like a hulk in the dark of the gym. He watched the young red haired woman at the edge of the ring. The sports bra was red. The capri-length sports tights were a darker red with a skull and crossed sabers high on the butt. The words on the sides did not represent the football team but what had become the name of affection for the Raft—Pirate Patch.

The two women fighting in the ring could have passed for Lucy Lawless and Linda Carter in their peak years. The muscles rippled, the moves were beyond cat-like and bordered on the blinding speed of a viper's strikes. Their intensity screamed extreme levels of professionals. A Wednesday afternoon sparring workout sparred with enough intensity for a heavyweight championship match.

The silence struck Blake the most. A dozen or so others in the gym and all were watching the match. Nobody was yelling. Even the combatants were almost silent except for the usual grunts and blowing breaths. In the videos, the screaming crowd had produced all the noise.

"Stop."

The Lucy held out her hand toward the Linda's right

leg. "Stop that. You make the same move every time. Your leg feints up like you're going to top kick my ribs, but then you stomp and spin kick with your left hoping to kick my head. If you do it in our real match, I will take you out in four moves. When we get home, I will steal your boy-friend, and take your dog for a walk he never comes back from. So just stop it. Now try again."

The lesson was delivered in a quiet, serious tone. It was not about choreography but similar to when Blake helped Christine become a better fighter, so the two bene-fited from a tougher workout. Blake's respect for the sport and the women was rising.

A tall woman crossed from the door to the lockers. As she passed under a couple of shafts of light, he could see the chestnut hair pulled tight to the head. He wondered how long the braid was in the back. The sports bra was black over another that was red. The two heavy-duty binders didn't do much to hide what was underneath. He liked her taste in the leggings. Nothing fancy, just shiny black with a few strips of matt black—basic and deadly. Blake could picture it all with the red boots.

"Hi, I'm Bridget. Clarence said you wanted to have me spar with someone?" She was all business. Her hands were wrapped, and she didn't offer one out to the large man.

Blake nudged his chin toward Noi.

"You're kidding, right? She's what... ninety-two pounds and maybe five-five?"

Noi turned and squinted into the dark at the talking.

"Oh, crud." The fighter stuck her hand out toward Noi. "Is she even old enough to be in here?"

"The door says eighteen. But don't count her out.

She's older than she looks. Besides she is five-seven and weighed in yesterday at one-twelve." He turned his mass and stepped slightly closer. The move allowed him to measure the woman, as well as intimidate. "Your job here is to not beat the snot out of her but to spar. I'm just a producer for an upcoming show." He pointed at Noi who was now ignoring them. "She, on the other hand, is the executive producer. So I would suggest you keep any headshots or kicks to a minimum. We're only here to take a look at your style and how you carry yourself in the ring."

He drew himself to his full six-three. He was barely over her—even in his loafers. He hitched his pants up. "So the real question I should ask is—are you willing to die?"

The woman's face was stone, pure hard stone. "Let's see what your little girl can do."

Blake, step-by-step, moved closer as the two disparately different women engaged, withdrew, circled, and engaged. Blake had casually sparred with Noi and had watched her and Christine spar, but the difference to now was running along the sand of a beach and the four-forty in the Olympics. After Noi had scored a couple of hits, the fighter realized she wasn't toying with a little girl. The fight became about finding the right level, and it kept rising.

The fighter caught the flashing ankle. "Stop." Noi froze. "You did this before. You will hit my thigh, but you were trying for a hip strike. You have been fighting mostly people your own size and got a bad habit. Look at the angle of your left foot. It never came around straight. Now feel what happens when I bring your foot up to my hip where you need to strike." She lifted the last five inches, and Noi fell over.

Bridget didn't laugh. She reached down and pulled Noi up. "Now give me your foot. Okay, now rotate the left, so it's pointing out." She brought the heel up to the strike point and then moved it back and forth, up and down, and in and out. "Can you feel how much more solid you are?"

"Yeah, thanks."

"Everyone focuses on the striking hand or foot. But the stance and balance are everything. Think of a car with a big engine. It's fast. But if the tires are shit, then the first time you get caught in the rain, you die. Now let's try it again."

As the sparring became more of a lesson, Blake thought about the woman inside the body. There was a true compassion and a willingness to share her knowledge with Noi. It would be a shame to lose a person such as her in the world.

A small dark man stepped from the shadows. "Your girl is good."

Blake turned and smiled with pride. "She's not my girl, Clarence. She is her own woman. But, yeah, she's better than I ever saw her fight before."

"I could book her in a fight this weekend, and by Sunday, she would have a few bruises, but she would have a few thousand in her fist."

Blake snorted softly. "You think she's good enough for the ring?"

"You just watched a match between a flyweight against a heavyweight. I'd say it was almost a draw. She had crazy speed with those legs, and her arm strength is off the charts. Where does she work out?"

"A private high school back east. But I'm now thinking she's been sneaking in more training somewhere else.

So what is Bridget's story?"

"Some good, some bad. She walked in here four years ago, with her two-year-old in tow. The divorce was messy only because they couldn't find the asshole who was a drunken gambler. He pounded on her when they dated in high school. She learned defensive moves but had to make them look like they had scored. In a fight, she looks like she's getting mutilated, but then she takes the other gal out, and you realize the one on the mat never got a solid hit in."

"So what is the good part?"

The man looked up. "Family. She has a crazy great family I would kill to be part of. Her daughter will be getting out of school in a few hours. Bridget's brother will pick her up in his police cruiser and take her the four blocks to her grandmother's place. The guy is crazy about his niece, and his wife is too. Last Christmas, they set up a huge tent in the grandparent's backyard and had everyone here join them for Christmas dinner. They even had presents for us."

"Hey, Blake." Noi hung on the ropes. "Are you ready to go to lunch with... um... Us?"

"Us?"

The redhead joined her at the ropes. "If your Kind is prejudice against Us... I'll understand."

Blake turned to the other man. His face was screwed up with crossed eyes.

Clarence chuckled. "Yeah, you're screwed and outgunned. You better go do what they say."

The lunch crowd at Musso and Frank's was light. They sat in a booth near the back. The waiter knew Bridget. He was a big fan of the local extreme martial arts scene.

Blake stabbed at his salad with his head down.

"So Clarence told you about my family."

Noi looked to Blake. He looked at Noi. "It wouldn't have mattered. She has a little girl and a big family she can't just walk away from. So her being one of you isn't the point. Besides, when I find the right body, I want to come back and workout with her."

"Bring her out to the Raft. Mom would like it too."

The redhead frowned. "Raft?"

Blake shrugged. "It's blown to shit right now, but it will get rebuilt. It's close to a square mile of catamarans all tied together. There is a lot going on out there, but basically, it's about cleaning up the Great Pacific Garbage Patch."

Her freckled hand came up and pointed. "The Swirl. It's supposed to be the size of Texas, but you can't see it from space. So some people doubt it's real."

Blake dipped his head. "It's closer to the size of Australia or Antarctica if you can see where the plastic is. The plastic gets broken up into flakes smaller than her baby toenail, but it floats in strata ranging from six inches deep to four feet below the surface. The fish and turtles confuse it for plankton. Once it fills their bellies, they can't take in food, and they die."

Noi continued. "The nets, beer can holders, hurricane or tsunami debris, or old boats and beds are just the poster children for the whole mess."

"Beds?"

Blake snorted. "The people weren't still in it. But we have pulled up some coffins and urns."

"Sounds like something I would like to see."

"When we get it all pulled back together, we'll have you out for a tour."

Noi giggled. "And some ass kicking."

Blake glared, but Bridget laughed. "It's all fun and games until we lose a planet. I'm in for all of it. So you are here looking for a…"

"I want my body back. You're a great match for the one I had for the last two and a half centuries. I liked being a woman, and I love Noi's mother. As you can guess, this body doesn't work on many levels."

"I might know a person. Can you heal spinal damage?"

"How bad?"

"She's in a chair, but can feel her feet."

"Backstory?"

"If she got up and walked out the care facility's door, she'd never be missed."

"Where?"

"She's down in Garden Grove."

"We have a car."

"Can I swing by and pick up my girl?

Blake read her face. "I assume your little girl knows this woman."

"She calls her auntie. She was my old sparring partner when I started about four years ago. We used to get billed as the Red Twins."

"Then I guess it would only be right. If I take the body, I'll want to know your girl, so she still has her auntie."

Noi clapped softly with excitement. "Yay, I get a cousin."

35 Jun is Loose

MANNY OPENED THE outer hatch door. As he started to step in, he looked back down the raft. There were large holes where some of the catamarans had been cut loose. Not one cat had gone unscathed. Only three of the masts spun well enough to produce electricity. Everything on the raft was down to minimum energy consumption.

By the fourth day, Ming couldn't stand the quiet and lack of a computer. She had called in one of the subs and commandeered a ride to Kona. She was eventually headed to Seattle to kick some ass and get the next four cats out the door.

Manny stepped into the dark. A single small light illuminated the young woman and the book she was reading. The four-watt LED was the only obvious use of electricity. As Manny walked near the cage, he could feel the hairs on his arms and neck prickle.

He sat in the other chair and looked over into the gloom at the bed, body, and box. It looked like a set from a dystopian play. "Any movement?"

"The body? No. Definitely vacated unless he truly died in there."

Manny shook his head. "Nah, the niacin and insulin have no other effect than they were used for. I mean, the insulin killed the body, but it was nothing exotic enough to kill the Jun part."

Nina held out her hand. "And yet…"

"Is it cold enough in here for Jessie to have gone into hibernation?"

Nita shrugged her face and shoulders. "You tell me? You've had the turtle for how many years?"

"Tortoise, and in the four years, he never hibernated."

"Where did you have him?"

"Mostly in my office or bedroom…"

"But I mean you had him here on the raft."

"Yeah…"

They both stared at the box, which had been unusually quiet for five days. Even if it was just Jessie, he should have moved because he was hungry. The walls of the box were only high enough to basically hold him. If he was really hungry, he could have tipped the box over.

The box just sat there.

The ping was soft but almost echoed in the room. Manny pulled out the phone. "Manny." He listened. "I'll be right there."

He stood and shoved the phone back in his pocket. "You want me to send over some dinner?"

Nina glanced at her dive watch. "Mom is bringing us dinner in an hour. I'm good, but thanks."

Manny turned and was halfway to the hatchway when Nina called out. He turned.

"Are we good?"

"About…?"

"All of it. About us not telling you Kinds about us."

Manny looked down at the deck as he thought. "The first night, I didn't sleep. Part of me was excited about maybe one day meeting some of my kids. But then, there was a part of me who wasn't so sure. It's a lot to take in all at once. But as for not telling us… crap, kid, who do you think your parents were? We have always lived in secrets. Who we are, what we are, where we have resources stashed, who we were, what we know, and the list goes on and on. You're just another secret on our list we didn't know was there."

He rolled his lips, as he looked into the black of the ceiling overhead. "Heck, kid, we were good the moment you told whoever it was to stay down. You're my kind of kid. Hell, I'd adopt you in a heartbeat."

Manny could see her shoulders slump in relaxation. "Good. I kind of like you too. Good night."

"Good night, kid." He turned for the hatch. At the hatch, he stalled for a second. "Just find out where Jun went… or I might have to find a blind three-flipper seal to kill you over." The hatch slammed shut with the sound of a heavy metal bell. The soft chuckle came a moment later.

MANNY SAT AT his desk doing paperwork. The raft was going to need almost as much to repair as it cost originally to construct.

He looked up at the row of clocks and smiled at the thought. He put the earpiece in and found the right number on the screen. He clicked on the green icon.

Brie answered. "This better be good, Manny. It is a wonderful day here in Singapore. I am naked on my private deck and getting the most amazing massage. What do you need?”

Manny laughed. “You better look at your security cameras then. Your apartment is swarming with police, and they are dusting for fingerprints. So what have you found in Beijing?”

“They better clean it up before I get home.” She knew Manny couldn’t see into her apartment and it was safe. She had ordered new furniture, carpet, and drapes. The work was being personally overseen by her new roommates and employees. Their day jobs had them reporting fifty-five floors below.

She moved a few things on her laptop and looked at the latest report.

“In Shanghai, we found close to five metric tons of a mix of metals. My team in Cathay is still cataloging, but they are suggesting close to ten tons. There are some odd bits here and there, but in China as a whole, I think we have close to sixteen or seventeen tons. Tomorrow I have an appointment with Hans Dorfman in Geneva. The security boxes all over the city will be flying open.”

“Good. We need money to rebuild. Keep me posted and have a nice flight tonight.”

“It better be. It’s Jun’s new 787 stretch.”

“Why would you need to stretch a Dreamliner?”

“Make room for the master bedroom.” She clicked off the connection. *Cops raiding my apartment, my ass.*

She called her apartment—just to check on the carpet.

Her phone chirped. There was a text from Manny. *I forgot to mention. Jun may have slipped his leash.*

"YOU SURE ABOUT this?" Blake had explained what was going to happen to the woman in the chair.

The woman looked up at the tall, athletic redhead. Tears tracked down the woman's face. The left hand on the wheel of the chair pulled slightly. The woman looked back at Blake.

"Did she tell you how we used to tag team back in our wrestling days? They billed us as identical twins. When we were in the ring, we moved like we could read each other's minds. After the matches, we would go out. We had our own table at Musso and Frank's Grill there in Hollywood. Nobody harassed us. We could go in there in our wrestling togs—bare feet and all. Nobody said a word except to ask how they could make us happy. We ruled the world."

She turned and reached out her hand. "Remember the time we fought in Tokyo?" They both laughed.

Bridget explained, "We wore our dress fighting boots with six-inch heels. We were about two feet taller than anyone else was in the room. We used to fluff our hair out so we had bright red manes. It scared the shit out of those Japanese guys. But you knew they also all had hard-ons at the same time."

The woman patted Bridget's hand and leaned over, so her head lay along the muscular arm. She drifted for a few seconds in the glow of old glories. Rolling her head only slightly, she looked at Blake. Her face was still wet, but her eyes were clear.

"I can't have that anymore. Not in this chair. But if what you say is true, at least my body would be there again. And I can live… well, die happy knowing Briggie and I can be together again."

Blake took a deep breath and leaned back in the chair. For once, Blake was humbled by the person whose body he was about to take over. His head ground around and looked at Noi. The girl nodded and fished in her purse.

"So what do I have to do?" The woman looked from Blake to her longtime friend.

Blake stood and loosened his belt. "Nothing. You just sit there. Noi here is going to give me a very large shot in the ass. In about five or so minutes, I'm going to take a little nap. Shortly after, I'm going to get up from your wheelchair and walk out of here. After a bit, someone will find you gone, and this body will have died of a heart attack."

The woman leaned back in the chair. "Just like that?"

Bridget nodded at her friend. "Just like that."

She looked at Noi poised with the large syringe. She nodded at the girl. "Don't miss."

They all smiled sadly.

Twenty minutes later, she pushed the wheels of the chair out the door.

Noi rested her hand on the handle of the car. "The damage was more than she let on, wasn't it?"

Blake nodded. She looked to Bridget. "Her spine was severed. It's lower than she knew, but it's where it will repair. But it might take more than a few days. I'll need a lot of protein."

"But it will work?"

Blake took the tall woman's hand. "Yes. Your friend was in a lot of pain, but most of it was being locked away in this body and in that hole of a life. Give me a few months to repair the damage and rebuild the muscle. We'll bring you and your daughter out to the raft, and I'll kick your ass for old time sake."

"She never could before. She was good, but I was always better. We just made a great team."

Noi snorted warmly. "And you two looked awesome while you kicked ass too."

Bridget nodded at the kid. "I like this kid more and more."

"Wait until you meet her mother. She's a chip off the old block."

"HAVE BODY. HEADED for San Francisco. Body needs work."

Manny stared at the text on his phone. He texted back there may be a problem, but he'd keep them posted.

36 Come Out, Come Out, Wherever You Are

NINA WAS BORED. For eight days, she had overseen a never changing set of dials and cage scene. What was inside the cage had only changed by beginning to decompose and smell. The reason she had volunteered for the job was, for some inexplicable reason, she liked the smell death. It reminded her of much happier times in other lives.

She smiled as she thought about plucking purses and rings from the fallen soldiers after Waterloo. The French had a habit of carrying all of their personal wealth in forms of gold. It had been the third day when, as a young lad, he spotted a torn open tunic. The soft reflection off the gold medallion and necklace had led her to retrace her path over the dead. The other human scavengers had taken guns, ammunition, swords, and food. By nightfall, they all had left to leave the young powder boy to sleep peacefully among the stench.

The haul provided her with a small place in the French Alps. When he was a dashing young man, he had progressed to the ultimate thief—a banker brokering international trade. When the nineteenth century had gotten control of itself, he learned to moonlight in the dark art of assassinations and stealing wealth by day.

She stood and walked around the large warehouse. A few empty wooden crates were stacked in one corner. The rest of the large space was as if it had been swept clean, except for the copper cage in the middle.

The laptop near the cage beeped twice. She flicked her left wrist and looked at the readout on her watch. It was the same as the laptop. The time was now noon local. She kicked one of the crates.

A long splinter cracked off the top of the one board. It hung by the staple at one end. Nina tore it from the crate and swished it through the air. She smiled at being almost sixty-two and still playing with wooden swords.

She dueled her way across the darkened space and her imagination.

As she neared the cage, she pinned her imaginary foe against the wall of wire mesh. With one last thrust, she pierced his heart, and the tip of her sword slid into the cage. The gap between wires was over an inch. Most of the sword was smaller.

Nina stood near the mesh and stared at the two-foot section of wood that was now inside the cage. Pushing the stick further, she buried the wood into the cage until it stuck.

The stick hung in the mesh as she stepped to examine her readings. She toggled back and forth from the current to an hour before. The stick in the Faraday cage made zero difference. The cage continued to consume the two-twenty voltage at a rate of eleven-point-three-two-seven amps.

Nina looked back at the crates. None would suit her purpose.

She fished her phone out of her pocket and dialed. "Hey, Manny, it's Nina. Can you find me something as non-conducting as wood and is about six feet long, but only three-quarters of an inch thick or thinner?"

She thumbed the phone off and slid it absentmindedly back into her back pocket. Thinking, she sat down as she stared at the stick in the mesh.

Several minutes later, the hatch door opened. Manny stepped through as a slender rod wiggled up and down with his walking. "I figured if you wanted six feet, ten would do."

He stopped at the stick in the cage. He thought about the significance. He was at a loss.

"The prince fought bravely but died heroically. I pierced him through his scarlet doublet and heart." She took the long rod. "Don't mess with a bored assassin." She examined the rod. "Fiberglass conducts electricity."

Manny sagged his head and looked at her through his lashes. "On the other hand, inert polycarbonate does not."

Her face lit up as she raised her one index finger. "Ah, great point." She turned and then turned back. "As well as great thinking."

She inserted the end as high as her head. The tip reached out to the edge of the cardboard box. She rested a hands length over the edge of the box and started to draw the box to her. It didn't move.

She withdrew the rod. Walking to the dark side of the cage, she inserted the rod at the height of her knees. She poked at the box. It moved. She kept pushing. The box turned. She pushed the other end.

Turn by turn, she inched the box across the cage. When it was near the wall of the lit side of the cage, she stopped.

Manny and Nina stood looking down at the unmoving turtle in the box. "What do you think?"

"I think your turtle is dead as the body on the bed."

"How can you be sure?"

"Without turning the cage off and going in there with a stethoscope? I can't." They stood looking.

A smile crept across Nina's cheek. Manny hiccupped. "I've seen evil grins like yours before."

She pushed him gently out of her way. She drew her former sword out of the mesh. Stepping over to where the box was, she reinserted the sword and probed the reptile.

The response was instant, rapid, and violent. The last two inches hung out of the right side of the tortoise's mouth. They were no longer attached to the rest of the stick.

"I think your beast is hungry and pissed off."

"But you can't see his aurora?"

She stepped over and hit a few keys on the computer. The cage stopped humming.

"Oh, shit. Not only is he hungry, but he is extremely mad." She stepped slightly closer. "Is little Junny Jim throwing a turtle tantrum?"

Manny stood looking at a simple pasteboard box with a California Desert Terrapin in it. "What do you see?"

"His aurora exceeds the box by at least three feet. Near his shell, there are streaks of yellow, but the rest is all pure angry red. There is nothing redeeming about this soul." She turned and studied the concentrating face. "Now what do you do with him?"

Manny snorted a soft, breathy laugh. "What any decent host should do—feed him. He must be hungry." He looked at her as he crossed to the door to the cage.

"You sure you want to pick him up without armor?" She held up the bitten end of the stick.

"Good point."

37 Electrifying

THE CONFERENCE ROOM was barely large enough to fit all the concerned parties. The centerpiece on the table was a thick acrylic case with holes drilled in it for air and passing lettuce. A California Desert Terrapin has no eyebrows. There are no facial features it can use to show disdain. Manny sat where he could see the head. He was positive Jun was scowling at him.

The affable stocky man entered the room. Everyone stood. Elon shied his head away. "Please, everyone, sit down. It's not like I'm the President of the United States or anything." He stepped over to Manny and shook his hand. "Good to see you, my friend. I heard the raft suffered severe damage in some areas."

"There was extensive damage, but we will eventually get her back together and up to steam."

"I have a couple of engineers I can lend you for a few years. They have expressed interest in coming out."

"We'd love to have them."

"I have to warn you about one of them. He putters about his lab muttering about a whale. I'm not sure he would be the best person to place on a ship in the middle of the ocean."

Manny laughed. "Is the man's name Grady?"

"You know him?"

Manny looked over at the woman in the wheelchair. They smiled. "Sure, send him. I'll even go down to an antique store and get him a harpoon." Manny turned. "Everybody, as I'm sure you know—this is Elon Musk. The wonderful cars we have been experiencing today are his invention." He turned. "Elon, this is Brie, Nina, Noi, Blake, Christine, Cole, and Red."

"As in the color red?"

"Is there any better color?" The man fluffed his beard with a smile.

"Well, welcome to all of you. I understand each of you were an integral part in bringing our guest here today." He nodded at the tortoise.

Nina snorted. She tucked her two middle fingers in and held up her hand. "Just don't stick your fingers in the holes."

Elon laughed. "Guaranteed."

Manny smoothed his hands on the large walnut table. "So, when do we leave for Lompoc?"

"We don't." Elon patted the man's hand at the shocked look on his face. "We leave in an hour for Cape Canaveral. The Falcon 9 is in Lompoc, but there is a better unit we secured for you down in Florida. After you had given us the payload specs, we retrofitted the carrier for the long flight, and this is a unit the government was kind of happy to get rid of in a useful way."

Manny's smile pulled up on the right. "And this disposable dog is a what?"

"The last of the great Saturn Vs. They had one always

for a backup. But now, with the changing times, it is so much scrap. But cheer up. We got it for a great price."

Drooping his left eyelid, Manny looked suspiciously at the man. "Define great price."

"How is free?" He laughed at the unchanged face. "When JPL heard where it was going, they asked if they could add some telemetric instruments. Then there was Cal Tech, Stanford, MIT, and finally, Cornel kicked in. In fact, your turtle here—"

As a host, everyone chorused loudly. "Tortoise. It's not a turtle."

"Excuse me." He waved his palm out. "Your astronaut here will be kept in cryogenic hibernation during the flight and monitored by Cornel, Cal Tech, JPL, and Stanford."

Blake cleared her throat. "Do they understand where it eventually is going?"

Elon rolled his lips together. "Well, something like a pass around the sun and, um… back?"

Christine coughed into her hand. "And if there is a problem?"

The man flattened his lips and shrugged. "Then, it will probably fall into the sun and burn up."

Noi muttered. "Ninety-four million miles away."

Musk and Manny nodded.

The question on everyone's mind was if it was far enough away.

THE WHITE ROCKET two miles away started to smoke at the bottom. The flames drove large clouds of smoke to the side. The roar finally hit the spectators as they watched the pillar become an inverted torch as it picked up speed. The wispy clouds were perfect strokes of white in the blue sky. The rocket cut the sky in half on its way to space. There was no cheering. The group stood solemnly watching today and thinking of tomorrow.

It would take almost one hundred years before the capsule burned up in the suns aurora. It may take as many years to make sure the evil doesn't return. Two hundred years. A lot could happen in that time.

38 One Year Later

THE SKY WAS a cloudless blue. Blake stood in her new blood red boots. In her right hand was a brand new sword—a gift from a friend. She had the blade made by a special sword maker. The steel was fused with metal from a meteorite. Forged into the side of the blade was a Nordic star.

Blake closed her eyes and turned her face toward the sun—the closest star. She could feel the new .50 caliber pistol in its holster at the small of her back. She rolled her shoulders. After months of ache and rebuilding, the muscles were soft and supple. She couldn't wait for Bridget to arrive in two more days. She could feel in her bones that this time, she would finally beat her mirror image.

Blake could hear the hatch open. The sound of the black boots on the deck was distinctive.

Christine slid her arm around Blake's waist. "I love the new color of boots. How do you like the new sword Noi sent?"

Blake hefted the sword and passed the blade through a figure eight in the air.

"The balance and weight are amazing. I also love the

pistol you gave me. You two really didn't have to."

Christine shrugged and kissed her on the cheek. "You know the old saying…"

Some days,
to save the world,
you need a pirate's heart,
a good sword,
solid back-up,
and a kick-ass pair of boots.

Other Books by Baer Charlton

The Very Littlest Dragon
Stoneheart
(Pulitzer Nominee 2015)
Angel Flights
What About Marsha?
Pirate's Patch

Southside Hooker Series

Death on a Dime – Book One
Night Vision – Book Two
Unbidden Garden – Book Three
Boomtown – Book Four
One Day Under the Grass – Book Five

BAER CHARLTON

About the Author

BAER CHARLTON GRADUATED from UC Irvine with a degree in Social Anthropology, monkeyed around for a while, and then proceeded onward with a life of global travel, multi-disciplinary adventure, and meeting the memorable array of characters he would come to describe in his writing. He has ridden things with gears, engines, and sails, and made things with wood, leather, and metal. He has been stitched back together more times than the average hockey team; his long-suffering wife and an assortment of cats and dogs have nursed him back to health after each surgery.

Baer knows a lot about many things in this world. History flows through his veins and pours out of him at the slightest provocation. Do not ask him what you may think is a simple question unless you have the time to hear a fascinating story.

You can find more about Baer at his website.
www.baercharlton.com

www.ingramcontent.com/pod-product-compliance
Lightning Source LLC
Chambersburg PA
CBHW020929120726
47905CB00008B/2443